# Written by

Silvana Miller

**Cover art by** Jaime Ricciardi

**Species art by** Kiuru Koponen

**Map cartography by** Chaim Holtjer

**Chapter art by** Jonas Spokas of Stardust Book Services

**Interior Formatting by** Sara Vertuan of Stardust Book Services

ISBN: 979-8-9898783-0-7

Dedicated to my grandmother, the original Silvana,
who supported me since the beginning. I wish you
were here to see how far I've come.

Gamorthes
NORTH strea
Hyrelli
SOLAR
ECLIPSE
Luraan
Elysian Falls
ELYSIAN Jungle
Fenre
Hyacinth oasis
SunLit cLouds
Crelano
Kezeno
Kipovandi
West Cirrus Ocean

Ocean
Mirion
Frozen Winds
Evaris
Arces
Admiral's Peak
Ramere
Kelic
Burning Talons
Khufhou
moon's eye cemetary
THE SHADOW Forest
Candor
Ademenos
Edwindon
PARadise Mts.
Long Shadows
The sleeping river
olden halln
eants
Elyton
Kearin
Dovetail Island
N
WYRD ISLAND
DReam Seers
Neeelon
chaim 2023

# LONG SHADOWS FIREPIE

**Physique:** short, average-bodied. They have large pupils and short wings

**Abilities:** fire breath and can ignite any part of their body at will. Silent flight. Good vision in low light

**Ruler:** King Wolf

# BURNING TALONS FIREPIE

**Physique:** covered in a thick layer of waterproof feathers. These extend down their legs in varying lengths, sometimes concealing the points of their short, curved claws

**Abilities:** fire breath and can ignite any part of their body at will. Waterproof feathers allow them to dive for fish without getting soaked. They can hold their breath for long stretches of time

**Ruler:** Queen Kenshaw

# GOLDEN HEARTS FIREPIE

**Physique:** powerful, muscled. Their body resembles that of an eagle more than a corvid. They have massive wings and huge, curved talons

**Abilities:** fire breath and can ignite any part of their body at will. Powerful wings allow them to fly long distances without exhaustion

**Ruler:** King Onyx

# SOLAR ECLIPSE FIREPIE

**Physique:** slim bodied with little muscle. Hundreds of years of uninterrupted peace led to the evolution of extravagant feathers over practical features

**Abilities:** fire breath and can ignite any part of their body at will. Resistant to most diseases and poisons

**Ruler:** Queen Raindrop

# FROZEN WINDS WINTERPIE

**Physique:** thin and tall, with pointed features. They have long claws with microscopic backward ridges. A white iris is present around their pupils.

**Abilities:** they can freeze any part of their body and any surface they come into contact with. Some can summon icicles from the ground. Thin pupils help them see in the harsh arctic light

**Ruler:** Queen Aisurida

# SUNLIT CLOUDS VENOMPIE

**Physique:** thin and tall. They have long claws and a snake-like tongue, along with barbs on their tongue or small fangs in their mouth. Scales are scattered randomly across their body

**Abilities:** they have potent venom in their fangs, tongue, or feathers, and a powerful resistance to heat. Thin pupils help them see in the harsh desert light

**Ruler:** Queen Rattlesnake

# DREAMSEER

**Physique:** a mix of traits from any of the known races. They are only seen in shades of blue, purple, pink, or silver, and have white pupiless eyes

**Abilities:** telepathy, future-sight, dream walking, or similarly strange powers

**Ruler:** King Omnipresence

# ALLEGIANCES

*Coyote Thieves Guild*
Owl Wings: Boss of the
Coyotes
Naom: Master Thief
Cyrill
Rose Heart
Legacy
Fortune
Misfire
Judgement
Thistle

*Jaguar Thieves Guild*
Vandal: Boss of the Jaguars
Xiketic: Master Thief
Honeydew
Lily
Parrot
Temporal
Inferno
Arctic

*Fox Thieves Guild*
Cottonmouth: Overseer of
all three guilds, Boss of the
Foxes
Cordovan: Master Thief
O'Hara
Cloudburst
Sterling
Quicksilver

## CHAPTER ONE

# MOONLIGHT

LEGACY BURST THROUGH THE HALLWAY in a whirlwind of red feathers, turning a corner and nearly slamming into the opposite wall. Large tapestries fluttered along the walls with the wind of her movement. Her claws ached with each dashing stride, a painful reminder that birds weren't quite made for running.

Her cloak, usually light and forgettable on her shoulders, weighed down heavily, the end whipping behind her at every turn.

Looming paintings of condescending royals watched her swift escape. Judgmental eyes frozen in time, mocking her attempt to outrun justice as she swung yet another corner, turning on her heels. She wasn't alone. Two other birds were running just the same, one barely a few wing-lengths ahead, the other just behind, all pushing forward with the same goal in mind: to get this heist done and over with.

They were so close. The Goldblood heist, the first full heist she'd been allowed to plan, every meticulous detail her own, and it was going flawlessly. She couldn't screw up now, not if she ever wanted her guild to respect her. Not if she ever wanted to surpass the others.

A large cloth bag, pregnant with gold, expensive jewelry, and rags to muffle the sound, hung heavy on her hip. Its contents were worth more than she was, possibly more than most of the fancy nobles roosting in this place. Among the treasures was a necklace stolen from Queen Ruby herself, adorned with dazzling jewels so rare Legacy couldn't even name them.

She took quick breaths in through her nose, enough to keep her going but not so loud as to alert anyone meandering about in their rooms in the late hours of the night. She yearned to fly, but she knew the flapping would be a dead giveaway that there was an intruder. After all, no noble was flapping about in here like their life depended on it—they were too proper for that. Even if their life did depend on it, they'd probably still resort to a dainty run. Can't breach etiquette when you're about to die, now can you?

The castle hallways were eerily empty, save for the thieves, lacking guards or civilians of any kind to block her hasty escape. That was thanks to Misfire, her crime partner and fellow Coyote Thieves Guild member. On the opposite end of the vast castle, he was meant to formulate a distraction, something to draw the citizens of this place away from where Rose Heart, Naom, and herself were making their getaway. The stark emptiness told her he'd succeeded.

*Success, something rare to come by these days,* she thought as she rounded the last corner, exit shining cold in contrast to the golden warmth of the castle. It was a wonder the heist had even gone this far without a hitch. It always felt like something happened right when things were going well. Either ungodly poor luck or, more commonly, one of the Coyotes screwing up a fundamental part of the mission.

No, she shouldn't even be thinking about it—best not to jinx herself.

Next to the aged archway sat a delicate golden cage standing barely eye level on a skillfully carved pedestal. Inside perched a bird, some type of fancy rainbow finch singing a gentle tune, blissfully unaware of the quiet chaos.

*You wish you had the brain capacity to break yourself out of there, but you can't even comprehend your own captivity.* The thought made her stop, ponder for just a fleeting moment. It was no harm to the heist; she had to catch her breath anyway.

There was still a long stretch to fly once she was out of here, and she'd have to fly like hell to make sure no one caught her.

A sultry voice broke her pondering before it began. "Good luck hauling that cage out of here, darling. It looks just as heavy as you," Rose Heart said, a red and pink blur bolting on past with grace. She outran her words, leaving them to settle in the dust she'd kicked up.

Legacy paid her no mind, though her claws twitched greedily toward the glittering bars. If the finch were as smart as the 'pies, the ruling race of Camorthes, it would take nothing more than a quick claw movement to flip open the fragile door and fly free. One claw flick for a life of freedom.

But the 'pies—the firepies, the winterpies, and the venompies—were alone in their sentience, alone in being the one race capable of moral dilemmas and the ability to grasp their own conscience. Sure, there were monkeys in the jungle capable of playing basic games, and their lesser crow cousins could solve simple puzzles, but it didn't hold a candle to what the 'pies were capable of.

It was nothing next to the birth of cities, law, and religion.

Her hesitation was short-lived, but long enough that when a figure slyly slipped around the corner behind her and her trio, she saw it out of the corner of her eye. A darkly cloaked fellow trailed the thieves, crimson eyes bright in the dimness. They carried themselves with a quietness more befitting of another criminal than a castle guard.

They could have been a sort of secret agent, some lawman who dealt with matters less forcefully than the common guards, but they kept nervously glancing behind themselves, like they were just as afraid to be caught as the thieves.

*Shit*, she thought as they quickly ducked into an empty room. Whatever they were, she didn't have the time to sit around and find out.

Her claws hit the floor as she sprung out the open archway, faint finch-song following her frantic bolt toward the exit gate. Far ahead, she struggled to make out Naom's black and blue feathers. They blended in with the darkness outside, and having Rose Heart halfway in between to block her from view did Legacy no favors.

Naom led the way powerfully, but Rose Heart lagged back just a few steps. Her face was crumpled in annoyance. Legacy felt a stab of embarrassment as she realized she was waiting for her to catch up.

The cloaked figure exploded past Legacy, a blur of bright feathers taking to the air with a pace a running cheetah couldn't match. They didn't strike Naom, as it looked like they were aiming to do, but instead alighted on the top of the gate, poised proudly. On their way by, Legacy spotted a curious emblem on their chest.

The symbol of a glowing white circle set over black. A full moon. This bird didn't just look like an assassin, they, no, he, *was* an assassin.

Silhouetted against the yellowed blood moon, she watched him reach for the lever that would bring the heavy gate crashing down.

"Naom!"

Legacy's cry was cut short as her face met cruel, cold earth. Dirt shoved deep into her nostrils while a powerful force grasped her shoulders and neck, pinning her mercilessly to the ground. A slender claw held her beak shut with a vice grip.

"What the hell are you trying to do? Get us caught? Keep your fucking beak shut or we'll lose everything," a voice whispered into her ear slit, alluring, smooth, and laced with potent venom.

Rose Heart.

Legacy struggled to kick off her companion, screaming as hard as she could but finding no voice in the frozen soil. *There's an assassin, a murderer. He's gonna kill her. By the gods he's gonna kill her.* Rose Heart, none the wiser, did nothing to release her grip.

Legacy's struggles ceased as the assassin, clearly visible from his moonlit perch, yanked the lever. Through blurred eyes she watched the heavy gate slam down, catching Naom's fleeing body with it. It looked unreal, the way her body flung down and crumpled under the weight of the iron gate. The way there was a clean, swept pathway, then blood shot out across the stone in one great explosion, the result of a bird being compressed, all its limbs and organs squished together in an instant.

Her stomach turned, but she couldn't look away.

The assassin sprung off immediately after, making for a hasty exit.

Rose Heart froze, grip loosening as she realized what was going on. Legacy flung her off with ease, spreading her wings and shooting into the sky after the assassin. Airborne, she moved miles faster than she ever had using her legs. She paid no mind to the dirt clumps clogging her face, blinking rapidly to fling the little grains off as they tried to fall into her eyes.

Fueled by fury, and having the advantage of a smaller, lighter body, she caught the assassin in seconds, grabbing the corner of his silky cloak and dragging him down to the midst of the royal gardens. The pair crashed to the earth below, a flurry of flying talons and feathers, rolling among the delicate flowers as they scrambled. She snagged his leg, pulled him to the ground, rolled on top, and pinned his soft throat against a stone barrier, pink dahlia petals floating around them. Blood dripped from a nick in the corner of his crimson eye, giving the eerie look that it was melting off his face. The moon lit their bodies in a pale glow.

Blue light filled her throat, fiery sparks darting off her tongue with every word. "A life for a life, that's how this shit works. This rivalry was all fun and games when it was just you lot taunting us, but now I ought to kill you for what you've done." The assassin winced as a spark struck his cheek, sizzling on his speckled feathers.

The rivalry in question was a strange one. A mysterious grudge between the New Moon Assassins and the Coyote Thieves Guild, two groups that should, by every right, be separate and unrelated to one another. No one was quite sure how it began, but it'd been going on since before Legacy joined the Coyotes. She just accepted it as a part of the status quo and tried not to think too deeply into the "why" of it.

Before now, it mostly consisted of stolen jobs. Of the New Moons murdering clients before they paid the Thieves, or the Thieves robbing clients before they paid the New Moons, but this was the first time anyone in either guild died. This was the first time it ever escalated to bloodshed on such a personal level.

"You don't... even know... if she's dead," the assassin croaked between breaths. His throat pulsed against her claw.

Fire flickered along her tongue, a messenger of the painful fate she had in mind for this fool. That was the signature ability of a firepie: the power to summon flames along their body in any place, at any time.

Different birds had different levels of power, denoted by the color of the fire. Hers being blue meant it could cook just about anyone except a purple fire.

This man was a winterpie, an easy observation to make now that she was close enough to see the white ring in his eyes. A thin sliver of snow around the deep black of his pupils.

He kicked his legs out, trying to sear her skin with his now-freezing talons, but his efforts were futile. Legacy was a halfbreed and had ice in her veins the same as him. She didn't have his same abilities, but she had the immunity to them.

"Because if you failed, this is all suddenly okay? Hell, if you're so sure she's still kicking, why don't you go peel her flattened corpse off the path and show me just how alive she is." Heat rose in her throat.

She was sure Naom was dead. Even obscured by dust and smoke from the falling gate, she knew a New Moon wouldn't be so quick to bail if he wasn't sure the job was done. And, as much as she hated to admit it to herself, no body could contort as sickeningly as that and hope to walk away as anything but a ghost.

She opened her beak and shot out a blast of flame, blue light engulfing the flowers, the dirt, and the assassin's fearful face. He screamed and lashed out, cold claws flailing wildly as he fought to throw her off. She held him tighter, claws digging into his shoulders, blasting fire until her throat was hoarse.

He was still screaming when armored claws pulled Legacy backward, pinning her down, cuffing her legs together, and tying her white wings against her body. She felt a rough tug as someone yanked the bag off her hip.

"You are under arrest, ma'am, for grand larceny. Better hope you have some clean money lying around or you'll be behind bars for a good long time."

# CHAPTER TWO

# A GUILD OF TROUBLES

A *GOOD LONG TIME* ENDED UP being a meager one week, a hazy period of time spent meandering around a dark cell in some dank basement underground somewhere in the Golden Hearts kingdom. The guards were quick to threaten Legacy with an eternity in jail but quicker to go back on their word when Owl Wings waved a hefty bag of gold in their faces.

The fury on his face made her wish he'd just left her in there instead.

She'd had one chance to prove herself to him, one grand heist he'd let her plan down to every minute detail and execute without a word of input from him or anyone else. It was her heist, her everything, a golden moment to prove she was better than the loons who made up the rest of the Coyotes, and she'd royally fucked it up.

At least she was out of that cell. The Coyote den was nothing to admire, but it was spacious, and even the smaller connected caves, one of which she stood in now, were warm and well-lit.

But failure didn't come without its consequences.

Now she was stuck being trained like some green-blood apprentice by none other than *her*. The Seducer of Kings to some, a whore with a silver tongue to others, the best thief in this guild, according to the Boss. Hence her new title of "Master Thief."

It used to be Naom, but it was hard to be a master at anything from beyond the grave.

It was supposed to be Legacy next. That's what the Goldblood heist was all about. Owl Wings was going to retire, Naom was going to take over as guildmaster, and Legacy would be the newest Master Thief.

Rose Heart huffed, twirling a slim black dagger in her claws once before tossing it to Legacy across the room.

"Catch," she said.

Legacy fumbled to catch the blade, only barely managing without running it through either her chest or her palm. She recovered quickly and pointed it toward the training dummy theatrically. It stood, emotionless and unmoving, between the ladies.

This daily training was a lot of things: a waste of time, a waste of energy, and a waste of thieves who could otherwise be doing actual jobs. What it wasn't, was useful.

She never learned anything from it, not one Darivan-damned thing. All she did was waltz in here, beat up a training dummy for a few hours, and tune out Rose Heart shouting redundant advice from the sidelines.

It wasn't relevant to their daily work. Basic knife wielding was a good skill set to have, she couldn't deny that, but she already knew enough to get by. They weren't warriors. They didn't need to be. That was the whole point of hiding in the shadows and doing all their work at night.

Assassins were much the same. When they struck, it wasn't usually a swinging blow for the target to see, much less defend themselves against.

The oddity of the events prior to her arrest nagged at the corner of her mind. The assassin then hadn't attacked in broad daylight, but he'd attacked by the light of the full moon, which wasn't much better.

An argument could be made that the thieves weren't much better, striking the heart of a kingdom by that same damning light, but it had been a carefully thought-out detail of Legacy's plan. The full moon was a night of revelry, partying, and birds staying up getting drunk. It was far more likely for a victim to assume their missing belongings were misplaced rather than stolen if they were intoxicated.

But the assassin wasn't going for drunken civilians. He was going for the thieves. Thieves who were stone-cold sober and could see his every feather. It had to be deliberate. It just had to be.

She just couldn't figure out why.

"Oh, for fuck's sake, get on with it," Rose Heart barked.

Legacy shot her a pointed glare.

And now, all this redundant training over one failed heist.

Granted, it was a huge heist they'd been planning out for months, that she'd been given the responsibility of running solely because she'd bragged that she could do it after Rose Heart botched one, but the problem didn't correlate with the solution. Knife fighting didn't come into play during this heist, and it probably wouldn't in the next.

She'd had that assassin in her claws. She'd already won. It was the fact that he'd interfered at all that ruined things, not incompetence on her end. This just felt like an insult.

She slashed at the dummy. The shining blade nicked the surface, splitting lines of straw.

*Thieves are supposed to plan for everything, no excuses* is what Owl Wings had said when Legacy begged for a second chance.

Yeah, sure, thieves were supposed to plan for everything, but how was she supposed to plan for *that*? Assassins were supposed to mind their quiet business in the shadowy corners of the world, unseen and unheard. It wasn't her fault they'd changed that mentality right at her shining moment.

She slashed again, missing by a hair. The weight of the blade was minuscule, but when it didn't connect with anything, she overshot and flung herself off-balance.

She didn't need to look at Rose Heart to feel the judgmental green glare digging into her back. In fact, she made sure not to. She kept her eyes on the target, shifting her weight between her legs.

Her fault or otherwise, the Boss wasn't too pleased to have to pay her way out of jail; the Coyotes didn't have much to spare. Not that much pleased him at all nowadays. Old age wore on a bird's patience, and he was well up in the six-hundreds. He still had about a hundred years left, but it was clear the previous ones weighed heavily on him.

Rose Heart nodded her elegant head at the dummy, as if Legacy needed to be encouraged.

"You are incredibly slow today," Rose Heart said simply.

The straw firepie stood dumbly, casting long shadows across the floor as it rested under burning gold torches. They'd been lit by Fortune, the only yellow-fire in the guild. She frequently whined about being the only one tasked with keeping them lit, but the Boss was firm. He oft complained that if he let everyone light the torches willy nilly, the clashing colors would give him a headache.

Legacy lunged forward, slashing cleanly across the dummy's fake feathered head. Hay and cloth bits fluttered to the floor.

Rose Heart's voice pierced the air without a moment's hesitation, sweet as honey, laced with shards of glass. "Darling, that was too wide. Swing like that and your enemy will have a few hundred years to think about their next move." She pointed a condescending black talon at the wounded dummy. "Strike again, and keep your blows close this time."

Legacy snorted and threw the dagger on the ground, the dusty thud reverberating off the close cave walls. "I already know what I'm doing, so can it and let me do my thing."

The last few hours of this wearying experience pulled so taut they snapped. It wasn't just the fact that the training existed that pissed her off, it was that Rose Heart was her mentor. Ever perfect Rose Heart, golden child of this guild. When she screwed up a heist, it was but a "mistakes happen" from the Boss.

Legacy would prefer anyone else in Rose Heart's position, even Misfire, famously incompetent, or Judgement, who was… there, like a decorative plant. However, the Boss ordered it, and his word, as well as the unofficial thieves' code, was the closest thing thieves had to law. So there wasn't much either could say in opposition. Not if they wanted a share of the meals and gold, or a home to stay in and a guild to bail them out when they did get caught.

Rose Heart stood at the other side of the small room. Her green eyes narrowed into furious slivers. The training dummy between them held its same blank face, marred by a long slash across one half of its head where lumps of bunched sheep's wool spilled out. Little strings of wool still dusted the floor and clung feebly to her feathers.

Rose Heart pointed at the dagger, snide. "Then leave or strike again, dear. I'm here on my time, and if you aren't going to suck it up for at least another hour, I couldn't care less about the consequences you'll face."

"Don't call me dear," Legacy spat as she picked up the dagger, twirling it around. The point glinted, sharp as broken glass. Its shadow flickered across the floor.

"I call everyone dear. If that bothers you, maybe you need to be less sensitive." Rose Heart grabbed the training dummy, shoving the stuffing back inside its head with more force than necessary. "I wouldn't be here training you if I had any choice in the matter, I assure you. There's many places in the world I'd rather be than talking to a hotheaded little bitch."

Legacy caught the dagger as she flipped it one last time, lunging forward to jab it at Rose Heart's throat. Not close enough to cut but enough to get her point across. Her voice lowered to a furious growl. "Care to repeat that? Is insulting me worth your life?"

Rose Heart reached up and rested her claw across the top of the handle, pushing it down ever so slightly to distance herself from the point. "It's not worth my life, dear, but I know you're too loyal to the Boss to kill me. All bark and no bite. A hotheaded little bitch, as I said. He'd kick you out in a heartbeat if you killed his favorite thief."

She wasn't lying there. She was, infuriatingly, the Boss's favorite. It wasn't due to her charming personality—she was this horrible to everyone, the Boss included, and her charm was exclusive to her victims. Nor was it her aptitude with a blade—Legacy was equal, if not better, and Fortune was undoubtedly better—but her talent at what they made a living off of: thievery. In the end, that's what counted.

Legacy knew she was at least equally as good, but until the Boss saw that, it meant nothing. The only bird who'd been better was Naom.

Rose Heart was a strange type for a thief, being a Solar Eclipse firepie to the letter. It was one of the four subspecies of firepie that existed on Camorthes, and the one notorious for having such ridiculous feather growths and morphs that it oft impeded daily life.

However, despite her Solar Eclipse blood granting her a tall, lanky figure with shiny red feathers and fanciful peacock-like crest growths on her head and chest, she was a master at disappearing into the shadows and becoming unseen. Like blowing out a torchlight. One moment she was the shining center of attention, the next she was gone, one with the rats and small critters who scurried between walls and under leafy forest floors.

She was also damn good at seduction, and she knew it. She could have any bird wrapped around her claw for a night before taking off in the morning with their valuables and their dignity.

That's what made her the Boss's pet. He didn't care that she was a pain in the ass who barely listened, that she had a bone to pick with nearly everyone in the guild, and couldn't spell "teamwork" if she tried. He cared that she brought in the gold.

But so did Legacy. She tried hard as hell to do her best, to follow his orders, but it just wasn't enough.

Legacy rolled her eyes, shoving the black dagger into her cloak. A second one hung symmetrically off her other side. That one was her own, reddish and more suited to her tastes than the scratched and worn training knife. The weight was a constant, comfortable reminder that she could defend herself at any moment.

"Whatever you say, *dear*. I won't kill you but, by Darivan, I can't stand another minute listening to you talk," Legacy said, her back to her fellow thief.

*Oh, sorry, Master Thief,* she thought, disgust curling her tongue.

The title mattered because the Boss's chosen Master Thief was the one who got to take over the guild when he died or retired. Usually, they died, but somehow Owl Wings defied fate and lived long enough that he was verging on retirement any year now. And owning the guild? Well, that meant profit. More profit than they were seeing now by a long shot.

It meant that even if the guild went under, you had a security blanket. The rest of the common rabble would have to figure it out on their own, but you could have a little bit of coin tucked away from the guild tax.

Rose Heart rolled her crimson shoulders. "Well, darling, make your choice: strike again or leave. I couldn't care less."

Legacy shook out her feathers. This wasn't a hard choice at all. As much as she wanted to avoid being the image of a pouting child, she wasn't going to spend another second near that pompous peacock of a woman. She silently turned her back to her fellow Coyote and stormed off, her loudly clicking talons echoing off the walls in the wide cavern.

Legacy's grim demeanor spread like poisonous spores throughout the damp cave that was home to the Coyotes. Not that it needed much to spread. This cave attracted a bad mood like spilled honey attracted gnats.

The Coyotes were one of the three thieves' guilds, all operating underneath the crime boss, Cottonmouth. The other two being the Jaguars and the Foxes. There also used to be the Wolves, before they went up in smoke.

They were all separate and yet the same. United by the same rules, supposed mutual respect, and the idea that thieves would work better if they didn't have to worry about competition with each other on top of worrying about the various law-keepers in Camorthes. Each guild had its own boss, its own Master Thief, and its own domain to work in, with Cottonmouth stepping in exceedingly rarely if something got out of hand.

Both the Foxes and Jaguars—and Wolves, when they'd existed—operated identically to the Coyotes, the big difference being location. That was the point of having separate guilds instead of sticking everyone in one hole in the ground. If the thieves' guilds were all together, it meant one mistake would cost everything. Now, if one guild went down, the rest were still functional.

Seeing all the arguing going on here, she oftentimes found herself wishing she had thrown her lot in with one of the other guilds instead.

*That's what happens when you shove a bunch of criminals together without thought or reason as to whether they'll get along.*

The Coyotes were notoriously the least stable of the three. Being the youngest guild, they were left with scraps when it came to finding recruits, since all the good ones were scooped up by the Jaguars and Foxes long before. It was up to the boss of each individual guild to recruit their own thieves, and while she trusted Owl Wings' judgment… it was obvious he didn't have much to work with.

The other guilds were better established, including in their ranks not only the best of the best but the children of prior thieves, who'd been taught the art from hatching.

*No,* Legacy thought. She owed it to Owl Wings to stay here. He'd recruited her, after all.

*Even if the Coyotes make me wish that I got left in that jail cell for a few more weeks. My cellmate was far quieter than this group.*

The Jaguars, nestled in the deep rainforest hidden right beneath the Solar Eclipse Kingdom's very nose, were the oldest guild. *Too bad they live in the jungle, a great place to be if you want to catch some mystery illness and die slowly before even getting the chance to rob a bird without a single coin to their name.*

The Foxes, planted right on the border of the Sunlit Clouds and Golden Hearts Kingdoms, were the smallest. They only numbered six thieves, but one of them was Cottonmouth, and three of the others were sisters. It led to few arguments, or disputes resolved so quickly it was like they'd never happened. Their cooperation was more military than criminal.

*They've got money, too, being right next to all the Sunlit Clouds' oligarchs. A shame it's stuck right next to a desert. Even half fire-blood isn't enough to make that tolerable.*

She reached up, touching the white ribbon marks streaked across her face, a symbol of her icy heritage.

The Wolves used to operate nearby, on the edge of the Long Shadows kingdom by the ocean, but someone, rumored to be one of their own, gave away their hiding place. A group of thieves was no match for the Long Shadows Guard.

*We're always at each other's throats, but at least we're loyal to Owl Wings, if nothing else. Better annoying than a traitor.*

Despite the drama and annoying company, the Coyote Guild was her home now. She was going to spend the rest of her life tucked away with them in a cave at the bottom of a valley, right inside the Burning Talons' territory. The climate was ideal, not too hot and not too cold; they even had all four seasons in full. The location was nearly flawless.

*Nearly, but not quite,* she thought as Naom's face flashed in her memory. Unfortunately the New Moons, a powerful guild of assassins for hire, also realized how lovely the weather was. They were holed up somewhere nearby, a little too close for comfort, and hated the Coyotes infringing on "their" territory.

*It's ridiculous; we're both living off land that belongs to the kingdoms, and we never even cross paths.* But it's not like she could say that to their faces and live. She might get stabbed, gutted, thrown to the wild dogs, or crushed into red mist under a moonlit castle gate.

Assassins being territorial wasn't something she'd expected, and to this day, she theorized that there was probably more to the conflict than met the eye.

Distant voices filled the air as she stepped out of the stone tunnel and onto the massive bridge in the middle of their cavernous home. Dying rays of golden sunlight from the holes in the roof above lit up dust particles in the air. Far down below, between towering spires of rock, some of the other Coyotes were shuffling about, talking in raised voices. The faraway crash of breaking glass raised the voices higher.

A life of paltry gold and constant arguments—that's what she lived now. Hopefully someday she could make enough coin to get herself a nice home far away from this place and live without walking on eggshells in every sentence she spoke. It was a lovely thought to entertain but far from achievable, not with their income waning by the day.

*The Boss is lucky I'm loyal as I am, else I would have dropped this shithole of a guild the moment the income stopped paying for my headache medicine.*

She hoped it was headache medicine, at least. She'd sniped them from a doctor and could only barely read the labels plastered to the colorful jars. When she found out they worked, she came back and bought a nice supply of them.

Water dripped from a high-up stalactite and fell past her beak. Her sky-blue gaze followed it down, down until it disappeared somewhere in the group of fighting birds below.

*It wasn't always like this,* she thought as the dripping sound was swamped over by angry voices. *Once we were all happier.* Sure, when the guild came together it was a hopeless mess, but there'd been a brief period after they settled in where everyone got along. Or at least got along enough to put their differences aside for their work.

It wasn't all buddy-buddy friendliness, but it was cordial. She liked that best.

She wasn't sure what started all the fighting anew. Long ago, disputes were few and far between. Then the atmosphere got tenser as the gold grew thinner and the New Moons grew stronger. Arguments multiplied until they became daily routine. Hating each other became the norm before any of them even saw it coming.

The payment was mostly at fault. Being a thief was high risk with unpredictable reward. The cracks in their lives shone through the less gold there was to fill the gaps. Living in the dark, away from society and the rest of Camorthes, was only fun when they had a semblance of the comforts of a real home.

She forced herself to tear her gaze away and focus on the gaping cavern at the other end of the bridge. That opening led to their personal rooms. She wasn't tired enough to sleep, but the atmosphere in the cave was stifling. *No better time to take a job,* she thought as she disappeared into the tunnel on the opposite side of the bridge, voices fading away behind her.

Twenty paces down the hall, fifth opening on the left. That was where the Boss's room was. She knocked hard on the enchanted stone barrier that made up the door.

That wasn't the work of the thieves; it was the last remaining magic of whatever group had lived here long before. It was the only door here like it and was impossible to break into if the designated owner didn't give it permission to open. How the door knew who its owner was, she had no idea.

As her talons rested against the cold stone, she wondered what happened to them, who they were, how they lived. Did they fight as much as the thieves? Was it even a group or just one lone magician? She made a mental note to grab a book on the history of this location next time she was in town.

*Hopefully they have something on it; it's a pretty obscure place.* Even if she didn't find anything, there was a charm to searching for books that made it a worthwhile experience regardless.

The door slid open, stone grating on stone and making a wonderfully ear-bleeding noise. Inside, Owl Wings and Cyrill stood around a cracked wooden table. Owl Wings looked up, brows scrunched. Cyrill kept his eyes on the table, yellow and empty.

The expression wasn't too out of the ordinary for Owl Wings—his age gave him a permanent half scowl, always looking like he was pissed off no matter who he was talking to—but it still made her spine shiver, like she'd done something wrong just by being here.

She tried to stash those doubts away as she bowed her head in greeting. "My apologies, Boss... Am I interrupting something?"

Owl Wings gestured at the table with a dark-brown wing. A pile of papers was strewn haphazardly atop it. "Yes, you are," he said, tan neck feathers rising in annoyance. "We're trying to put together a heist that'll save our asses, while you lot waste the day yelling back and forth over meaningless bullshit." He pointed one short black claw at the papers, yellow foot barely visible underneath the heavy brown feathering on his legs. "It's not the lack of plans or opportunity screwing us, it's the fact that I can't trust your sorry asses to pull any of them off."

Legacy glanced over the papers, littered with furious scribbles and half-written sentences, a few diagrams thrown in for good measure. "Don't lump me in with them, Boss. You know I'm good at what I do." She was no Rose Heart, but she wasn't bad by any means. Her jobs had at least a ninety percent success rate, if she had to throw out an estimate.

Owl Wings sighed, stepping back from the table as his feathers lowered. "Ah, I suppose you're right. You and Rose Heart are the only two keeping this guild together." He picked up a vial of ink and swirled it around like a fine wine. "So don't do what Naom did and get yourself killed. Cottonmouth is on my ass about how much gold we're bringing in, and we can't take another loss. Now what did you need?"

She picked up one of the papers, trying to puzzle out what it said. It was a near-incomprehensible mess of poor penmanship and an ugly little scribble of a crown in the corner. For all his skill in thievery, Owl Wings was no artist. "I came to find some work, just a small job I can do tonight."

He set the inkwell down and grabbed the paper back from her, setting it in the stack neatly. "Not in the mood for sleeping? I'd have thought training would tire you out some."

"Eh, got nocturnal blood, y'know?" she said. That was more or less a joke, the lack of sleep being attributed to insomnia and stress rather than anything to do with her heritage. The Long Shadows kingdom was nocturnal, but it was a learned lifestyle, not something to be passed down in blood.

"Well, I've got a little work for you, then. Got a client looking for some nice peryton furs, says the trading caravan already sold them off before he got the chance to buy, so now it's up to us to make sure we… intercept the caravan and snag those furs before they make it to their original buyer."

He grabbed a sheet off the top of the paper pile. "It's gotta be done by tomorrow night. I was gonna do it myself before I leave, but I'd rather you handle it. Gives me time to work shit out. They're in our area, so it shouldn't be too much legwork."

*Leave? What's that about?* She opened her beak to ask, but the look on his face said that an explanation would come in time. *Better to wait, then*, she thought as she grabbed the paper.

# CHAPTER THREE

# TO BE A THIEF

L EGACY CLUNG TO THE DARK branches. Her cloak hung heavy over her shoulders, masking her red feathers so she looked like just another shadowy pocket of forest, impossible to see for anyone who wasn't looking. Her breaths were so small they didn't even shift the leaves pressed wetly against her face. Her heart knew now was the time to quiet its powerful thumping. That was one of her first lessons as a thief: control yourself, control your body and your mind, so not even life itself would give you away to the target.

Life was loud—thumping hearts, deep breaths, rushing blood—and a thief had to maintain absolute control to ensure none of them outed her before she was ready to swoop in. Even one misstep could spell, at best, a failed mission, at worst, a dead thief. She wasn't a fan of either outcome.

Her target tonight was a band of traveling fur traders huddled together far below, two deep asleep, a third on watch. Being creatures of the elements, neither firepies nor winterpies actually needed the furs to stay warm. Firepies could cast a flame whenever they felt a chill, winterpies were creatures of the ice, and venompies rarely left their arid desert land for any reason. Furs were nothing but a symbol of status, a way to flaunt your wealth for everyone around to see you and think "Damn, I wish I had a fur cloak like that." That, and sometimes they lined beds, furniture, or were used in alchemy. It was mostly cosmetic, though, and one of the most popular items the Coyotes had to steal alongside jewelry.

Wild animals were easy to catch, but the skinning and tanning to make quality fur is what made them so prized. It wasn't a common skill set, and those who made them weren't fond of sharing their secrets outside their circles.

She watched the group below, with eyes sharper than broken glass, as she waited to make her move. Three hours had passed by now, and she was feeling the dangerous twinges of impatience wear at her brain.

Being a thief wasn't what most birds thought it was. It wasn't a cloaked and handsome rogue dashing through alleyways, snatching a coin purse, and running into the night never to be seen again.

No. Not at all. Being a thief was mostly waiting... and watching... and watching people while waiting, and waiting while watching other people. Sometimes she passed the time by pretending she was a majestic gryphon about to pounce on an unsuspecting deer. Or a sleek she-wolf stalking a rabbit. Maybe it was childish, but no child could do the work she pulled off. Besides, if it made the job go faster, who would give a damn.

Finally, the third fur trader, the one chosen to stay awake on watch, began falling victim to the heavy temptation of sleep. *It only took three hours.* Now that he was distracted with keeping himself awake, Legacy was allowed to be alive again.

She kept her wings pinned tight to her body as she crept backward toward the base of the branch. Ever so slowly, she stretched a leg down and grasped the branch lower than the one she was on. Step by agonizingly slow step, she made her way to the damp, mossy ground below. Plants were quietly crushed beneath her claws as she crept toward the sleeping group. The watchman's back was to her, and everyone else was asleep.

The perfect situation for an easy game.

A dog howled in the distance, though it sounded more like a throaty half-bark. The watchman perked up, now-sharp eyes focusing on the shadowed trees. With his attention drawn to the sounds, Legacy bolted toward one of the carriages, angling her body so that if he looked back toward her, she'd be hidden by the large mass of a sleeping gryphon. It was a muscled creature, but a harness bound its huge frame to the front of the carriage. Even if it did stir, it was too confined to be a threat. Besides, it was a carriage gryphon. Chances were it was more tired than the caravaning birds from hauling their goods about all day.

Legacy darted inside the largest carriage, looking backward every few seconds to make sure no one followed. Clear. She rifled through bags, feeling each fur within for the distinct half-feathered texture of something off a peryton. Her claws brushed various pelts. *Deer… that one was rabbit, or maybe jackalope… something soft, feathered… a peryton. Golden.* She grabbed the bag and scanned the camp one last time. Two birds asleep around the empty campfire, one facing the wrong way, eyes fixed on the trees.

Even if he saw her now, there was no way he'd give chase and abandon the caravan. Not for any longer than she needed to escape. She set off into the air, praying to Darivan the bag wouldn't be too heavy.

Darivan was favoring her today. It was gloriously lightweight, thanks to being mostly peryton furs, and she was able to rise past the treetops above before the caravan even knew what hit them.

⁕ ✦ ✦ ☾ ✦ ✦ ⁕

Soft moonlight glowed over the treetops, lining each pine needle in delicate silver. Nothing moved or stirred, every diurnal creature tucked in to sleep for the night. The nocturnal were too quiet to be sensed, no louder than shadows, no more present than ghosts.

She glanced back to double-check no one followed her. Though even if they did, without their gryphons at their side, the fight would be in Legacy's favor. Caravans could be hit or miss when it came to battle technique, but with the armor the guard was wearing he'd have a hell of a time catching up.

She would know; caravans were always stuffed full with goodies, and that made them a popular target for Coyotes. This was the kind of job she'd done a million times before and she felt like she knew how they operated more than they themselves did.

Her eye caught something just as she turned her head to face forward, and she whipped around to try and catch what it was. In doing so, she saw the swift dash of sky-blue feathers retreating into the trees. Damn. The caravan watchbird wasn't a bright blue like that, but she hadn't paid close attention to the rest of them. Someone must have seen her.

It was strange for one to give chase. Normally, even if they did notice something amiss, they'd cut their loss and carry on with keener eyes. Ditching the entire caravan for one bag of furs was rarely worth it.

She dipped down and set the bag on a sturdy branch before turning tail and diving into the trees where she saw the mystery bird take cover. Revealing herself wasn't the ideal plan, but if someone was giving chase, she'd rather they be dead than risk leading them to the Coyote den.

Not that death was likely, not with this type of bird. She'd fought many a caravaner before, and even their guards were mediocre at best, too weighed down by their showy armor to be fast enough to strike a figure lithe as herself.

Her wings beat the air softly as she descended, one claw inching toward the dagger on her belt as she used the other to land gently on a branch. It dipped under her weight, the creak loud, but was swallowed up by the multitude of other creaking branches as the wind swished between them.

She squinted down, trying to see where the bird went. They had painfully bright cerulean feathers, hard to miss in this muted environment. Between the tight-knit leaves, she could barely make out some kind of scene just below her.

Two birds sat together on a needled branch, huddled together and engrossed in each other's eyes. One with sky-blue feathers held a bleeding jackalope in his claws, which he was tearing into hearty pieces and offering to his partner. She looked just as out of place as he did, all bright blues, pale purples, and stark, unnatural whites. There were a few spots of crimson where the jackalope blood spilled onto her heather chest feathers. Legacy couldn't quite tell what race she was, though she looked too tall to be a Long Shadows bird.

Neither of them was from the caravan, but she couldn't sigh in relief just yet. Not when the male was a man she'd seen not long before and certainly not under the best circumstances.

An assassin, a New Moon, the one who killed Naom. His name was still unknown to her, but the mere sight of him made Legacy's stomach turn.

He looked bad, with half his face contorted into a grisly mess of raw tissue. There was a gaping hole where his right eye should be.

Despite the simmering anger in her chest, she told herself it wasn't worth a fight now, not if she could slip away. She had furs to haul back home, and they were hard enough to carry without being wounded.

Just as she angled her primaries to fly off, the assassin looked up and locked eyes with her. One bright red eye, flashing with recognition.

*Shit.*

With a whoosh of feathers, before Legacy could blink, he leaped off the branch. His jackalope fell to the ground far, far below. He grabbed a long, frighteningly pointed dagger off his belt, aiming it at her face as he shot toward her.

Legacy grabbed her own just in time to block the attack, tearing it off her belt with such a force it ripped the buckle. Her dagger glanced off his with a horrible metal-on-metal scrape. The sound echoed through the looming trees.

Behind the assassin's shoulder, she caught a glimpse of his lover, golden eyes wide as saucers. Her sharp yell pierced the silence of the Shadow Forest. "What in Camorthes are you doing, Skyflake? Do you know her?"

*So that's your name, you bastard.*

The assassin, Skyflake, struck again, aiming for Legacy's neck. She dodged the blow with ease, diving in to stick her dagger right in his wing. The blade slid off, only managing to shear feathers. The shaved blue plumes were carried away in the wind.

"It's nothing, Louisa, just a personal matter!" he yelled back, barely escaping a second strike at his wing. He retaliated with a jab of his dagger, connecting with Legacy's back and leaving a deep red line.

"Sonofabitch," she gasped, flight faltering as pain seared through her body. "It'll take more than that to off me, assassin!" she screeched as she struck back, blade slicing Skyflake's chest cleanly. Feathers burst from the strike. His wings missed a beat, and he dove to avoid being struck again.

As Legacy aimed to score his back, she noticed something odd. Whatever she just said, Louisa now looked a strange mix of terrified and furious. More than she had already, at least.

"Assassin? Skyflake, is there something you haven't told me?" the girl screeched.

*Oh, this is good*, Legacy thought with a grin as she wheeled around and landed on the branch, shoving the tip of her dagger against Lousia's white-feathered throat before she could scream. Skyflake froze midair, talons tense around the handle of his blade.

Legacy put a wing around the girl, a smile splitting her face. Her carefully positioned dagger kept Skyflake from moving any closer. One wrong move, and she'd score his lady's throat. She leaned in to speak to Louisa, though her eyes were fixed on Skyflake. "You heard that right; your little boyfriend here is an assassin. One of the New Moons, in fact. You know, the famous horrible evil ones. And if he moves one wingbeat closer, you'll suffer the same fate he's put countless others through. Makes you think, doesn't it?"

The words held no emotional weight, not to herself. Legacy didn't give a damn about who did or didn't murder others, and the ethics of it bored her, but it gave her powerful leverage to get her sweet revenge. Manipulation was just as powerful as brute force.

Skyflake balked, stuttering with fury. "Let go of her this instant! I swear, Louisa, I can explain this later." He fluttered frantically back and forth, visibly aching to lunge forward but too scared to risk his love's life.

Legacy grinned wider, turning her full attention to Louisa. "You know, his last victim was my best friend.

He killed her just a few miles from here. In cold blood. Slit her throat and tore out her heart right on the river shore." That was a three-quarter-lie. The location was sort of right, the method was entirely wrong, whether it was in cold blood was debatable, and the "best friend" part was complete bullshit. She couldn't stand Naom when she was alive, which made it all the more frustrating that she couldn't get her crumpled, mangled body out of her head.

Louisa bought it hook, line, and sinker, yellow eyes welling up with tears of shock. Legacy noticed that she had a string of pearls strung across both sides of her face, held up by her beak. If those were real, they might be valuable. "I can't believe this— you— anything! Skyflake. Is she telling the truth?" Louisa shook like a leaf, voice weak. She sounded desperate, like she was begging Skyflake to deny it. It made sense—who would want to be dating an assassin? If you yourself weren't also one, it seemed like it was more effort than it was worth to try and make things work.

Then again, she was a little biased. Whether she liked Naom or not, anybody who killed a Coyote earned her ire on principle.

Skyflake fiddled with his dagger, looking like his mind was screaming for him to rush forward and attack, regardless of the hostage Legacy held. Her blue eyes stayed locked on him in case of any sudden moves. She shifted her balance, the stinging wound on her back growing more painful by the second. There was an uncomfortable wet warmth where blood seeped out, trapped against her skin by her feathers.

"She's lying! I swear!" Skyflake paused, taking a breath. "I am an assassin. I was going to tell you myself. I promise. But I had no part in the murder of her so-called friend!" He pointed his dagger accusingly at Legacy, the tip red with blood. "She did that all herself; I'm just her cover-up." His words tumbled out oddly, sounds muddled, stumbling over each other until he was near-incomprehensible. He couldn't lie more obviously if he tried. "Louisa, please believe me."

Louisa said something back, sounding as though she were underwater. Legacy shook her head, readjusting her balance.

*Maybe he wasn't messing up his words,* Legacy thought as she found herself losing track of the conversation. A dizzy blackness crept into the corners of her vision.

*Maybe I'm just bleeding out because this damn assassin got in my way before I managed to drag my sorry ass home,* but she barely finished her thought before everything blurred, and she felt herself freefalling through the air while the world disappeared around her.

～☺✦ ✦ ☾ ✦ ✦☺～

Legacy jerked awake as something sharp jabbed into her back, right between her wings. She blinked blearily as she cleared the foggy remnants of sleep from her eyes. Her side, where she lay, was horrendously wet from the grass beneath. Soft light seeped in through the faraway tops of massive trees. Moss crept up every trunk and rock, and fungi nestled in the shadows of stumps.

*Still in the Shadow Forest, then.* That gave her a small measure of comfort.

Another jab between the wings. She winced. Memories of a wound on her back, and the squabble

51

that came with it, flooded back into her head piece by blurry piece.

"Quit poking me—hurts like a bitch," she said, though she wasn't sure to whom.

Wait, wait. She mentally backpedaled several steps. Why was some stranger touching her? And why was she letting it happen? She tried pathetically to pull herself up, but her body refused to cooperate.

Maybe she needed to start slower. She wiggled each claw, then her foot, then tried shifting her leg.

A soft, kind voice came from behind her, vaguely familiar. "Oh, thank Diyos you're alive. I was so worried."

Diyos? No one she knew worshipped that goddess. She jumped up and spun around, feeling like a nail was being driven through her spine as she did. Still, she stood strong, wings poised high, ready for another fight if need be.

Facing her, brow furrowed in annoyance, was Louisa. Her cheeks were still damp from her earlier tears. She reached forward to try and ease Legacy back down to the ground.

"Careful! Please, I just sewed that closed; I don't need you tearing it open again."

Legacy turned her head to look at her back, eyes going wide at the clean, stitched line running from one shoulder to the other, wrapping around her back and stretching down each wing. The work was impressively clean, though the thin threads looked like they struggled to hold together her brutally inflamed wound.

"What—no, why the fuck are you helping me?" Legacy swung her head back around. Her body was still sore, but more cooperative than it had been a second ago.

"Watch your mouth. You're just as bad as Skyflake." Louisa crouched beside a small leather pack, rummaging around within. Right, Skyflake, who was nowhere to be found while his apparent lover tended to the bird he'd tried to kill.

"Speak of the bastard—"

"Watch your mouth, I said, not even a second ago," Louisa interrupted, producing a worryingly large syringe from the pack. She then grabbed a small vial of deep-blue fluid, pouring it into the tool. "He's not around. I chased him off."

"Isn't he your lover?" Legacy took a step back, eyeing the syringe skeptically. "And you still didn't tell me why you're helping me out." Maybe this was an organ harvest, and Louisa was some kind of black-market dealer.

Louisa gestured at the soft ground, voice firm. "Sit."

Legacy sat. Then wondered why she did.

Louisa fiddled with the syringe more as she talked. "I'm helping you because I work as a healer of Diyos. It's my mission to never turn away an injured bird, no matter who they are. Skyflake may be my... partner, but I'm more than a little peeved with him today, so I sent him off." She raised the syringe.

Legacy stood back up, scrambling away. "Oh no, don't even think about sticking me with that. It's not even a normal color—looks like something off a poison toad." If she died, it wasn't going to be lying down and letting someone take her organs.

"Frog." Louisa corrected, not missing a beat.

"Keep that shit—"

"Watch your mouth."

"—away from me." Legacy backed up several paces, back pulsing in periodic bursts of agony.

"It's long past deadly. You'd be surprised the ingredients that go into most modern medicines." Louisa gestured at the squished moss patch. "Now sit and let me do this or die of that pretty little infection. Your choice."

Legacy relented, sitting down with a melodramatic huff. She didn't like this one bit, but the location of the wound meant an infection could cripple a wing, if not both of them. Worse than dead would be alive and unable to fly. If the wound were on a leg, it would hardly hold her back being her race spent most of their days in the sky. But a lame wing? That spelled disaster. For a thief, at least. Hard to steal from others by walking up to them, taking their stuff, then sauntering away.

She winced as a sharp, cold needle jabbed into her spine. "Damn, do you have to be this rough with everything?"

Louisa frowned, extracting the syringe delicately. "Do you have to complain about everything? Honestly. I could have let you bleed out."

"You just told me that you'd never turn away someone injured, so no, you couldn't." This time she held still as Louisa poked and prodded her wound. "You seriously didn't know your boyfriend was an assassin?" she asked, changing the subject.

"Ah… no. We only started courting recently, so I suppose he was waiting for a better time to break the news. I knew he was hiding something from me. I just assumed it was out of embarrassment, not the fact that he…" *Kills birds* went unsaid.

"Embarrassment?"

Louisa shrugged, looking down bashfully. "I, ah, assumed he worked as an escort, with how he dodged conversations about work and disappeared so often for jobs he'd never talk about." She gestured for Legacy to stand back up, replacing her tools in her medical pack. "I would have preferred it to an assassin."

"I can't imagine anyone wanting to pay to sleep with him, but to each their own." Legacy stood up, ruffled her feathers, and winced. "So are you breaking up with him, then? He's a real bastard even outside his work. If that's worth knowing."

"Hey, he's still my partner, so watch your tongue. Besides, I can tell you aren't quite clean yourself." Louisa swung her bag over her back, settled between her wings, and buckled it across her chest. "I only helped you because you were hurt. We aren't friends. I don't know you or owe you information."

*Damn, I should have been a little more tactful with that,* Legacy thought. Not that tact was her thing. Thievery required a broad range of talents and jobs, and no one thief was good at all of them. That's why guilds formed: to take advantage of each bird's individual strengths while making up for their pitfalls with their guild-mates. Legacy was good at sneaking, hiding, and disappearing into shadows, but she was terrible at charm. Once she opened her beak, things usually went to shit quickly afterward.

Rose Heart was the exact opposite, excelling in seduction and charm but falling short in the sneaking department. Ornamental feathers weren't easy to conceal. Misfire was interesting because he was bad at everything.

Why he was even part of the guild, Legacy had no clue. There was also Judgement, who never worked without Thistle at his side, which led her to wonder if he even did anything. Potentially he just shared credit for work he didn't do.

"Ah, I'm sorry…" Legacy tried to think of any redeeming qualities Skyflake might have. "Well I'm sure he has his… upsides, I guess. Like being good at murder." Louisa winced.

Legacy spread her wings, hissing quietly as her wound stretched. "Anyways, I should be off now. You've fixed me well enough, and I've got work of my own to handle." Flying was going to suck; there was no way to circumvent that, but she didn't want to spend too much time getting friendly with a stranger if she could help it. That, and her bag of fur was still on a branch somewhere in the trees, and every passing minute risked someone flying by and snagging it. Best to put up with the pain and retreat back to the den now, before she lost her hard-earned goods.

It made her think. The Coyotes had no real healer or doctor. She was on her own with this wound now. She'd better hope the stitches held until the wound healed, because she wasn't getting more of them.

# CHAPTER FOUR

# THE BOSS IS GONE

"Boss is gone," Fortune said.

"What?" Legacy replied, having just landed on the bridge that spanned the center of their den, the heavy bag of fur thumped down beside her. Several blood drops splattered at her feet.

"Boss is gone. Took a trip with his so-called right-wing man. No idea why or when he'll be back—"

"He left me in charge," Rose Heart said as she landed beside the two, a smug smile gracing her beak. She extended a slim, black-scaled leg palm up toward the ceiling. "So hand me the bag."

Legacy recoiled backward, voice taking a sharp turn from confused to furious. "Like hell I'll give them to you. Not until I figure out what's going on here." Rose Heart *probably* wouldn't scam her out of a job, but she could never be too careful.

The Boss being gone was no great shock. She'd heard him mention leaving before she took off on her own job, after all. The real surprise was that he took Cyrill with him and left Rose Heart in charge. Normally in situations like these, his co-leader, or right-wing man, or whatever Cyrill was supposed to be, stayed behind to manage the guild in his absence.

Granted, Cyrill was awful at the job. Every single time, he just holed himself up in his office and let the guild have rein of the place until Owl Wings came back. More injuries and general mishaps happened under his watch than at any other time. The Boss probably got sick of it and had the sense to choose someone different.

It was just a shame he'd chosen Rose Heart, of all birds. Even Judgement would do better, and he was just Cyrill with a drinking problem.

Rose Heart frowned, retracting her claw. "Need I explain anything that isn't already obvious? The Boss took a trip and left me in charge. He can't trust you buffoons to run this circus without an authority figure, and Cyrill hardly qualifies."

Legacy's neck feathers bristled. "Cut the pretentious talk. 'Need I explain' my ass. I'm asking *Fortune specifically* if we've got any new information outside of the obvious." She let out a deep breath, leaning her weight heavily on her less injured side. The flight back was a rough one, but at least the furs were untouched where she'd left them.

Fortune stepped in front of Rose Heart, her dark-gray feathers taking up most of Legacy's vision. The golden stars on her wings and tail glittered even in the dim cavern light. "Not a word. He said 'Cyrill and I are leaving. Listen to Rose Heart while I'm gone.' Then they took off into the sunset. Probably just wanted some alone time with his little lover—"

"They've got nothing going on," Rose Heart interrupted. "Not of a sexual nature, at least. You can't tell me Cyrill has ever been laid in his entire life and have me believe you."

"Just because he doesn't flirt and preen like you doesn't mean he's a virgin." Fortune held up one claw, making a circle that she slowly shoved a long primary feather through.

"Flirt and preen? The man barely talks. I've seen furniture with more personality," Rose Heart snapped.

"You're just mad he doesn't have to try as hard as you," Legacy added weakly. The blood loss had finally crept up on her as she stood on shaky legs.

"Whatever, just give me the bag," Rose Heart said, voice sour.

Legacy relented, passing the bag over with a soft grunt. "Just don't lose it. I bled for that shit." So much for a quick and easy job; she was going to feel this one for a while.

Rose Heart, bag in her grasp, took off with a smooth beat of her crimson wings, leaving the two birds alone again. Fortune squinted her yellow eyes at the long, hastily stitched wound spanning Legacy's back.

Now that the initial shock had worn off, it was stinging painfully and ached with every movement.

"What'd you get into?" Fortune said, reaching out to touch it gently, long golden talons brushing the swollen edges of the wound. Her voice was crass, but her face creased in worry.

Legacy recoiled at the touch. "Ran into one of the New Moons on my way here, hanging out with his little girlfriend. I stopped by, threw him around a little bit, and probably ruined his relationship, so I'd call it a success."

A bat fluttered by her head, squeaking all the while.

"No way you stitched that yourself," Fortune said, swatting the bat down and cracking its neck. Warm yellow flames engulfed it as it sat limp in her claws. The smell of hearty, roasted meat mixed with bitter burnt fur wafted into the air.

"What, no confidence in my medical abilities? Guess I can't blame you." Legacy rolled her shoulders, the skin stretching painfully in an almost cathartic way. "You gonna share that?" she said as she lunged for the bat. Fortune lifted it just over her head, between two long claws, out of Legacy's feeble reach. Tiny droplets of fresh blood bubbled out its nose, spattering the stone.

"You're dodging the question." Fortune stretched even taller, her impressive height easily holding the furry snack out of Legacy's grasp. Legacy swiped again in a vain attempt to score it, claws brushing empty air. Her back twinged painfully at the motion, stitches being pulled to their limits.

"If I answer, do I get the bat?"

Fortune nodded.

"It was Louisa. Now give me the bat." She let out a grunt of defiance as her friend held it impossibly higher. The savory, meaty smell was mouthwatering. Long jobs like tonight's always left her stomach an empty void, crying out for even the smallest morsel of food.

"Am I… supposed to know her?" Fortune said, bat lowering as her leg grew sore. Standing on one leg wasn't too much of a task and was very common while a bird used their free claw for tasks requiring more dexterity than wings could provide, but it could tire you out if you did it for more than a few minutes.

"Nope. Your question was answered." Legacy swiped again. "Bat. Now." There wasn't a real reason to keep this information sacred. Louisa was just some girl who happened to be dating a New Moon, but it still felt weird giving out too much on the encounter. The moment had been too… intimate, too close to speak so freely about.

That, and she didn't want to confess she got her ass kicked and had to be nursed back to health by the guy's girlfriend.

Fortune shrugged, tearing a wing off the bat with her beak before tossing the rest to Legacy, who caught it gleefully. "Fair enough, none of my business anyways. You should probably dodge work for a few days though. Looks pretty nasty even all stitched up. I'm shocked he got such a number on you." She circled Legacy, dark feathers shining in the torchlight.

"Yeah, I guess," Legacy muttered.

Fortune was a peculiar bird, a cocktail of several Camorthan races haphazardly mixed into one creature that looked a lot like none of them.

She stood frighteningly tall, towering over every bird in the guild like a feathered pillar. Her plumage was a deep, charcoal gray that absorbed more light than it reflected, dotted with the occasional gold feather here and there. Her wings and tail were a starscape, brilliant speckles of gold scattered across them like a living night sky. On her shoulders and neck were scales of a similar color, the mark of venompie blood. Her talons were long, curled, and ridged, a distinct winterpie trait. Yet her elemental ability? Yellow fire, proving that she had close firepie blood to top it all off. What race of firepie, specifically, was unknown, lost among the muddled and mixed traits she expressed across her body.

"I'll get him back for it," Fortune said. "Don't worry. Next time I see him, I'm dragging his bloody corpse alllll the way to the doorstep of his stupid guild. Let them know exactly what I think."

It sounded righteous and brave, a thief avenging her wounded partner in crime, but Legacy knew better. Fortune was well-known across the guild for her bloodthirsty tendencies, and she would always jump at the chance to… eliminate… anyone.

*No matter, at least she'd stopped asking questions*, Legacy thought as she dove off the bridge, wings barely holding her aloft as she flew to her room. It was one of the many open caves along the walls of their underground ravine. On a good day, she liked the height—it made it feel more private despite the lack of a door. But on a day like this, it was just extra work to try and lift herself to the entrance. She landed roughly, legs nearly giving out, and collapsed inside on the mound of furs that made up her bed.

# CHAPTER FIVE

# THE BOSS IS BACK

AFTER A WEEK OF LOUNGING around doing a whole lot of nothing, Legacy's wound was kind enough to ease up and stop hurting.

It wasn't a willing bed rest, but one enforced by Rose Heart. She'd refused to give Legacy a single job until she "looked less like she'd spent the night six feet under," much to Legacy's dismay. Now her wound looked mild and innocent, a flat pink scab nestled under the feathers of her wing. The appearance was the least of her worries. She was really just happy she couldn't feel that nagging ache clinging to her like a burr.

She stretched her wings wide over her head, the clean white feathers sliding against one another in perfect harmony. Far below the entrance to her room, the other Coyotes milled about in the cavern.

Judgement was perched on one of the many spires of stone, eyes closed and supposedly napping. It was the same thing he'd do every day when he wasn't eating, on a job, or otherwise occupied. Sometimes Legacy wondered if he was narcoleptic.

On the bridge, Rose Heart was standing with her back to Misfire. He looked like he was trying to hold a conversation, while she did everything in her power to ignore him.

The others were nowhere in sight, probably off on jobs or holed up in any of the rooms. For how dusty, unkempt, and dry it was, this cavern was generous with its space, and the Coyotes had more rooms than they knew what to do with. Almost half the caverns stayed empty, filled with cobwebs and bats until someone found a way to use them or until another thief moved in and needed a place to stay.

It'd been a while since that happened. Judgement was the newest, but his presence… hadn't added much to the guild, so he didn't count. He was pretty enough to be a statue—a spot of deep blue and white among the dusky oranges and browns of the den—and moved even less. Even now, she wondered what compelled Owl Wings to recruit him. Maybe desperation, or to add to the atmosphere.

Whatever, not something she needed to worry about. Owl Wings had his reasons. He always did.

Legacy jumped off the ledge, breathing a sigh of relief as her wings caught the air and easily drifted her down to the lowest part of the cavern.

The kitchen loomed before her. A sizable arch entrance that opened to the biggest cavern in the guild. It was littered with tables and stray dishes. At the center was a fire pit, currently unlit. Several shelves were pushed against the walls, stocked with more cobwebs than food. It was bare bones, but it got the job done. She strolled up to the shelves, lighting the fire pit with a small blast of blue flames on the way.

They were dusty and barren, save a few old herbs hanging on a string. Then she looked inside the cupboard, gingerly pushing aside empty glass jars to try and find anything but dust bunnies.

The last cupboard was her lucky one, a little cleaner than the rest and housing a few dried strips of meat. They looked painfully unseasoned and overcooked, but it was food.

She sat herself at one of the tables, muttered a small prayer to Darivan, and got to work on her meal. It tore effortlessly, despite its tough appearance. She could easily rip it into chunks small enough to swallow without gagging on the dry texture.

Keeping good meat for long in the warmer months was hard, so it was usually up to the Coyotes to hunt for their heartier meals. The unappetizing dried stuff was for anyone unlucky enough to be stuck inside, such was her case.

When she'd first joined, it wasn't like this. The shelves had an array of spices, and meat was treated with skillful techniques to preserve the flavor.

Now, she counted herself lucky even to find torched strips of mystery meat.

"The Boss is back!" a loud voice cried from the entryway. Legacy jolted as Misfire barged into the dining area, an orange bolt of painfully bright cheer. In his rush, he knocked his hip into a bowl and sent it clattering to the floor.

"Ah, oops, didn't mean to do that," he said.

Legacy huffed at him. As shoddy as the meal was, the peace and quiet had been nice. Now it was gone, a leaf on the wind, swept away by someone whose lack of ability made Judgement look good at his job.

"Come on, get up. Let's goooo," Misfire said as he jabbed an off-white claw at the exit. His pale blue eyes shone with energy.

"I'm eating. Tell him I said hi," Legacy said.

*So the Boss is back, big whoop. He may be the authority around here but giving him a king's welcome seems overkill.* She shoved down the last chunk of meat, feeling it catch on the sides of her throat as it went down.

Misfire's claw drooped, and he leaned over to pick up the bowl in his beak, voice muffled through the wood. "He… uh, he asked for all of us, actually. Seemed real serious about it too."

"All of us, huh? What's he got, a new heist for us?" Legacy said, a small hope rising in her chest. Maybe The Boss finally took her pleading to heart; maybe she'd finally get another shot at proving herself.

"Not quite. It's uh. It's… a…" Misfire set the bowl down, tapping his claws against it as he struggled to find his words. His forked blue tongue flickered out as he spoke, the color a sharp contrast to the deep brown-orange of his beak. "You know what? He'll probably explain it better than me, mostly because I don't actually know. Not a heist, though."

Misfire was average height for a venompie, with a perfectly average body. His feathers were the color of a faded orange, speckled with pale red scales so similar they almost blended in entirely. His wings and tail alternated shades of darker orange, tipped in the same off-white color that graced his stomach, secondary feathers, and a thin white line underneath his eyes.  He wore a faded, brown, hoodless cloak with a snake embroidered across its surface like it was constricting itself around him, held up by an onyx pendant at his chest.

He stood confidently, wings held out and chest puffed like he knew his way around.

He didn't.

"Alright, fine. I'll go, but this better be as important as you say or I'm kicking your ass," Legacy said. She swept the remaining crumbs of meat off the table and stood up.

He flinched and stayed several wingbeats behind her as they took off out the door. They weaved around a few stalactites as they flew to the bridge, a silence heavy with curiosity and confusion between them.

Misfire must have been telling the truth. On the bridge was not only Owl Wings, tapping his black claws impatiently, but Fortune and Judgement. Judgement couldn't be damned to abandon his midday nap for a meeting unless it was important, and Fortune would ditch even if it were. Both of them together sent a chill of anxiety up Legacy's spine.

*What the hell is going on?*

Legacy landed soundlessly, Misfire thudded down beside her, sending up a puff of dust. She sidled up to

Fortune, speaking in a low voice. "You know what's going on?"

"Not a clue," Fortune replied. "Owl Wings said he'd explain when everyone got here." The two looked over at him in tandem.

Owl Wings paced back and forth, with uncharacteristically high energy. On his side hung a worn leather bag, secured to him by a strap stretched across his chest and weighed down by something heavy. It thwacked into him with every step.

The faint sunlight trickling in from above cast a feeble shadow that moved back and forth alongside him.

Legacy looked around, tallying who was here so far. Herself, obviously, Misfire, Fortune, Judgement, and Owl Wings.

*Rose Heart,* she added as the slender firepie alighted on the bridge, a perplexed expression on her face.

They were missing Naom, Thistle, and Cyrill.

*Thistle and Cyrill,* she corrected.

The latter of whom was probably in the know already, since he'd left on the same trip.

It was unlikely he'd show up. Even if he hadn't gone along, he was the Boss's right-wing man, meaning he got inside information before a breath of it ever reached the Coyotes.

"Where the hell is Thistle?" Owl Wings spat, impatience grating his voice. Misfire flinched, though the words weren't directed at him. "I said everyone. That doesn't mean everyone except him."

Owl Wings wasn't famed for his patience, but this energy was excessive even by his standards. Whatever he had to tell them must be big, because he was nearly frothing at the mouth. She'd seen rabid animals more relaxed.

His pacing grew more insistent, a loud *tap tap tap* of his claws in her ear while she peeked over the bridge, seeing if she could spot Thistle.

No sign of him. The cavern, save the bridge, was still and empty.

Though empty was a generous term. The den was clean enough, but having so many inhabitants took its toll. Dusty rags were scattered on the ground far below, bits of bone and animal parts that couldn't be eaten peeked out from small crevices, and the shining disks of fake coins littered every pool of stagnant water.

Real coins, called scelons were made of gold or silver. While those other ones made a suitable imitation, they'd never get by any vendor worth their salt. Good for nothing but empty wishes—or flicking them at Judgement.

Even now, Judgement stood stone still, only moving when Owl Wings bumped into him and unceremoniously shouldered him aside.

The fraud coins used to work, hence the massive amount of them all over the floor, but new technology was a bane to thieves. *Stupid fancy mages and their stupid fancy gadgets.* Nowadays, just about anyone who sold anything invested in a bit of jewelry or an article of clothing that'd alert them to a fake. Even Owl Wings supposedly had one. It was one of his four earrings, not that Legacy knew which one.

He'd never actually told anyone; the Coyotes just found out when Fortune tried to pay her guild due with fakes and got subsequently banned from every job for a month.

Owl Wings huffed as a scrawny gray-purple figure slapped down onto the bridge, looking like he'd just woken up from the dead.

Owl Wings whirled on him immediately. "About damn time. When I say I want all of you here, I want all of you here *now*. Not in five minutes, not in an hour, *now*."

Thistle averted his green eyes, hunched on the very brink of the bridge like he was going to take off any second. Owl Wings shot him a fierce glare before shedding the bag he'd been wearing, carefully drawing out a massive book while he spoke.

"Now, Coyotes, I have something here that could, no, will change everything." He paused, either catching his breath or for dramatic flair.

"Fuckin' spill it, then," Fortune whispered. Legacy prodded her in the side.

If Owl Wings heard, he didn't acknowledge it. "No more fighting rats for stray gutter coins, no more shitty, unseasoned food, and no more getting my ass chewed out by Cottonmouth for having a guild that performs worse than a gaggle of fucking geese." He laid the book down in front of himself. The pages were haphazardly glued in, all sticking out at painfully different lengths.

The Coyotes, save Thistle, who hung back with a skeptical glare, crept forward to get a closer look.

It didn't look particularly special. It was a poorly bound black leather book. A stylized golden sun graced the cover.

"This," he said, laying a claw on the cover, "is a calling from the Dreamseers."

Misfire sneezed, sheepishly covering his beak when Owl Wings glanced his way.

*I think I might still be loopy from the blood loss*, Legacy thought as she tried to mentally pick up what he was putting down, only for it to slip and slide out of her grasp and splat on the floor.

The Dreamseers were the strangest and most powerful kingdom of Camorthes. Not powerful in military might or monetary influence, but in sheer respect. No bird with a working head on their shoulders would refuse what they told you to do. They existed to keep Camorthes together. Though individual kingdoms may have strained relationships, they ensured it would never progress to a threat to the world as a whole. They could see the future, or bits of it at least, and use that knowledge to act as an organization of living guardian angels.

They never explained why they did things, if the things they did were even public enough to be noticed, but what in Darivan's name did they want with a bunch of thieves?

"I… beg your pardon?" Rose Heart said, strained, like she was afraid to question what was happening.

"The Dreamseers called me, in regards to all of you, to carry out a sort of…" Owl Wings' voice trailed off, like he couldn't find the right term. "… job they have."

Thistle huffed, doing his best to look disinterested, but Legacy saw his eyes dart to the book.

Owl Wings kept his speech flowing, rambling off more before anyone else could get a word in. "Now, I'm not gonna pretend to care about their righteous cause or reason for doing this, or whatever, because I don't.

What I care about is the reward they're gonna give us for doing it."

Rose Heart, along with most of the guild, just looked more confused. Except Judgement, who was looking at the floor, and Thistle, who looked either nervous or furious. It was hard to tell with him sometimes. The massive eye bags and incredibly messy feathers made him hard to read. It also made him permanently look like he was recovering from an unfortunate lightning strike.

"I'll explain what we're doing as we go along," Owl Wings said. "Just know it's going to involve a lot of traveling, a lot of danger, and a better life for the lot of us."

Misfire pushed in closer, sky-blue eyes wide.

Legacy tried to speak, choked on a frog in her throat, then pulled herself together. "I'll follow you through anything, Boss. I really will," she forced out. "I just have a question. I mean, I have a lot, but this one seems more important."

"I'm sure you do. I'll answer what I can," Owl Wings answered gruffly as he flipped through pages of the book, touching it with unusual gentleness. The pages moved too fast for Legacy to see what the scribbles depicted.

He stopped on one page: a curious drawing of a crescent moon surrounded by four stars in a diamond pattern. It was the same pattern the Dreamseers used on their flag.

It stood out in how it was painted in the deliberate strokes of someone taking their time to get it right, unlike the panicked scrawls that filled the rest of the book.

"Why us?" Legacy asked. "A bunch of criminals, I mean. Couldn't they find some young bastard with a sword to do it?" There was no shortage of young bastards with swords in Camorthes. Legacy read a lot of books, and those were usually the prophecy-fulfilling types.

"You know how the Dreamseers work. They don't like attention. They don't like to be seen. It's in their best interest that as few birds learn of this as possible." He tapped the book. Legacy tried to peer at the words scribbled underneath the drawing but couldn't quite make them out from where she stood. It didn't help having Misfire's stupid orange head blocking her sight.

Owl Wings continued, looking not just at Legacy, but at all the Coyotes. "This is only a job that we, who work from the shadows and have names known to no one, can do."

Thistle scoffed as he shoved past the other thieves, purple and gray feathers bristling in fury. More bristled than they already were, at least. "And I'm supposed to just roll over and go along with this? I joined this guild to steal, not run around fulfilling prophecies and doing chores for the ones who think they're too high and mighty for it." The long muffs of his legs splayed across the floor, claws tensed underneath. "What are we doing, and why are we doing it?"

Legacy took a few steps back, the other Coyotes following suit.

"I already told you why," Owl Wings said, standing tall, his pale form looming over Thistle. They were the same race, both Burning Talons firepies, but Owl Wings was older, bigger, and more muscled. He kept one claw protectively over the book. "We're doing their chores because they're gonna pay us more than any single one of you has ever earned in your lifetime. Don't you get it? We'll be richer than rich."

Thistle took another step, but it looked like he was shaking. "And you think—"

"Now," Owl Wings said, voice hardening as he locked each of the Coyotes in a cold stare, "this is the deal. If you want to complain and stomp your feet and whine about it, I couldn't care less, but if you refuse to take part in this"—he jabbed a claw at the book—"you can leave, or I will force you. This is a billion-in-one chance; I won't have it thrown away by someone too childish to suck it up for a few odd jobs."

"You still didn't tell us what we're doing," Misfire interrupted.

Legacy had a feeling this was more than a few odd jobs. It sounded risky, but she wouldn't be here if she didn't want to take risks. Her previous anxiety swelled into excitement, already turning over ideas of what she'd do with the wealth.

"What he said— you dodged the question." Thistle said.

"It does seem… strange." Judgement's voice was so soft it was muddled underneath the others.

"Give him a damn minute," Legacy said, fixing a glare on Thistle. The Boss would explain, but only if they could shut up and let him talk.

"By Darivan, one at a time. Wait until I'm done talking before you all keep spouting shit at me, please." Owl Wings rubbed his forehead, sighing. The dark mask of feathers on his face made his disappointed expression even darker.

Thistle huffed, a spark of purple fire puffing out his nose as he whipped around. "Fine, I'll go along with this little game. But it's only because I've got nowhere better to go." He dove off the bridge, taking flight to his room and leaving the rest of the Coyotes in their dumbfounded silence.

Dumbfounded at the situation, that was. Thistle's outburst was nothing new. He'd had it out for the Boss since day one, and no one really knew why. If he was hoping to ever be a Master Thief himself, he was going about it in the worst way possible.

Judgement took off, landing back on his spire a ways away from the bridge.

Owl Wings packed up the book, sliding it into his bag. "If I knew that's all it took to shut you lot up, I'd have prophecies by the day." He laughed to himself.

"One more question," Legacy said. "Why us? I mean, you said why already. It's because we're sneaky and behind the scenes and all that, but why the Coyotes specifically? Did we not just fail a massive heist?" *That was my fault, but we don't need to get into that.*

"They didn't choose us specifically," Owl Wings said. "They told Cottonmouth to choose any of the guilds, so she picked the most expendable one."

"Oh." Legacy deflated a little at that. She'd hoped that maybe where the other thieves didn't see her potential, the Dreamseers had.

"Makes sense, I guess," Misfire mumbled.

"It does not. Have some confidence, man," Fortune shot back at him.

"I'm pulling your leg," Owl Wings said. "The gold is the real reason. Piles of wealth breed laziness, and that's what the Foxes and Jaguars are sitting on. They might be able to do this with some efficiency, unlike you guys, but they have so much gold sitting around, why would they? We're broke and desperate, so Cottonmouth knows we won't flake, plain as that."

"Ah," Legacy said, not feeling any better with that explanation.

"So you're saying we're being bought off?" Rose Heart added, unimpressed.

"Precisely! You get it." Owl Wings laughed again. "We're broke as hell, and if dragging our sorry asses in circles around Camorthes is what it takes to get back on our feet, that's what we're gonna do."

# CHAPTER SIX

# VICTOR SER VYNN

S EVERAL DAYS OF SILENCE FOLLOWED after the strange announcement. Not complete silence from everyone, that wouldn't happen unless they all collectively keeled over dead, but from Owl Wings, who kept stringing the Coyotes along, saying "I'll explain more soon."

Just as the excuses started to wear on the guild's patience, change finally happened.

Change that meant Legacy now stood at the top of a worn stone staircase in the damp darkness of the Shadow Forest. Beside her were the others, the entire guild, excluding Cyrill.

In front of her, imposing stone walls loomed over the forested hillside. A peaked and pointed roof caught rays of rising sunlight as it reached toward the sky far above her head. Lesser birds—crows, jackdaws, sparrows, and the like—fluttered about bushes nestled at the foot of the structure, pecking, singing, and doing all the manner of things birds did when they didn't have to worry themselves silly over politics and prophecies.

It was a magician's castle, in all its wondrous, ethereal glory, resting before the thieves as if to mock them for what they could never have.

Thieves didn't get the luxury of castles; they got dens and caverns, damp holes in the ground where guards would never think, or dare, to poke into, and common folk knew well enough to stay away from. They got cisterns rife with dirty animals. On a good day, Legacy was grateful the Coyotes got a slightly dusty cave instead of a sewer.

But standing before this castle, it was hard to tamp down her jealousy.

*One day I'll be a Master Thief, top dog of the lower dregs of society, and I'll have a pretty magical mansion to sleep in while my underlings do the fieldwork*, she thought as she craned her neck to take in the massive structure. Silvery clouds drifted through the sky, reflected in the tall windows.

Beside her, Fortune and Rose Heart chatted quietly, Thistle paced back and forth, and Judgement stood silent and still.

Orbs of faint, peaceful light bobbed around towers, casting a soft glow on night-blackened stone. Stars pinpricked the sky far above, fading by the minute as the sun rose.

In truth, Master Thief or not, she'd never get a home quite of this scale. That needed magic a bird had to be hatched with, something bred through careful lineages of magicians to ensure they had generations of power, growing greater by the decade.

Money could buy a lot of things, but that wasn't one of them.

And this was not just any magician's castle. It was Victor Ser Vynn's castle. *The archmage.* The most powerful magician on the surface of Camorthes—there were likely a few rivals alive in mysterious hell dimensions and otherworlds, but no one ever came back from those. There were rumors he could do just about anything, should he desire it.

That in itself was nerve-racking enough, but even more was that no one really knew what those desires were or what moral compass he followed.

Growing up, she'd heard plenty about him from her foster mother, Vinmara, who'd frequently expressed annoyance that he took no apprentices and seemed content to have no children, stunting his impressive magical line right at its most powerful.

It was an odd sentiment from Vinmara given that she wasn't even from his family. She was hatched from the Hir Lanas, while Victor was a Ser Vynn. Magician families were at constant odds when it came to being the archmage, each family hoping their clutch of eggs would bear one more powerful than the current. Encouraging each other to succeed was unusual.

Perhaps that was it, though. Bloodlines. Being a mother to the next archmage would be life-changing, and Legacy heard Victor was quite handsome. A shame Vinmara died before she ever won his heart, if that's what she'd been after.

Still, none of that explained why a gaggle of thieves was at his door, huddled together on his ornate porch.

"I'd be willing to bet he has his fancy claws in all sorts of politics; is that why we're here?" Legacy asked, turning to Owl Wings. He stood, unmoving, at the vast doorway. It stretched several wing-lengths over even the tallest bird's head. She wondered why he didn't knock.

He tipped his head in her direction, eyes still fixed on the door. "Eh? Not a bad thought, but no, we're here for… something else. You'll know when we talk to him."

Legacy huffed, craning her neck even farther to look at the windows staring out every wall, reflecting the rising sun with soft golden streaks cast across their surface and reflecting onto the tops of shadowed trees.

The door opened slowly, but the pitched creak broke the silence so startlingly she jumped.

A man stood on the other side. He was tall, endlessly tall. He had legs like slim pillars that held up a well-formed body, with a small, angular head atop a slender neck. His white feathers, cleaned to the point of shining, were only broken up by the occasional stray patch of delicate heather plumage.

A warm grin split his dark purple beak. "Hello, hellooo, my dearest Coyotes." He spoke in a deeply accented voice, words rolling off his tongue like marbles. "I take it you're here for the enchanted gear your boss so generously paid me for?"

Owl Wings grimaced.

*Generous?*

"Aren't we broke?" Misfire said.

"The hell did you get that kind of money from?" Fortune spat.

"Ugh, and I've been eating unseasoned chunks of stale chicken? You could have put some of this toward food," Rose Heart added.

Victor gave a smile to the group as Owl Wings turned around, voice strong in his explanation. "We are broke. If you want to say it like that." He glared daggers at Misfire. "I had to dip into the emergency stores for spare coin, but I assure you, this will be *well* worth it." He shook his head. "I've seen you bastards try to pull off a heist, and it's not happening without magical intervention." He patted Victor, who didn't drop his smile, on the shoulder. "Now, I got this pretty little magician here to enchant us some gear, as he said. I'll let him take over for now."

"Pretty?" Legacy whispered questioningly to herself. He looked average at best, though maybe the rumors and hearsay just hyped him up too much. Victor's smile twitched down.

*Oh shit, he heard that.*

He locked eyes with her for a brief moment, grinning less in an "I'm happy to be here and can't wait to let a bunch of criminals into my home" way, and more of an "I know more than you think" way.

It was over in an instant, as his features softened into something more genuine.

"Come in, after me, all of you." He gestured at the guild, who followed after him with varying degrees of hesitancy. Legacy and Rose Heart followed Owl Wings, close and obedient. Misfire trotted after, eyeing Victor warily. Fortune hung back but reluctantly went in.

Thistle stayed planted as though glued to the ground, feathers bristling. Judgement grabbed the corner of his green cloak, tugging him along.

Inside, the massive living space sucked up any words Legacy might have had. Engraved marble pillars held up the roof far above their heads, set in a floor that shined beyond anything a normal deep clean could accomplish. Slim vases filled with delicate, rare flowers perched on nearly every table, soft petals damp despite the dry air of the room. Windows taller than any living creature stretched high up along the walls, carved with colorful stained glass images that told stories of birds and magic and the like, lighting up the marble and stone interior with a prismatic rainbow.

A grand staircase stood as the centerpiece, one large stair splitting off two ways at the top, then four, then six, connecting to a series of doors and walkways far above that led to Darivan-knows-where. It looked less like a home and more like a miniature city.

Soft spheres of light hovered around the room, gathering above the thieves to illuminate their path as the Coyotes were guided up the endless staircase. They warily trod after Victor as he led them up several flights of floating stairs. He stopped at a wooden blue door connected to no wall.

"Is this safe? Like, is this gonna trap me in some alternate dimension?" Thistle said, backing away from the door until his back talon hung off the top stair. His unkempt feathers betrayed his trembling.

"Shut the hell up, Thistle. We've been through a lot sketchier, with a lot less reward to boot," Legacy shot back, accidentally bumping into Misfire. She'd grown up around magicians. They did weird shit like this all the time, and sometimes it was better to just go with it than to question every little thing.

It was all for show, a display to flaunt their power when other magicians visited.

Not to mention, she was near vibrating with curiosity and had no patience for Thistle's skepticism. The top of this staircase was also unpleasantly crowded. The sooner they got inside that mystery room, the better. Anything to get Rose Heart's tail out of her face.

Victor coughed smoothly, drawing the attention back his way. "I kept them in here to ensure they wouldn't get stolen; one must be careful when dealing with your type. I assure you, this room is safe." He winked at Owl Wings.

It was then she noticed something curious about his face. His eyes specifically.

One, the right eye, was a delicate shade of winter-leaf green, pale with the typical ice-blood ring around the pupil. His other was lemon yellow with the same ring. *I wonder if he enchanted them to do that or if he was born that way.* She'd never seen a bird with two different eyes before. It was such a small but fascinating detail.

The door opened, and the thieves poured inside in a messy line. Save Thistle, who hung back until Judgement whispered something in his ear, prompting him to join the rest.

The room was… unexpectedly plain. Stone walls, stone floor, and it wasn't more than twenty wing-lengths long in either direction. A lack of windows meant the only light source was two glowing orbs floating playfully above a single, long, mahogany table in the center of the space.

On the table rested a heap of… things. A dagger poking out the corner of a cloak, a small slip of black cloth that would barely cover a beak, a longsword, a floral painted vase, and more, huddled in a messy, haphazard pile. It didn't look like junk, but it also didn't look like it had any coherent theme.

Legacy eyed the pile, tensing up to move quickly when she was given the word. She'd hate to miss out on something good just for being slow.

Victor gestured at the pile with a swooping wing, pale purple primary feathers making a small *whoosh*. "Go on, Coyotes! Take your pick. All of it's enchanted, and there's quite a lot to choose from." He glanced at Misfire, who was reaching to put the cloth over his face. "Ahh, don't put anything on yet, or swing the blades around. Just think, let the item choose you. Take your time with it."

Legacy darted over and ran a talon along the table's edge. Her heart raced, telling her to grab something now, quick, before the other Coyotes got the good stuff, but her brain held her back. It told her this was a chance she'd never get again. *I have to make it count.*

When she was younger, she'd had all manner of enchanted objects to play with. Some actual toys, some weapons, some seemingly random garbage enchanted for testing purposes, but ever since leaving Vinmara's she hadn't had a chance to use them again. Magicians could be stingy with their things. Acquiring them was nearly impossible without connections or a steep fee.

A strange sensation came over her, a darkening of the room around, a brightening of the table. It was subtle enough that she couldn't tell if it was in her head or a result of the light orbs fluctuating. Her claws twitched toward one object, brighter than the rest despite being deep-brown cloth. A cloak, identical to the one she wore on most of her jobs, to the one she was wearing *now*, scuffed silver buckle and all. The other thieves were talking, but they sounded muffled as she reached for the cloak.

She halted as she felt a pressure on the back of her neck, the warm touch of another bird fiddling with the buckle that held her current cloak up. The ever-present, comforting weight of it slipped down her shoulders, off her body, pulled away by graceful claws. "You don't need this anymore…" a voice whispered next to her ear. She shivered.

Then it was gone, the voice, the warmth, her cloak. She reached for the new one, beckoning her from the table. It looked the same, but it felt worlds different. The fabric wasn't hastily stitched over-sunned stiffness, but soft supple silk that sat in her claws weightlessly.

Her feathers rippled as a shudder ran through her body, washing away the strange sensation and leaving her clearheaded again.

*What the hell was that?*

She looked at the others, nosily peeking at what they'd grabbed. Fortune, Thistle, and Rose Heart all held daggers. Fortune had an exact replica of her usual dagger. In her case, it was even more noticeable, having engraved the original with "Killer" across the crooked steel. The same word was scrawled in her messy penmanship on the new one.

Misfire, like herself, chose a cloak. Judgement held the tiny slip of black fabric Legacy had noticed earlier. The longsword, and a few other items, remained untouched. Not quite right for the work of thieves.

Not that Judgement's choice was. *All the weapons and cloaks available, and you chose a rag.* Even possessed by the curious, mind-bending will she just endured, she was sure she'd be able to resist grabbing something that stupid.

*His loss.*

Owl Wings held nothing. Either an item for himself was a stretch too far in their funds or he'd got something back when he paid Victor to do this. Maybe a new earring. He had four now, and Legacy was fairly confident he'd always had four, but it's not something she paid much attention to.

*I'd look damn good with an earring or two.* The problem lying there was the metal: that's all it could take to botch a good job, a lone glint in the depths of shadows. Even the buckles on her cloak were scuffed to prevent such shining. She could scuff earrings if she got them, but then they'd look dull, and there'd be no point in wearing them at all.

Owl Wings only had his earrings because he was technically retired. He bossed the Coyotes around, told them what to do, where to go, and planned their biggest heists, but he rarely went out in the field. "Bones are too creaky. They'll hear me coming a mile away," is what he said when she'd asked why.

"Lovely choices, everyone! Grand, lovely choices," Victor said, as if his magic didn't influence those very choices. "Now, you all have a long journey ahead, so I'll graciously invite you to stay a night."

He swung open the door, long tail swooshing along the ground. "Follow me, and I'll guide you to your rooms."

"All I ask in return is that you stay put, no wandering about. Magic is finicky and all," he said, airy laughter echoing through his mansion.

⁕ ✦ ✦ ☾ ✦ ✦ ⁕

Legacy woke from the best sleep of her entire life with a long, dramatically drawn-out, beak-stretching yawn. The nests, fashioned from the finest blankets she'd ever had the luxury of touching, hugged tight to her body like a warm embrace. Even Vinmara's hadn't been quite that good. The temperature was perfect—not too hot, not too cold, not humid or dry. Part of her wanted to stay here forever.

The other part of her was humming with nerves. Now that she held her enchanted cloak, she felt the reality of the prophecy, the journey ahead, all of it boiling underneath the surface until she wanted nothing more than to bolt on ahead to their first trial.

It was anxiety, but of the weirdly motivating kind. The kind that made a bird excel at whatever was ahead rather than shrivel up in fear. She ran a claw over the cloak, feeling the supple fabric on the sensitive pads of her palm.

"It'll turn you invisible; not a bird alive can see you, but only when the hood is up," Victor had explained on last night's walk to their room. "That way, you don't have to struggle in and out of it every time you want to be seen, or likewise." She tried to overhear what he said when he explained to the others what their items did, but he was good at keeping his voice just low enough that she couldn't catch it.

She stood up, heart beating with anticipation. She wouldn't claim to be an early bird, but when she woke up with a task at hand, she was well and thoroughly awake the moment her eyes peeled open.

It's not that she wanted to do this inane prophecy but right now, things were moving at a snail's pace. The sooner she got this over with, the sooner their lives went back to normal (and the sooner she'd be swimming in scelons).

That, and maybe, just maybe, she could use this as a chance to redeem herself for the mistake that was her last heist. If she could pull this off, the Boss would be over the moon.

She looked around, peering to see if anyone else was awake, but they all seemed to be contently snoozing.

Except for Thistle, who she almost missed for how unmoving he was, green eyes bright and alert from where his head was half tucked under a wing.

It struck her then that she'd never actually seen him asleep, or even close to it. He was always so jittery it was hard to imagine.

It was also odd seeing the Coyotes all sleeping together without Naom among them. She felt a pang of emptiness and looked to the side. The two were never friends. In fact, the two argued more than talked and barely saw eye-to-eye on anything, but that didn't mean Legacy wanted her dead.

She'd likely never even gotten a burial. The Golden Heart's officers probably just scraped her flattened corpse off the road and threw it to the dogs.

The air stirred as Owl Wings walked in, having slept in a different room than his guild. Above him floated several glowing orbs, lighting up the peacefully dark room and rousing the rest of the gang. Thistle stayed stone still, Judgement's eyes opened but the rest of him stayed put, Misfire yawned in an overexaggerated manner, and Rose Heart stretched, rolling her shoulders gracefully. Fortune stayed asleep.

"The plan for today," Owl Wings started, not bothering to open with a *good morning*, "is to decide who's coming along for our first mission."

"You haven't even told us where we're going," Misfire said blearily, stretching one leg, then the other. He glanced at Rose Heart, and his face fell when she didn't even look his way.

"Or what we're doing," Rose Heart added, preening her long, flowing tail. "I'm still not completely sure what being part of this prophecy means. I mean I get the gist, but the gist is hardly enough."

"Ahh… right…" Owl Wings cleared his throat. "The short and sweet version is we get to run our asses around Camorthes, fixing all the kingdom's problems."

"All of them?" Misfire asked. "They, uh, have a lot."

"No, not literally every problem, you dunce. I just mean the large, potentially world-ending, war-starting ones. Anything that could escalate to a total kingdom collapse."

"Total collapse? Sounds fun," Fortune said, finally rousing. It was likely she'd been awake for a while and only feigned sleep to be left alone.

Owl Wings sighed so deep it sucked the air into his lungs and left the room a little bit colder. "Once one kingdom falls, it's over. Each one is dealing with issues that seem trivial now, but can and will escalate to greater perils until… until one cracks under the pressure. That's what will set off the end of the world, supposedly."

"It's basically a checklist, if that helps. The Dreamseers already tipped me off to where to start and dropped a few hints about what to look for," he continued.

He reached into the bag strapped to his waist, pulling out the book. "As I said, here, our King Omnipresence has written the prophesied end of the world. Smaller signs are already piling up, but he claims it can be avoidable if we can avert some of the key turning points."

"The hell you mean 'as I said'? You never said any of that," Fortune said under her breath.

He picked up the book again, shut it, and shoved it back in the bag. "Supposedly, the largest avertable sign is the total collapse of any of the seven kingdoms. Once that happens, very little can be done to turn back."

"I wouldn't mind if the Sunlit Clouds ran into the ground, personally," Rose Heart said, still preening herself. It was starting to get excessive.

"Hey, I ain't done anything to deserve that," Misfire replied, hurt.

"Now listen," Owl Wings continued, eyes locked on the Coyotes and their skeptical expressions, "I don't know how accurate the end of the world part is. And you know what? I don't give a damn. What matters is that if we pull this off, we're gonna be the richest thieves this world has ever seen; *that's* what I care about. King Omnipresence has more wealth than he could dream to use, and nothing is better than being paid by a man with more gold than he knows what to do with."

One of the light orbs flitted up to his face, and he swatted it away with force. "Our first trial is the Golden Hearts

Kingdom. I don't have a damn clue what their problem is, but it's the closest kingdom to us, so we'll start there."

"Aren't we closer to the Long Shadows?" Thistle piped up, eyes narrowed. He did have a point, given the mansion they stood in now was right inside the border of the Long Shadows territory.

"The closest kingdom I want to go to," Owl Wings corrected. "The Long Shadows is… finicky, in many regards. Not a good starting point," is what he said. But Legacy heard *it's a lot harder to fix, and you're probably going to fail and get horribly demoralized for the rest of the journey if we start there.*

She could be wrong, maybe there was a different reason, but that seemed like the most likely one. She'd grown up there after all, and knew its problems intimately.

"Now," Owl Wings said, "the journey is our main priority until we sort this bullshit out, but I can't just abandon the guild either. Some of you gotta stay behind, do some normal work, make sure no one breaks in and all that. Or just sit on your ass because you think I won't notice." He glared at the Coyotes sternly. Misfire stretched out a tan leg again, "accidentally" poking it into Rose Heart. She pecked him, and he recoiled.

"Legacy, Rose Heart, and… I suppose we don't need more than that. Two should be fine. That way, if this is some fucked-up trap, I don't lose all of you at once."

*Excuse me?* Legacy stood up, stiff legged. "What about Fortune? She and I work well together." The two were more distant as of late, but they'd worked together before, and Legacy could at least tolerate her. Hell, she'd even take Judgement over Rose Heart.

"Fortune has a snake's tongue and scales on her back. She may not be a pure venom-blood, but she looks like one, and that's enough to get on the Golden Hearts bad side."

*Right, they hate venompies.* It was all over a stupid dispute regarding Dovetail Island, a lovely spot of land floating in the West Cirrus Ocean, planted between Wyrd Island, the desert, and the Golden Hearts Plains.

"You two are my top thieves, not to mention we have our friends, the Foxes, in the area. If things get hairy, we can borrow a couple of them for a time."

*And a price.*

It didn't sit right with Legacy how freely Owl Wings was tossing their funds around. Even if this prophecy had a chance at making them rich, he was diving headfirst very eagerly into something none of them quite understood. What if none of these riches came to pass and they ended up more broke than before? The Dreamseers could see the future, sure, but it was susceptible to constant change. That's why there needed to be a whole kingdom of them to keep watch over it. It felt like a risky gamble for a group that could hardly do the bare minimum.

No, she had to trust in the Boss.

The guild was everything to him, to all of them; he had to have a good reason to take such a risk. He was older, wiser, and she had to trust he knew what he was doing.

"Rose Heart and me it is, then," she said begrudgingly.

Owl Wings gave a small smile at that, which almost soothed her anger at her unpleasant companionship.

*Almost,* she thought as Rose Heart flashed her a venomed glare.

# CHAPTER SEVEN

# A QUIET JOURNEY

THE TRIP WAS SO UNEVENTFUL it was frightening.

Where birds often spoke of wild animals, hostile border guards, or hunters opposed to other races in their land, not one came by to interrupt the two thieves in their journey. Not a single territorial Golden Hearts 'pie or hungry gryphon on the prowl. Something about it felt eerie.

Actually, one thing did stand out: the lack of anything. Not just a lack of adversaries, but a lack of stray jackalopes hopping about, and a lack of perytons daintily hopping through wheatgrass fields. Food was scarce, as though any edible creature for miles had been plucked from their grazing grounds and whooshed away, never to be seen again.

Luckily enough, the girls were able to scrounge up a few scrawny mice and rabbits, but it was the kind of meal that left someone wanting rather than sustained.

Now, under the cool moonlight, nestled in the rolls of endless fields, Legacy and Rose Heart camped. They were planted just near enough they could see the looming stone walls of Kalin, but not so close anyone would bother them about it.

Endless waves of golden spring grass flowed softly in the breeze, dotted with purple heather and spots of yellow dandelions.

It was a scenic view if you weren't stuck in a soggy ditch by a rippling creek. When you got up close and personal with the view, there were a lot more bugs and a lot more mud puddles hidden under the golden fronds than you might expect.

Legacy wasn't happy with the plan, if you could even call it a plan, but the Coyote duo didn't have much of a choice. The journey from Victor's mansion to here was a long and arduous one, even as uninterrupted as it was. Neither had the impressive wingspan of a Golden Hearts 'pie, and twelve hours of flying, with the occasional stop to nab a scrawny animal for lunch in between, was grueling. It left the duo looking haggard, worn, and somehow more pissed at each other than they'd been at the start of their journey.

Tense and travel-worn was not the best first impression they could make coming into Kalin, and a quick way to get profiled as criminals before they'd even done anything. So now the plan was to sleep in a dingy ditch and recuperate before setting foot in the city.

Not that Kalin was *that* prestigious. It was a pretty normal place. It was also the capital of the Golden Hearts' kingdom, but outside that title, it wasn't anything to sneeze at. Birds often called it the Ashen City.

Given four of the seven kingdoms were inhabited by firepies, each filled with an array of cities, it struck her as strange only this one got such a nickname.

Just one of those things someone said offhandedly that stuck, she supposed. Or maybe it had historical context, but kingdom history wasn't her forte. She scoffed to herself, turning her attention to the creek in front of where she stood.

Her reflection in the pool stared back at her, marred by glittering ripples and stones just beneath the surface of the shallow water.

She flipped her cloak hood up; the reflection shuddered, blurred, then was gone. The moon stood, alone and pale, in her wake.

She flipped the hood down. Her own blue eyes shone up to greet her from below her feet.

She flipped her hood up. Her image shuddered, but a bird still stood reflected in the water. This one was taller, lankier, with funny growths on her head, and standing a few wing-lengths back.

"Are you done? We have places to be," Rose Heart snapped.

Legacy guiltily slid the hood back down, face rippling back into view. "Yeah, yeah, we do, but you can't tell me you haven't been playing around with your knife."

Rose Heart shrugged, not confirming nor denying, which was a confirmation in and of itself.

"Why do they call it the Ashen City, anyways?" Legacy said, walking over to root through her bag. It sat in a heap beside the patch of squashed grass where she'd be sleeping tonight.

"I thought you read books, darling. 'Kalin' means ash," Rose Heart quipped, sliding her dagger out of its sheath and holding it up in the moonlight, eyes trained on its sharp, rose-pink edge.

"I read fun books, not weird cryptic shit in other languages." Legacy didn't know the translation of it until now, but she did know that Kalin was one of those old Ezelan words. A language that, though lost long to time crept into the names of birds and cities and the like.

"You probably just look at the pictures," Rose Heart said, shoving her dagger back in its sheath and unbuckling her travel pack. "Whatever, I'm going to sleep. It'll make tomorrow come sooner."

*She has a point there, I guess.*

Legacy rolled onto the grass, feeling her back chill against the damp sprigs. High above, the stars glittered against the endless night, peppered between soft clouds. The moon shone pale, watching over the world below.

She stared until the stars began to blur, and her eyes drooped closed. Beneath the sky, just a small red dot in an endless field of wheat gold and sage green, she sank into a restful slumber.

The next day, the girls, woken by the bright sun rays, packed their things and set out on the small trek to Kalin, so close they didn't even have to fly. Wings were

Darivan's blessing, but flying took more energy than walking, so any chance to do the latter was appreciated.

Legacy breathed in a deep sigh of relief as she crossed the bridge, tasting fresh grass and damp wood on the back of her tongue. Rose Heart trotted beside her, head high. They both had to look sure of themselves, like they were here on important, completely legal business. Which they actually could be. After all this planning and traveling, Legacy still didn't have an inkling of what they were going to be doing. It *probably* wasn't legal, because there was no point recruiting thieves for anything but, but it wouldn't be the strangest surprise she'd been hit with so far.

The aged wood thudded under her feet in time with her steps. The Golden Hearts was a classic type of kingdom, the architecture inspired by the first image to come to mind when someone said "castle" without providing further details. It was the kind of stone and brick building style that graced children's storybooks all across Camorthes.

Kalin was the most poignant example—circled by impenetrable stone walls, fitted with a moat of water to keep animals at bay, and a long wooden drawbridge to finish it off.

It'd take no more than a few wingbeats to soar right over the walls, but that was a one-way ticket to getting shot down by their powerful sentries, who stood vigilant.

Far above Legacy's head, a pair of them marched along the top of the wall. Their massive crossbows barely weighed them down, the angry tips of their bolts visible even from ground level.

Water rushed below the bridge.

"State your business," the gate guard said as they approached, idly toying with a long, ornate sword. It looked like something built to hang on a wall and show off to guests rather than a weapon to wield in battle, but Legacy supposed that was the point. Should any trouble arise, the guard only needed to hold her own long enough for the sentries to come hailing down. They would ensure the problem was swiftly dealt with.

"We'd like to have an audience with King Onyx. Please. I'm not quite sure how to go about it, but I was told to tell someone official, and you look the part," Rose Heart said, perfecting the tonal balance of "this is urgent" and "I'm a naive young girl who doesn't know what I'm doing." It was infuriating how good she was at it, using her voice as a tool to pry what she wanted out of any conversation.

Legacy had tried before, but instead of charming birds with her girlish innocence into giving her free stuff, they just looked embarrassed for her. A lot of them also thought she was homeless.

The guard huffed. "And I'd like to end my shift and go home right now, but we can't all get what we want. He's a busy man, with all the troubles of late. No time for idle conversation with strangers like you two." The guard flicked her claw dismissively.

"Ah, but that's what we're here about, to help him with those troubles," Rose Heart continued. Legacy listened in with earnest curiosity. She was no green-blood when it came to thievery, but hearing the way Rose Heart would speak, the way she'd bounce her words off of others to pretend she knew what was going on, showed there was always more to learn.

*If only I weren't learning it from her. Ugh.*

The guard looked unconvinced. She lowered her voice, and Legacy had to strain to hear it. "Listen, I think you're full of shit. But lucky for you, I'm not paid enough to care, so go on, go inside. If you start stirring up trouble and people start asking who let you in, don't you say it was me. I swear, if you do, I'll find your prison cell and strangle you myself."

Rose Heart looked over to Legacy and smirked, chest puffed at her success. Legacy rolled her eyes, staring ahead as the massive portcullis blocking their path slid upward, the mechanical sound creaking through the air.

Legacy's chest tightened at the awful noise, but she darted through the entrance as swiftly as she could. She didn't think the guard was lying, but she still breathed a sigh of relief when she made it safely to the other side.

"Now, let's find the inn Owl Wings booked for us," Rose Heart said, keen eyes examining the surrounding streets. She looked out of place among the crowd of muscled Golden Hearts birds. Her slender frame made her look small, despite her height. She walked with her head high regardless, seemingly unaffected by being the odd one out.

CHAPTER EIGHT

# THE STRANGER

LEGACY HAD NO DOUBT THAT, despite his calm demeanor at Victor's mansion, Owl Wings was getting nervous about spending all their money too fast. The tavern he had so generously rented a room in, dubbed the Chilly Pegasus by the half-rotten sign hung outside, was…. well, it spoke for itself. Or at least the puddle of mysterious liquid in the corner did.

An odd smell wafted through the air, some kind of must mixed with liquor, then mixed with liquor that had been partially digested and expelled from someone's body. Hopefully unrelated to the aforementioned puddle. Candles lined the walls, flickering just close enough to the wood to put the patrons on edge.

100

Rose Heart looked as disgusted as Legacy felt, huddled in close and keeping her wings tight to her body, her proud stance long gone as she tried to avoid touching as much of this place as she could.

Legacy walked up to the counter, a cracked stretch of wood stained with various colors that she didn't even know drinks came in.

The bartender himself was exactly the type she'd expect to be working here, stumbling on his feet and slurring his words. Either half-dead, exhausted, or drunk. Maybe some cocktail of all of the above. He fit in so well that it took her a moment to realize he wasn't even a Golden Hearts firepie. In fact, he wasn't even a firepie. His tall, lanky figure, ridged claws barely visible around the neck of a glass, and snow-white feathers gave away that he was a winterpie.

Legacy looked back briefly to make sure no one was close by. Even doing innocent things, like checking into a room, had to be discreet enough that they couldn't be traced. Flies buzzed around spilled beers and plates left uncleaned. The majority of this small nation of travesty was drunk, and those who were sober looked like they wished they weren't. Her foot made an uncomfortable sticky sound every time she lifted it from the floor, and she opted to stand as lightly as possible.

"You take the bed. I think I'm gonna plant my ass outside and take my chances sleeping on the street," she whispered to Rose Heart before turning her attention to the bartender. "Reservation for Owl Wings."

The bartender swung his head, swirling a glass of some bubbling drink in his claw before slamming it on the counter. He laughed, low and mocking. "We don't…

we don't do reservations. That's for the posh bastards at the"—he paused, flicking his tongue as though he'd lost the word and was desperately trying to scare it out of the corners of his mouth—"Toasty Unicorn. That place. Yeah… Our rich, pompous cousins. Same owner, if you can believe it."

"Bullshit," Legacy spat, reaching forward to grab the bartender by his beer-crusted vest. He dodged the attempt with surprising dexterity, sliding nimbly to the side before sinking back into his drunken stupor.

She spared a glance at Rose Heart, who nodded in silent agreement.

Something was off here.

Call it a thief's intuition, or common sense, but no drunken man should be that agile. He was bluffing, but why?

"Sorry, sweet," he continued, slipping back into his performance flawlessly, "no money, no room… no reservation. Nothing for… nothing for you gals. Especially after that sorry attempt on my life." He hiccupped.

"Even if I hypo… hy… hypothetically did take reservations"—he swung a wing lazily over the counter, stark white feathers a heavy contrast to the dark oak—"neither of you happens to look like Owl Wings. So… so scram or buy a drink. I'm not all that picky."

White… it was just then Legacy noticed something odd. Not just the color but the way it shone in the light, preened and well-groomed in a way that no man in his state should be. His apron was dirtied and stained, but not a drop of ale tainted the feathers beneath.

Legacy leaned in close, voice seething. "Weird for a bartender as tipsy as you to remember what one in hundreds of customers looks like, no? We're with him, so give us the damn room before I throttle you in front of your—"

"Legacy, darling, I hate to interrupt, but shouldn't we be… a bit less…" Rose Heart gestured in an odd manner, flapping her claw around in a feeble attempt to get her point across. *High key* is what Legacy was able to glean from it.

Something flashed on the bartender's face, thin eyes widening a minuscule amount. They were white too—clear, unbroken white that matched his feathers.

"Ohoho, trying to stay on the down-low? I see, I see." The bartender's voice changed suddenly. A sly, whispering contrast to his slurred drunken act. "Well, O'Hara can understand that."

Both Legacy and Rose Heart gave a start, immediately looking at each other to affirm what was just said.

O'Hara barreled on. "The room is yours, and give my regards to Owl Wings, or don't. I'm not particularly bent on it." Now things were clicking into place. This was O'Hara, a notorious recruit of the Fox Thieves Guild. Not much was known about him, given he'd only joined a few months ago, but names got around when it came to the guilds. No doubt he'd recognized Legacy's, hence his sudden turn of character.

"Wait, since we're all…" Legacy spared a glance at the patrons perched at various tables in the bar. They all seemed lost in their own cups and conversations. Good. "Since we're all… companions, maybe you can help us."

"Not a chance. O'Hara is a busy man; things to do, people to scam." He gestured at the patrons in the bar. "Real bartender is drugged out of his ass upstairs. I have to make the most of this moment now, before he wakes up and kicks my sorry tail out." He leaned dramatically against the counter, the slur returning to hang off his words.

"I just need you to answer a question, maybe even two, but that's it. I'll only take a moment. Please." Some birds were above begging; some thought themselves too dignified or too sophisticated to stoop to wide eyes and a pleading voice.

Legacy was not one of them. It's not that she enjoyed begging, but she did enjoy money, and sometimes the most money came from a blow to one's dignity. The same was applicable to information—which often led to money, in a thief's case.

"O'Hara does not have a moment. Now go on, go upstairs before he remembers that we don't do reservations around here." He picked up a clean glass and started wiping it with a rag, turning a cold silver-speckled shoulder to the Coyotes. Legacy noticed he kept alternating how he spoke about himself, like he couldn't settle between the third-person or first. Quite possibly he was struggling to stay in character as a bartender now that he knew he was talking to other thieves. It'd make sense, since it sounded like he was more comfortable referring to himself by name, and was only forcing himself to speak normally to blend in.

"Fine, then, be a dick about it. But don't come crawling to us if you need help," Legacy said. The threat was stupid, lacked any teeth, and she was embarrassed she even spat it out. The guilds didn't frequently rely on each other for anything, let alone need each other's help in their own home territories. Still, she always had to have the last word; it was instinct.

Before she reached the stairs, one of the patrons sitting in the corner motioned her over. A book sat on the table next to his drink. On his beak was a pair of tinted glasses. She would have ignored him, but Rose Heart nudged her toward him before taking off up the stairs. He met Legacy's eyes with a welcoming grin. *Thanks, asshole.*

She hoped this stranger hadn't heard any of her interaction with O'Hara. She mentally rifled through how incriminating the stuff she'd said was as she reluctantly sidled up to his table. The corner was dim, but the weird smell was less poignant, and she could breathe the slightest bit easier without gagging.

"You're a pretty little thing. Care to sit with me a moment?" he said, gesturing at the chair across from himself. His feathers were coal-dark, not quite black but almost too dark to call gray. The only reason she could tell so surely was that true black scales shone underneath his feathers. This was an odd place to see a venompie, and she was surprised he'd even been let in the castle gates.

She was less surprised he'd snagged a room at the inn. O'Hara was not here to play on the side of the Kalin citizens and probably let anyone with a coin to their name in while he was up front.

"Care to sit with me a moment?" he asked.

"Not really," she said curtly.

He looked crestfallen, and Legacy barreled on to catch her slip up. *He might know something, just pretend you're really into this conversation.*

"Ah, I mean, for a moment I guess I can," she said, stepping onto the seat and sitting, chest feathers over her feet. It's not that she wanted to spend time with this guy, or would feel bad for giving him the shoulder, but this was an opportunity best not wasted. "So… what brings you here? Probably nothing good; can't imagine coming here willingly."

His brow twitched. It was hard to read his expression behind the glasses. *Why is he even wearing those inside?* They were a common accessory for venompies, used to lessen the striking brightness of the desert, but this was a poorly lit inn lobby. "Mm-hmm , you could say that, but what brings me here is hardly important." He leaned in, one wing resting on the table. "What I care about is you."

*Ugh, creep,* she thought, but what she said was, "You flatter me. I'm just… here on business."

"Business? What a coincidence: so am I."

"Yeah… um… just here to help with what's going on and all that." She took a sip of her drink. Then she remembered she didn't have one and that she'd, in fact, drank his. It tasted sour, and the bitter aftertaste clung to the roof of her mouth.

Thankfully her words piqued his curiosity, enough he either didn't notice what she'd done or didn't care. The corner of his beak quirked. "Oh, you mean the gang? They've been quite the pain, clearing out the locals' food, harassing people in the streets, being general problems."

*Gang?* Now invested, she leaned in. "Yeah, that, that's what I'm dealing with. It'd help if I knew more, though; you are all real cagey about it."

"You all? You flatter me, but I'm not from here. I'm merely a visitor," he said as he laughed. "I think you've just been spending time with the wrong birds; I can't imagine anyone being too up in arms about it," he said, confused. "It's pretty common knowledge, even to outsiders. The Kirran is just sort of there, everywhere, out to stir up trouble, and we're not sure why."

She shrank in her skin, embarrassed. The consequence of pretending you knew what you were talking about when you didn't was that the blow to one's image and dignity, when you got caught in the lie, was a hard-hitting one. At least now she had a name to stick to the problem she was supposed to solve. The Kirran.

Another old Ezelan word, but not one she knew the meaning of.

"Where've they been hanging out at? If anyone knows, of course," she asked.

He threw back the last of the drink before he answered, smacking his beak at the unpleasant flavor. His forked tongue flickered out. "Oh, we all know, because anyone who gets too close either doesn't come back or comes back in tatters." He chuckled. "They're in the canyon up north. Can't miss it for the big stone spires. Looks like the back of a porcupine."

She stood up, brushing off her chest feathers. This was all she needed. The rest could be puzzled out on the way. "Ah, well, thank you. I should be getting back to my room now, though. It's getting pretty late, and I've got a lot to do tomorrow."

"Leaving so soon?" he said, disappointed. "You know where to find me if you want another chat."

Legacy was already walking away. His words muddled to background noise as she rolled over the plan for tomorrow in her head. A canyon of spikes, like a big porcupine, should be easy enough to find.

## CHAPTER NINE
# THE KIRRAN

THE INN BEDS WERE AS uncomfortable to sleep in as one would expect. Legacy didn't know it was possible to make a bag of wool-stuffed fabric stiff and unyielding, but the Chilly Pegasus proved her wrong.

Now, getting into the meat of her journey, she was off to a start both unpleasantly sore and bruised. Not the best state to be in on a task that needed her full range of movement, and then some. If what the stranger said about birds coming back in tatters, or not at all, wasn't an exaggeration, she could have a fight on her claws.

On the bright side, the girls did find the canyon. On the darker side, it seemed bent on trying to kill them.

*Well, I guess he wasn't exaggerating. Kind of assumed it'd be the Kirran who did the mauling, though, not the weather.*

Wind whipped viciously at her face, pulling, tugging, and ruffling her dusty red feathers. The sharp air stabbed at her eyes and yanked at her cloak, making every beat of her wings a momentous effort.

She never thought she'd envy the speed of a snail, but she'd kill to be going that slow now. Hurtling forward at falcon speeds above an endless field of massive stone spikes was heart-racing in the worst way. She muttered a prayer to Darivan that the winds didn't whisk her into getting spiked in the abdomen.

To her right, Rose Heart wasn't faring much better, if not worse. Her ornamental feathers flopped around into her own eyes, while her massive, flowing wings hindered her every move. The soft tips bent weakly in the wind rather than catching it. Her flowing tail drug behind her like a weight, the long feathers messing with her balance more than helping.

The headwind was brutal and merciless, trying with all its might to throw the pair of thieves into its jagged mouth below.

The canyon ran deep. It faded to shadowy black before the bottom met the light, like an ocean of dirt and rock. Rising from these depths were massive spires of sun-bleached stone, crooked and gnarled as an old bird's talons, reaching up high in a vain attempt to snag any creature unfortunate enough to fly too low.

This was where the Kirran lived, supposedly, if the man she'd spoken to knew what he was talking about.

On one hand, this was good—less searching around in the dark and less worries about the gang finding them and making a move first.

On the other, that meant the Kirran were so confident in themselves and their security that they didn't need to hide their location. They welcomed their enemies with open wings and, no doubt, loaded weapons.

Rose Heart caught her eye and gave a small nod. Picking up the cue, Legacy curled her wings in, took a deep breath to steel her nerves, and plunged into the nest of spikes below.

The sheer force of air pinned every feather down tight to her skin, while her cloak turned pointed behind her, flattening to her tail and forming her entire body into a shape as near to a living arrow as she could get.

The speed was as intoxicating as it was frightening. She could only pray no spikes appeared out of the obscuring black sea where she was diving. The thought of crashing headlong into one made her stomach turn.

Darivan favored her today, because flat, rock-ridden ground met her sight far below. She slowed her descent with raised wings, carefully landing amid the stone forest with a *whoosh* of her cloak.

From down here, the sky was nowhere to be seen. The looming nature-grown pillars blocked out the sun, the clouds, every trace of blue and white far above, masking it with a heavy gray. She shuddered, a strange unease crawling across her bones and nesting in her throat.

It was odd. She should be used to a sunless world, having been raised in the Long Shadows kingdom, but this was in every way the opposite. The Shadow Forest was dark but lush, filled with greens and heavy browns, damp with moss and whispering with wildlife. This place felt cold and dead, devoid of plants and sound. Even her own footsteps were swallowed by the vast cold, muffled as though she were underwater.

She shook her head as if physically shaking away her feeling of unease, then flipped her cloak up. There was no apparent change with it, no ripple of magic or shudder in the film of reality, no sense that anything was different than it was before, but she knew now that she was entirely invisible.

She prayed to herself a third time, because it seemed to work the first two. *Darivan, guide me.*

Voices echoed through the stone, muffled and distant but with an airy playfulness, a comfortable, joking familiarity that only shone with dear friends, lovers, and family. Her breath ghosted into the air, frigid cold condensing it into a little cloud above her nose. The words were lost to the spires, but they drifted closer.

She tensed up, breath stilled deep in her chest. The voices neared. Now she was able to pick up brief snippets, nonsensical phrases taken wholly out of context.

"No, no, not at all…" A female voice, annoyed.

"Well if… did her damn job…" A second female voice, this one more airy. Legacy tried to catch the name she said, but it slipped away before she could make sense of it.

"Your airheaded sister couldn't stay focused long enough to walk the length of her room, let alone the border. Nensho said someone was out here, so there's someone out here, regardless of what your sister says."

The voices stilled, the birds coming to a stop to put all their energy into complaining.

Legacy crept in, pinning her body to the spire to keep her movements minimal. She tried to take short, shallow breaths, unsure if the condensation she breathed was included in her invisibility or not.

"Agreed," said the second girl. "Useless creature."

Legacy filed away everything she heard at rapid pace, trying to keep up with the conversation as the voices grew more heated, words scrambled with indignation. The gang considered the spires their territory, and someone had been seen around said territory. This could mean something. Or nothing, but better to know useless information than to let something important slip under.

"You shut up about my damn sister," a third voice, male, barked.

*If only they'd say something useful; I don't care about this asshole's sister.*

"Well, maybe she should do her job, then. I haven't a clue why Nensho hasn't kicked her out yet," said the first girl, "especially after she lost that necklace. It was huge; how the hell do you lose something like that? Especially to a skinny little winterpie."

Legacy inched closer, her view of them blocked by one particularly wide stone. It sounded like they were just on the other side.

Nensho. That marked the second time someone mentioned that name. They must be someone with power if they could kick out members at their discretion. Maybe even the leader of this group.

"Take that back!"

"Take what back? I'm just telling you the damn truth."

They were getting sidetracked. Legacy had the perfect chance to sit around and have information fall into her lap, and they chose to talk about this guy's sister instead. She evidently wasn't someone of note, and this was frustratingly pointless.

An idea struck her, sudden, sharp, and brilliant. She picked up a stone—nothing too big, nothing that would hurt too bad but enough it would unmistakably feel deliberate—ducked around the corner, and lobbed it at the back of the first girl.

It clocked her in the head. *Close enough.*

The girl jumped nigh three feet in the air, amber feathers bristling and muscles tense. "What the hell was that?" she screeched. Her companions huddled in, their eyes suspiciously darting around the spires.

"Could it be the stranger Nensho mentioned?" the second girl whispered, a nervous quiver in her voice.

Legacy leaned in, cocking her head to absorb every word. The stranger's identity was unimportant, but finding out how the Kirran treated outsiders in their territory was worth bringing back to Rose Heart.

"Who the hell else would it be? Let's split up and look around before they take off," added the male, his silver chest puffed authoritatively.

Territorial, that felt like the best word for this group. One stranger, who was probably some young buck on a dare, and they went all-out on looking for them. She grimaced; this complicated things. It's not that she expected it to be easy, but knowing even one stray set them off like this meant getting on the inside without confrontation would be a fight and a half.

She had her invisibility cloak, that helped, but convincing an entire gang to uproot and move out required some face-to-face conversation, which wasn't easy to pull off when one party was transparent.

She could, alternatively, try scaring them out, but if they mistook that as antagonism from the Golden Hearts, she could easily escalate the situation she was supposed to be remedying.

*No matter; I'll figure it out. Just gotta play it by ear.*

The birds took off then, and she could hear their beating wings echoing off the stone.

She spread her wings to fly after them but froze at a loud thud behind her, followed by the distinct noise of footsteps.

# CHAPTER TEN

# CHANCE ENCOUNTER

A BIRD BURST FROM BETWEEN THE spires.

A mess of bloody white feathers careened into Legacy. The ensuing thud sounded like a bag of flour being dropped, complete with several objects comically flying off. The heap of feathers staggered back up to its feet, swiped the dust off itself, and looked around with confusion. Male, Legacy noted, a winterpie, all white save a few gray speckles on his shoulders and wingtips, with no trace of color in his eye—oh… she knew this man.

"What the hell is a *bartender* doing out here?" Legacy snapped.

The thief-faking-bartender—O'Hara, she remembered, though it was hard not to with how often he said his own name—jumped nigh six feet in the air and whirled around, braced for a fight.

"You heard me, O'Hara; what are you doing here? Did you follow me?" She ripped her dagger from its sheath and jabbed it in his direction.

"Ah! I am too young to be hearing voices!" He scrambled to pick the ejected objects up from the ground. The first: a large black hat with a vast brim and a small silver string tied loosely around the base. The second: a shining piece of jewelry. A large gem, yellow diamond maybe, set in a delicate golden chain. He shoved the necklace in a bag around his waist, threw the hat on his head, and spread his wings to fly away.

*Shit. He can't see me.*

Legacy grabbed the cloak and pulled the hood down, revealing herself in a swift movement before O'Hara could run. "No, no, you aren't hearing shit, at least not this time. It's just me. Don't go anywhere."

"Ah! Where did you come from? O'Hara did not see you." He backed up against a pillar, wings spread just enough to give him an easy out. "Are you here to steal these?" He gestured at the small pouch he'd just stuffed the necklace into. "You can try. O'Hara may not win the fight, but he will ensure we both come out of it equally dead."

He had a way of talking that grated on her brain. He just kept going and going without letting her get a word in edgewise, even talking over his own questions before she could answer.

"Ugh, no, I'm not here for you. I'm doing my own thing." She re-sheathed her dagger. "I'm trying to learn about this gang myself since a certain unhelpful thief wouldn't tell me anything." She glowered at him.

O'Hara laughed, light and carefree. "Ooooh, I assume you are talking about O'Hara. Well, he has his own work to do, so bye for now. Tell your rose-red companion he said hello. He must be off now."

He jumped up with a powerful flap of his wings, his winterpie blood giving him a vast wingspan. The beats on the air were so strong it felt like the wind had snuck down into the canyon with her.

Legacy caught a glimpse of a dark figure high above, diving closer by the second. Before she could shout a warning, it plowed into O'Hara.

With a startled yelp, he careened to the ground, the figure landing heavily on top of him. Dust billowed up from where they landed.

Legacy reached to pull her hood over her head, but something grabbed her from behind, shoving her down and tightly gripping her claws. She struggled back, trying to kick free, but the bird holding her was far stronger, the weight of their muscles alone enough to keep her pinned.

All her struggle did was waste breath.

"O'Hara is too young to die!" O'Hara screamed, voice muffled from where Legacy lay pinned. She could barely catch a glimpse of him struggling just as hard, long legs kicking out at his attacker.

A third figure, another large, muscular Golden Hearts firepie landed between the two, frowning deeply.

"I told you there were intruders. And here they are," she said to the others. Legacy couldn't see who held her down, but she recognized the one speaking as one of the gang members she'd been spying on earlier.

"You two are going straight to Nensho," the bird in the middle said, yellow eyes bright and dangerous. "I'm sure she'd love to get an eyeful of the thieves who stole her necklace."

There were a lot of things Legacy didn't know. But one thing she did know was that if these were just lackeys, she definitely didn't want to meet Nensho herself.

Hopefully, this was one of those situations where the leader was some scrawny twig of a bird who hid behind the muscles of their compatriots.

Legacy tried to glare at O'Hara, but the bird holding her shoved her head down, beak ground into the dry dirt.

She made one last attempt to struggle as they lifted her up from the floor. Massive eagle-like talons dug into her shoulders. Every movement stung with pain.

The bird trying to carry O'Hara was slim and the smallest of the bunch, struggling to grasp his smooth winterpie feathers. She watched with wide eyes as O'Hara managed to kick him off, grab his bag back, and shoot off into the sky like a bolt of lightning, blood droplets splattered the ground in his wake.

"Wait, don't leave me here!" she tried to yell, but he was gone in a matter of seconds, the two unoccupied gang members frantically flapping after him.

The bird carrying her tightened her grip. "Don't even think about it," she said, hauling Legacy higher and higher until they rose above the gnarled stone pillars, fresh wind breezing into their lungs.

Legacy pulled against her grip, but all it did was dig thorny talons deeper into her shoulders. With a hiss of pain, she lunged around and tried pecking her leg, getting a firm grip on a scale and pulling it off cleanly.

Her attacker's wingbeats faltered, and her grip loosened for just a moment. But it wasn't enough to get free. Legacy lamented as she pecked again.

The Kirran bird released one talon after another vicious peck, but before Legacy could twist around and break free, something hard slammed the back of her head.

It all went dark, and the last thing she saw was spires of stone growing ever smaller beneath her.

Legacy woke up to nothing but black. Darkness filled her vision in every direction she looked. Her head felt so fuzzy, it took her a moment to realize why this was bad, and then her first reaction was to panic.

She jumped to her feet but stumbled back down as she felt hard resistance on both her ankles. She grunted as her body met the ground again in a cruel thud.

The clanging sound of chains echoed back into her ears. Her legs were chained down tight, and she couldn't even lift one high enough to rip off whatever was blocking her vision. She shook her head, roughly yanking it side to side in an attempt to dislodge it, but it was on tight. All she managed was to make herself more disoriented than she'd been before.

Cool gusts of air blew into her side, offering a small consolation that she was probably outside and not in someone's basement. Beneath her claws was stone, but it felt warm, like the sun had been shining on it.

"She's awake. Take it off," a voice said from behind. They had a strange, slithering lisp.

Then her vision went white. Her eyes barely had time to adjust to the onslaught of light before a bird's face came beak to beak with her. Large, furious yellow eyes set in a massive skull. A bulky neck led into a huge, hulking form with muscle rolling underneath the navy-blue feathers. No doubt a Golden Hearts firepie. That meant they were probably still within Golden Hearts' territory. Hopefully.

Because otherwise, this was some twisted trafficking attempt, and she preferred to keep her organs.

She tried to get a glimpse of the surroundings, but the bird's boxy frame blocked her view. All she had for reference was the heat beneath her claws, the wind battering her side, and the faint smell of sage in her nose.

"Nice to meet you again, little thief," the bird said. Female, but her voice deeper than any Legacy had heard before.

She tried to back up, but the chains held her tight. Something wound around her neck, it nestled underneath her feathers and dug into her skin.. A thin wire that felt like it was being held by whoever was standing behind her. She pulled against it, straining her ankles and neck as she lashed in fury.

"I have no idea who you are! Now let me go, ass—" Her yelling was cut off by a cruel yank of the chain, squeezing her airway shut for just a moment before it let up. A warning.

She coughed, and tried to reach up to rub her throat, but her claws couldn't go above her chest.

"Playing dumb; you really think that's gonna work on me? 'Cause it won't," the large bird said. She had a strange drawl to her voice and sounded kind of like a farmer. She looked like one too. Powerful, muscular, body littered with scars and, Legacy noticed now that some distance was between them, a straw hat on her head.

"Ugh, I'm not playing dumb you—" The chain pulled tight again. She whipped her head around to glare at whoever was holding it.

A stranger, no one she'd seen prior. And a venompie, too. It was weird to see another one so soon. Maybe they were near the Sunlit Clouds border. He had coppery feathers that shimmered between brown and green, almost like scales. Real scales, pale yellow, dotted his neck and shoulders. On the bridge of his beak sat a pair of tinted glasses.

"I really am not," she continued, facing the bigger bird and trying to force a more polite tone. "I have no idea what's going on or who you are."

"She sounds genuine," the venompie said reluctantly.

"Yeah sure, but I ain't fond of her talking so bold to my face. And, whether she's the shithead who stole my necklace or not, she still reeks of thievery."

Legacy froze, limbs turning ice cold as the words set in. A stolen necklace. A thief.

This was Nensho, leader of the Kirran, the feared gang member tormenting an entire kingdom.

Legacy spat in her face.

# CHAPTER ELEVEN

# TERMS AND CONDITIONS

IT WAS A DECISION SHE regretted before she'd even done it. More so when the chain around her neck tightened again, digging into her throat and aggravating her almost healed wounds from Skyflake.

Nensho jerked back, eyes wide in shock as Legacy thrashed, turning to bite the venompie holding her. She jabbed him hard in the neck, not enough to draw blood but enough he loosened his grip, and she was able to slide her neck out before he could tighten it again. Then she spread her wings and leaped up, toward the sky, toward freedom.

Her ankles were still bound, chained to circles of metal in the stone, and she crashed back onto the floor in a heap of red. Her face burned in shame as she felt the chain slip around her neck, and she pecked the man holding it hard in the foot.

"Quit that, will you? You aren't getting out of here, so stop being a pain," he snapped, rubbing his sore foot with the one still holding the chain. He looked to Nensho, wheat-yellow eyes simmering behind his glasses.

She was laughing, wide-mouthed and deep-chested, barely able to contain herself. "I've never seen that before!" she screeched, wiping her face with a claw before standing in front of Legacy again, this time farther back. "You're a sparky one, aren't ya?"

Legacy bristled at being spoken to the same way one might speak to a dog, but she kept her temper reined in. "Whatever, just explain what's going on. I don't know what necklace you're talking about, and I'm no thief." She did know what necklace she was talking about—she'd seen it fall out of O'Hara's bag. And she was a thief. She hoped that, on top of it all, she was a good liar too.

"One of you little criminals stole my necklace." Damn, Nensho was too committed now to believe Legacy was anything but a thief. "Now, I ain't some frivolous peacock missing her jewel; I couldn't give less of a damn about that. It held great value to me, sentimentally, you understand. It came from my grandmother, and I'm not all too happy to have it gone." Her expression was mostly mild, but Legacy saw her smile turn downward at the mention of her grandmother.

Legacy tried not to think about all the sentimental objects she'd stolen in her lifetime. Instead, she finally dared to look around to see where she was, and if she even had a chance of flying away if she got these damn chains off.

They were on top of a cliff, looming high above a field, made of nothing but hard stone, something she was now painfully aware of. She longed to rub her sore joints after having them bashed into the ground several times now. She could only imagine how the bruising would look if her feathers didn't cover it.

Golden fields and small hill rises spanned out for endless miles, broken only by the occasional shining spring or farmhouse. Occasionally a lone tree. She saw no cities or castles, not even a little town. This was truly the middle of nowhere. At least she was still within Golden Hearts' borders, but that didn't help much with how massive each kingdom was.

The tallest thing for miles was the cliff they stood on, and it almost felt out of place, like some careless god dropped it out of their pocket on their way to plant mountains in the Burning Talons kingdom. It didn't connect to a range. It was just one peak alone in the wheat.

"I know at least one of you little bastards took it," Nensho said. "On a bad day, I'd chain you here and hold you up until my culprit came forward, but I have a better idea, since you seem to think you're pretty funny, and irritating as it may be, I admire the confidence. I think I'll let you go, following certain terms, of course."

Legacy stood up straighter, more than a little shocked. It was this easy to get away? It felt wrong, like she was forgetting something. Like if she agreed to this, it would mean some kind of fresh hell later on.

She'd never dealt with a gang leader before, but she knew that they didn't get their positions through kindness and generosity.

"What's the catch?" she asked, eyes narrow.

"Suspicious, ain't you?" Nensho said, twirling a long wheat stalk between her claws before setting it in her beak. "You shouldn't be. You aren't the one who stole it and, thief or no, I don't think myself the type to shed blood just for the fun of it."

It hit her then what she'd forgotten. The mission. The whole reason she was chained up atop a cliff to begin with. "Ah, wait, actually I have a question about that." Legacy spoke fast, hoping to catch an answer before Nensho got mad or changed her mind. "Why are you so invested in all this? The gang shit, I mean. Isn't the whole point that you guys like violence or whatever?"

It was badly worded, but everything she'd heard about gangs prior painted them as bloodthirsty groups with rigid ranking systems and a taste for the gorier things in life. There wasn't much else to offer. Since living outside the Camorthan kingdoms was so hard, she found it difficult to grasp the concept of anyone just striking out on their own for fun.

The Coyotes did, sure, but they were thieves. They had a goal. This gang was just… sort of here.

"I said you could leave, not ask me stupid questions." Nensho chewed on the wheat stalk. "If they didn't tax the piss out of me, I wouldn't care, but I ain't much a fan of having half my income hoarded by the king so he can throw stupid fancy balls instead of fixing any of the 'lesser' cities' problems. If you ain't from Kalin, he don't give a shit, so I decided I'd had enough, and now I'm my own queen, and I make his life hell. That answer it for ya?"

It actually did. It answered a lot of things. As thieves, they had a tax both for the guild and for Cottonmouth, but that was to pay for their living arrangements. Food, water, escape if any of them messed up. Things the thieves benefited from.

The thought of that extra money going to stuff that didn't even affect her, or just into some rich king's pockets, was irritating. Of course, Owl Wings always took a small cut for himself, but he did manage their jobs and heists behind the scenes, not just sit around on his ass.

She bitterly shook her head at the thought of her recent failure, the most recent use of those "taxed" funds, as though she could shake it off her shoulders and be rid of it. All it did was make her shoulders ache and the venompie tug on the chain. She shot him a glare.

"Ugh, I guess I get it, whatever. What are your terms for letting go of me?" She needed to figure out how to get the Kirran off the Golden Hearts' territory, but it was looking more impossible by the minute.

Force would fail in an instant. Though right now it was just her, Nensho, and this venompie, she knew that an entire gang lay hidden somewhere, likely as strong as their boss, and likely far less willing to talk anything out. Nensho alone looked like blades would just bounce right off her, and the scars across her body told a story of birds who'd tested that theory before.

Talking things out was a risk she wasn't going to take here, not chained up and at Nensho's mercy. If she was going to talk her and the Kirran into leaving, it was going to be when she had a viable escape plan beforehand.

Nensho let out a "hmph" sound, like she was thinking it over. Finally, she took in a long, exaggerated breath and sighed it out, focusing her golden gaze on Legacy. The sun was rising, lighting her feathers up in a soft purple hue. "I want you to bring me my necklace." It was far from a surprise—send a thief to steal from a thief, since they'd know all the tricks, but it still sent a shudder of worry down her spine.

*Damn O'Hara. If it weren't for him, this would be easy money. Now I'm stuck on another shitty failure-bound job.* Her stomach twisted at the thought of disappointing Owl Wings again.

Rose Heart wasn't even here, but if she messed this up, there was no chance they'd both be blamed. Legacy would take the fall, again, and then she'd never be a Master Thief, if he let her stay a Coyote at all.

"I can do you one better," she said, blurting it without thinking.

"Hm?" Nensho replied, curiously twiddling the wheat stalk, dented and bent from her grinding it in her beak.

O'Hara's obnoxious face flashed in her mind, smiling and smug and altogether unhelpful. It was his fault she was in this mess. Not to mention abandoning her to the gang without even a glance back.

"I can bring you the thief who took it."

# CHAPTER TWELVE
# A LIFE FOR A LIFE

"I F YOU AND YOUR GANG can promise to leave this kingdom, I can bring the thief to you. He trusts me, sort of, and I have a better chance than any of you at finding him. Takes a thief to find a thief," Legacy said.

Nensho balked. "Promise to… what? Why the hell would I do that? An' why do you care if we sit up here or not? Y'ain't civilians. Or the king." A look of uncertainty flashed over her face, like she was rethinking whether Legacy was actually a thief, or if she might be some government spy instead.

Legacy nodded, then winced as the wire pushed into her wounds. "I swear, if that necklace is really so important, and you really want revenge on him so badly, let me do this. Let me bring him to you, and you can leave this kingdom alone."

Nensho leaned in closer, the wheat stalk brushing Legacy's cheek. "It's a brave offer, 'specially from someone chained up on my cliff, but you're gonna have to do better than that if you want me out of here. That thief's a pain, but he's not worth uprooting all my hard work over. Steal the king's crown too. That might change my mind."

*Well, this is gonna be one hell of a job.* Legacy tried to keep a straight face, as though she caught thieves and stole crowns every day.

There was a chance Nensho was lying, that Legacy would show up with the crown and the thief and get kicked to the curb with nothing to show for it, but it was a gamble worth taking. If she could pull this off, if she could single-handedly do all this, Owl Wings would have to make her the Master Thief. At the very least, she'd regain her lost respect from the Goldblood heist.

And maybe the others would stop glaring at her like she was the one who killed Naom.

That'd be nice too.

She knew that they knew she wasn't really at fault, but Naom had been pretty well-liked within the guild, even by the weird ones, like Thistle.

*If Rose Heart had been in charge, she'd have done it smarter. She'd have never gone under the drawbridge; she'd have killed the assassin and gotten away instead of being arrested. So really it was all Legacy's fault. She planned it, after all.*

"Hah, you think I can't?" Legacy said, puffing out her chest. "Watch, I'll bring that thief right back here, with a shiny crown on his head and everything."

"Heh, you're a bold one. We'll have to see if you have the skills to back that up or if you're all bark and no bite. Let her go, Copperhead." Nensho motioned to the venompie, who hesitantly released the wire on her neck. He came around in front of her, small key in his claw as he nervously eyed her chained ankles.

She wanted to peck him one more time, because it'd be funny, and it'd get back at him for the strain on her neck, but then she risked not getting let go at all. As long as her legs were stuck to the floor, there wasn't a whole lot of places she could go if he didn't unlock the chains. Being killed was bad, but the thought of being left to starve here was even worse.

The situation felt very off, though. It simmered in her mind like an expired meal in her stomach, the vague sense of things being not quite right but not so blatantly wrong she could do anything about it.

She'd never say it out loud, lest she give Nensho any more ideas, but why had she bothered with the negotiation at all? She was the massive leader of a massive gang. With enough power and influence, a whole kingdom was afraid of her. Yet she seemed surprisingly grounded.

Why hadn't she just forced Legacy to do this? Was her gang really as strong as she claimed, or was it all a facade?

Realistically, she probably just wanted a thief indebted to her. The guilds had underground connections no gang could match. But it felt like too easy of an answer. The reward not on par with the price.

The venompie, Copperhead, finally dipped down. He deftly unlocked one foot, then the other, before leaping backward. His pale yellow tongue flicked nervously as he eyed her, waiting for her next move.

Nensho waved a claw at the open field. "Alright, go on, git. You've got a job to do and so do I. Just bring the goods here when you get 'em. I'll know when you're up here." She paused, a simmer in her next words. "I'll also know if you try and pull a fast one on me, so don't even think about it. No god can save you then."

Legacy stretched out her wings, looking over the landscape to try and get an idea of where to go. Before she could, she felt a rough shove from behind.

"What the hell!" she yelped as another shove pushed her straight off the ledge, into the wide, open sky. She struggled to catch herself in the air, sore, wounded, and a bit blindsided by being hurtled off a cliff. She managed to catch a drift of wind below her primaries, enough to soar safely above the wheat fields rather than careening into them.

That was a close one. She prayed thanks to Darivan that Nensho was understanding enough to let her go, rather than slitting her throat and throwing her dead body to rot in a ditch somewhere. Now she just had to make it back to Kalin, where she could get on with her mission.

Despite the near-death experience, if you could call it that, she felt a hopeful thrill beat in her chest. Where before she felt like she was scrambling in the dark to figure out what to do, now she had a clear goal in mind. All she had to do was steal a crown.

And a thief.

That part was more worrisome. Where the crown would no doubt have its own set of challenges, it wasn't something totally foreign to her. Her own failed heist at this same castle was for royal jewelry. Not quite the king's crown, but the queen's stash of jewelry, which was just as pricey.

She beat her wings, the sun glowed warm on her red feathers, and simmered into her open wounds.

Catching O'Hara was going to be the hardest part. Not only did he seem distrustful of fellow thieves, meaning even getting close to him would be hard, she would be violating the thieves' code just a little, tiny bit in the process.

The thieves' code was simple, parroted to her and all the Coyotes and Jaguars and Foxes again and again by their guildmasters.

*You do not turn your back on a fellow thief, you do not steal from, injure, or betray a fellow thief, you do not betray the guild, and above all else, listen to the word of the grand guildmaster.*

The grand guildmaster was Cottonmouth and had been for a long time prior to Legacy being hatched.

She wheeled in closer to one of the decrepit buildings dotting the countryside. Rotten wood barely held the place together, the roof careening dangerously to one side and the door half-collapsed. Dry mosses and overgrown weeds stuck up around the sides, some poking out from inside the building. It looked like an old barn, based on the massive doors and peaked roof.

To catch O'Hara and turn him in to Nensho would no doubt count as a betrayal of a thief and break the thieves' code. Depending on what Nensho did after, it could fall under the death or injury clause as well.

Legacy didn't consider herself the type to break rules. *But no one has to know.* She could send Rose Heart to get the crown and deal with him on the side. It shouldn't be too hard. He wasn't even part of the Coyotes, so maybe it wasn't too bad of a betrayal compared to what happened to the Wolves.

It's not like she was handing him over to the guards or doing anything to endanger the guilds themselves, so this was probably okay. It was better for everyone in the long run. Once it was over, it was over; no loose ends.

She touched down at the crooked barn door with a thud, landing awkwardly as her wounds burned in her skin. A mix of small and large cuts littered her neck and shoulders, stinging with every movement.

She walked over to a pool of stagnant water, angling herself to try and get a better look at them. Several flies buzzed around her face, and she swiped them away with a wing. Most of the cuts seemed surface deep, though it was hard to tell beneath the feathers, and her cloak had saved her shoulders from damage entirely. They were sore, but as she tugged the cloak down enough to peek, she could see nothing broke skin; it had just aggravated the older wounds she'd gotten from Skyflake.

Amazingly, the cloak itself was unharmed, not even a frayed edge or small tear to show for how roughly she'd been grabbed and tossed around. It felt equal parts amazing and unnatural, in the usual fashion of magical items.

Her neck scrapes were worse. At least one gouged deep between the feathers, enough it was still oozing blood through the crusted and dried edges. It stung like hell too.

Magicians had it easy; they could just wave a claw and do away with things like this. It's why they never had scars, or wounds, or anything that showed they'd been alive for as many hundreds of years as they usually lived.

Vinmara used to cast those spells on Legacy, enough so that when she first joined the Coyotes, Owl Wings thought she was younger than she really was because of the pristine state her feathers and skin were in. Thievery wasn't often a first choice for anyone, and most of the birds coming around had some degree of scarring or mussed feathers to show for their prior lives.

The shock of going from a comfortable life freeloading in a magician's mansion to a shithole cave filled with obnoxious boneheads wasn't easy. She hadn't thought about it much recently, or much at all since leaving, but it was all for the better.

There was nothing for her at her first "home," nothing long-term, anyway. She could have stayed and lived an easy, comfortable life, but she'd have been about as useful as a house cat—being that not only was she non-magical, but she wasn't even biologically related to any magicians. She and her bloodline had nothing to offer to a Hir Lana household.

And she didn't consider herself the type to sit still and look pretty.

It'd be nice to have a mansion someday, of course, but she wanted to earn it. She wanted to be the best damn thief the Boss had ever seen and climb her way to the top by her own merit.

The thought gave her a burst of energy, and she spread her wings and shot into the air again. It was sunrise, and while her body ached and her neck hurt no matter how hard she tried to keep it still, she had a job to do that couldn't wait a moment longer.

The air was pleasantly cool and smelled like dew and wheat. She took in a deep breath, filling her lungs and soaring higher and higher until the barn became a small dot far below. She wheeled in circles for a moment, swooping and diving absentmindedly as she racked her brain to find out where she was. The lack of mountains meant she was nowhere near Camber—that place was right next to the Burning Talons, who had a territory of nothing but mountains. Kenrin was probably far too. It was right by the sea, and two massive rivers surrounded the area it sat in. She couldn't see the rivers or the sea, so she had to be by the Sunlit Clouds border.

Her best bet was to fly north until she found the river that passed Kalin. Even if she didn't run directly into the city, she could follow it as a guide until she ended up there. That or she'd go the wrong way and end up at the ocean, but she was confident she could figure it out.

She beat her wings, the air unyielding as she took off north across the plains. The winds were mild, the sun just far enough to the side it didn't hurt her eyes, and the temperature was perfect. It felt almost as if Darivan herself was urging Legacy to move forward, to restore her reputation as a thief. With a surge of confidence in her heart, she flew towards her destiny on light wings.

# BACK IN THE ASHEN CITY

Hours passed. Her wings, no longer light, ached with every flap when the river finally came into view. It wound across the plains and sparkled cool silver in the sunlight. Her sigh of relief was so deep she nearly plummeted down into the water. Her neck was sore beyond belief, and it felt like the wind was throwing her around more than she was gliding to its beat. The blood stopped dripping hours ago. It was no doubt going to scar, but what Camorthan didn't have a few scars?

The magicians, actually. They were too stupid and magical and perfect for that.

She wasn't one of those, though, otherwise she'd be living an easy life back at Vinmara's, probably still working alongside her stuffy apprentice.

She huffed, spreading her wings to catch the air and lift herself just a bit higher. The world felt vast and frighteningly endless from up here, spanning in all directions until it faded blue with distance. It was nothing like the Shadow Forest, where you could barely see a few wingbeats in front of you for all the trees and plant growth. She preferred it that way. The closed-in feeling was comfortable and controlled, whereas out here she felt vulnerable and visible from all sides, like nothing she did was secret even from the prey animals darting below.

Her stomach growled, reminding her she hadn't eaten for several days, not since she and Rose Heart camped outside of Kalin. It could wait, she told herself as a faded figure rose in the distance. She was almost there.

*Almost there*, however, was easier said than done. She didn't have the massive, burly wings of a Golden Hearts 'pie, and the hours of flight wore on her joints. Despite her mixed blood, all of her traits were identical to a Long Shadows 'pie, short wings not meant for long distance included. The winterpie blood in her barely showed, though from reading books on the matter it sounded like that was the case with most winterpie crosses of any kind. They were a selfish, secluded lot, even stingy with their genetics.

When she finally made it within what must have been a mile of the castle walls, she had to half-crash-half-land on a muddy bank by the river, chest heaving with effort and wings limp at her sides. She lay down on the bank, legs stretching out as she took a moment to bask in the sun, as though it could replenish her energy and heal her wounds. It didn't, but it did soothe them, and soon enough she was able to pull herself together enough to limp across the field, claws catching on damp grass and overgrown weeds, across the moat, with the water running calmly below, and up to the castle gate.

She knew she looked damn pathetic when the guard, different than the one who'd let her in previously, didn't even ask why she was there, just opened the gate with a pitying look on her face and waved Legacy on inside.

Going back to the Chilly Pegasus seemed a good start. Even if O'Hara had moved on, the sun was starting to set, and she needed to stop and breathe a moment.

Her legs moved like lead as she hauled her weary body into the inn, up the stairs—knocking her claws painfully on one of the steps as she stumbled—and to the bedroom door.

She tried turning the knob, and frowned as it almost got stuck, but a little more force and it reluctantly complied. The door creaked open, the hinges doing their best in their old age.

She was greeted by a scene of scattered feathers, blood, and a whole lot of yelling.

Rose Heart had O'Hara pinned to the floor, dagger to his neck, while he talked a mile a minute underneath her. The feathers around the room were his, little spots of white strewn about like snowflakes.

"O'Hara swears he has nothing to do with it! Maybe if your friend was better at escaping like O'Hara, she would not have been captured, yes?"

"And maybe if you were better at keeping your damn mouth shut, you wouldn't have a dagger to your throat," Legacy spat, causing both the others to freeze and look her direction with wide eyes. She leaned heavily on the doorway, eyes bright with anger. The trip back was so grueling she almost forgot O'Hara had left her for dead. But now it all came crashing back to her—the anger she had at his betrayal, the soreness of her wounds, and the exhaustion from spending so many hours trying to drag her battered body back to this dingy tavern.

Rose Heart, with a final glare at O'Hara, stepped off to allow him to stand, though she kept her dagger pointed at his chest.

"Legacy, dear, you've been gone for days; where have you been? And more importantly, was it this bastard's fault?" she asked, concerned.

Legacy felt an answer bubble in her throat. She wanted to say yes, that it was this bastard's fault she'd been caught, but she hesitated.

She needed O'Hara's trust. That didn't mean she had to suck up to him, but it did mean that if she took his side here, he'd feel indebted to her, if the odds were in her favor. It was another gamble in a series of gambles where she felt like everything was hanging in the balance between her own skill and sheer luck.

"No, it wasn't. We got caught together, and the bird carrying me was too fast for him to catch up with when he broke free." Legacy glanced at O'Hara. His eyes widened a minuscule amount, no doubt surprised she took his side.

"However, I did learn more about the Kirran, a lot more, in fact, and we may need his help to pull off what I need to do."

Rose Heart lay across one of the soft bed mounds, head tilted curiously. "Do tell. I was too busy trying to find you and didn't learn much here, I'm afraid."

"Hah, I'm surprised you even looked. Couldn't do this job alone?" Legacy said, allowing herself to flop down on another bed, the soft cushion wrapping around her aching body like the wings of an angel.

"Oh, shut up. Don't get a big head about it. Owl Wings would be pissed if I came home alone, that's all. Now tell me what you learned and this thing you say you want to pull off." Rose Heart flashed a glare at O'Hara as he tried to sneak out the door, and he paused sheepishly with one claw on the handle.

"Right. I was able to talk to Nensho herself. The boss of the Kirran," Legacy said, feeling her chest swell in pride. "She let me go on one condition, and I was also able to bargain with her about taking her gang elsewhere on the same condition."

"Spit it out, darling, I don't have all night," Rose Heart said, picking at her claw.

They did have all night, in fact. At least Legacy did. She couldn't do anything right now if she tried.

"We've gotta steal the king's crown," she said, gesturing to her head. The movement sent a sting down her shoulder. "She's pissed at him for taxes or something, and if we steal that and maybe a good chunk of his most valuable possessions, she won't mind leaving."

Rose Heart didn't speak for a moment, like she was waiting for Legacy to say more.

"Is that it, really?" O'Hara said from the doorway. "Seems a little too simple." *Damnit*, she'd hoped they wouldn't question that too much.

"Really is. Nensho wasn't as big-bad-wolf type as I thought she'd be—seemed more like an angry farmer than a gangster—and she really has it out for King Onyx, so whatever we do to him will make her happy, I guess." She played up her shock at the simplicity of it, just enough to sell it to the others that she was truly baffled that all they had to do was steal a crown.

Then again "all we have to do" were bold words for a job like this. Onyx's crown didn't often leave his head, and if it did, she had no doubt it was in the same room he slept at night, meaning whatever they did, they'd have to get pretty close and personal with him to grab it. That, and security was likely upped since she got caught on that heist last time.

"Hm, that is strange, but if you say it's what she wanted, I suppose it's worth a try. It's not like we have any other leads, and seeing you like that tells me another face-to-face with Nensho will be no easy task." Rose Heart pointed at her bloody neck. "You should clean that up before it gets on the bed. Not that they're going to notice one bloodstain among all the other mysterious stains here." She grimaced at the bed she was lying on, looking suddenly uncomfortable.

"So, boy, are you helping us or not?" Rose Heart said to O'Hara.

He clicked his tongue. "It depends on what is in it for O'Hara. He is not fond of silly missions like this; he prefers to con unwitting drunkards and gamblers."

"It'll get Nensho off your back," Legacy said quickly. "She was mad as hell, and it didn't sound like she was going to give up hunting you down anytime soon. If you do this, maybe she'll leave you alone."

"O'Hara is touched she spoke of him. A shame he has no interest in making amends." He went to turn the door handle. It got stuck, and he spent a moment fighting with it.

"And we can let you keep whatever you steal from the royal treasury on the way. Nensho didn't seem to care about the actual objects, just ruining the king's day, so I'm sure whatever you take is fair game," she added before he could leave.

That made him stop, a glimmer in his eyes. "Ah, he supposes he could help you, then. It would make Cottonmouth very pleased to have a wealth of jewels, and O'Hara has not been much in her favor lately." From what Legacy had heard, no one alive was in Cottonmouth's favor, but if it's what got him to tag along, she wouldn't complain.

"Thanks. We tried robbing that castle a little while back, and it's much better as a three-bird job. Feel free to tag along with us. Tomorrow we're gonna figure out how to actually do this." She closed her eyes, body sinking deeper into the cushion.

"An offer to spend the night with a lovely lady? O'Hara supposes he can accept."

She was too tired to bother with an argument, but she still bristled at his comment. She wasn't sure if the "lovely lady" in question was her or Rose Heart, but either would make her equally annoyed for different reasons.

She was almost asleep when she felt a heavy weight crash onto the other side of the cushion. "Hey, wait a second. What the hell. I never said you could lay next to me. Piss off," she protested, neck feathers fluffed in anger as O'Hara made himself comfortable on the other side of the bed. The beds, round cushions with a dip in the middle, were not meant for multiple birds at once, not if they wanted to stay far apart enough that they didn't touch.

O'Hara just yawned and stretched out, taking up more than half of the space. "You did invite O'Hara in to stay, and there were only two beds to choose from." He looked across the room at Rose Heart. She wasn't sleeping. She was lying still with her eyes open like some kind of guard dog. "He is afraid to come near that one—she looks like she bites," he said. He wasn't wrong. She was a deeply unpleasant person with a dislike of men in particular.

"Ugh, whatever. Just shut up and sleep," she said, curling into herself as tightly as she could to avoid any contact with him. Falling asleep was easy, and it took her barely a few minutes to lapse into a deep, dreamless rest.

⁕ ⁑ ☽ ⁑ ⁕

Despite her exhaustion, Legacy was the first to wake up. O'Hara was on the floor, upside-down with his hat underneath his head. Rose Heart hadn't moved an inch, the only change being that her eyes were now closed, and her breaths were deeper, giving away that she was fully asleep. Did she always sleep so still? It had to cause some soreness to stay in the same spot all night—it did when Legacy slept like that at least.

She slid off the bed, claws clicking against the wooden floorboards even as she tried to step quietly. She walked up to the window, adjusting her cloak as she did. It rubbed on her wounds, and she winced.

Outside, the streets were just beginning to glow with the sunrise, the golden light making even the run-down, trash-filled alleys look kind of pretty. The occasional bird shuttled back and forth below, each on their way to their normal, boring, mindless jobs.

The smell of morning dew filled her nose, mixed with the heady scent of the wooden window frame.

Light conversation drifted on the air, friendly greetings and jovial hellos being shared as the working birds shuffled on to their jobs.

Being a thief had ups and downs, but one of the ups was the fact that it was pretty exciting job, that didn't follow the same structured routine that most others did. It also sounded cool. A lot of birds stole, of course, but there was a big difference between casual theft and being a thief. She puffed her chest out, cool air seeping into her feathers and causing a chill to run down her spine.

Just before she turned around to wake the others, something caught her eye on  the street below. It was a bird, but one who stood out from the rest who'd passed by. They wore a long, concealing cloak that covered not only their body but so much of their face she wondered how they could see where they were going. Where the other birds moved swiftly and confidently in their comfortable routines, this one dashed down the alley, throwing constant glances behind themselves and staying close to the wall. They paused just at the end of where Legacy could see. They hugged tightly to the shadows, avoiding the spreading sunlight like a disease. It was almost thief behavior, but exaggerated to the point it was comical. Like a caricature of what someone thought thieves did. Instead of blending in, this stranger stood out like a sore claw.

Could they be another of the Foxes?

No, no way, not with a technique like that. Dashing around in a cloak only worked at night when it actually made you harder to see. In the daylight it just made you look weird. When there was such a bustling crowd, holding your head high and acting like a part of it was the best way to go undercover.

They could be an assassin. It was the only other occupation she could think of that needed that kind of getup. With them, once the job was done, all that mattered was concealing their faces. Unlike the thieves, they could just kill anyone who got in their way.

Not that thieves couldn't kill. She glanced back briefly at O'Hara before looking at the stranger again. It was just generally advised against. Murder brought a whole slew of consequences with a different avenue of preparation needed to avoid them. It was far more dangerous, and the guards would never let it slide like they sometimes did with petty theft.

The stranger turned the corner, ducking out of sight. Legacy sighed and went over to Rose Heart, pecking her shoulder pointedly. "Hey, get up, we've got shit to do."

They left the tavern as a trio, Rose Heart side by side with Legacy, and O'Hara out of sight. It would raise suspicion if he followed them directly, since he'd been playing bartender, so he opted to take the window while the girls walked out the front door.

Just as they left, the door slamming roughly behind them, a figure darted past, cloaked head to toe and moving at a swift pace. Legacy gasped, recognizing the stranger she'd seen moments ago. Up close revealed nothing—they moved too fast to try and peek underneath their long hood—and they disappeared into the tavern before she could try and catch a closer glance.

"What is it?" Rose Heart said, a concerned arch to her brow.

"Oh, nothing important. I just remembered I forgot something back at the room. Go on ahead. I'll catch up in a moment."

It could very well be nothing, just some lone bird creeping around, *or maybe a drug dealer*, she thought as she ducked back inside the tavern, trying to move as quickly as she could without looking too noticeable. But it could also be another thief, someone to help out on their mission. She dashed up the stairs, following close behind the other bird. It could even be Skyflake or one of his fellow assassins, out to cause trouble for the Coyotes again. She paused at the top of the stairway, but before she could do anything else, the bird spoke.

"What are you, some kind of sick stalker? I thought better of you, but this all seems awfully suspicious." The voice was familiar, a female, but the name and identity escaped her. The girl kept her back to Legacy, which was entirely unhelpful.

"No, I just thought you were someone I knew, so I doubled back," Legacy stammered, mind blanking on what to say.

The bird turned around, flinging back her woolen hood.

"Yeah, sure you did. Seven kingdoms in Camorthes and here you are, poking your beak around the tavern I frequent. Sounds like a stalker to me," Louisa said.

The feathers on her neck bristled.

"No, no, I didn't mean it that way!" Legacy said, trying to save some face. "I didn't even know you lived here or that you go to this tavern. I thought you were… well… someone else." She trailed off awkwardly, not wanting to name Skyflake in front of her. Not after already getting on her bad side by insulting him.

Louisa's anger cracked, a glint of confusion in her eyes. "You didn't— Never mind, you seem genuine enough, I guess. Let's talk in here." She gestured toward the room she was next to. Right, this was maybe not a good conversation to be having in the middle of a hallway where anyone could hear, even if they were too drunk to track any of it.

Inside the room, Legacy tried to plead her case again. "My companion and I are on completely unrelated business, I swear. I'm more curious what you're doing here. You don't strike me as someone poor enough to rent a room in this shithole." She noticed now that Louisa wasn't wearing any of the accessories she'd had when they first met. Even the pearls on her face were absent. Had she been kicked out of her home? Fallen into poverty? There were a million possibilities.

"Language. Okay, I'll explain, but you seriously, absolutely cannot tell a soul you saw me here, alright?" Louisa looked at her with a frantic desperation in her eyes. Whatever the reason for her being here, it must be pretty serious. It also explained why she was so blatantly open about dashing around in a cloak. If she wasn't a criminal, hiding her face from passersby was all that mattered. Not much stealth needed since the guards likely weren't involved.

Likely. Louisa didn't seem like a criminal type, not after her breakdown upon finding out Skyflake was an assassin, but maybe he'd been a bad influence on her.

Louisa looked out the window sadly, claw resting on the windowsill. "I'm sneaking out. Thanks to my position, I'm not supposed to leave like this, but by Diyos, am I tired of being cooped up at home. It's stifling." She turned around, a brightness in her eyes. "So I don't stay cooped up, I take off whenever I please and pray they don't find out. I've been lucky so far, but I've had a few close calls."

Her position? Legacy turned over her brain, trying to remember what that was. She also wondered who "they" were, maybe coworkers.

"You're… a doctor, right?"

Louisa's brows quirked. "All that and that's what you have to say? Ugh, really, I'm a healer, so close enough."

"Oh, sorry, sorry. I was just wondering what kind of strict doctors you had here that you can't even leave the kingdom as you please. Seems kinda weird, y'know?"

"Healer," Louisa corrected. "And being one is a bit heavier than being a doctor—we deal in more religious and spiritual matters, so I'm not supposed to stray far from the church."

Legacy remembered how blatantly she'd been dashing through the alleys. "You aren't very good at sneaking out," she said.

"I beg your pardon? Well, I'm sorry I'm a healer and not an expert criminal thief like you," Louisa spat. "Some of us have actual jobs."

Before she could retort, the door opened. Both girls jumped, eyes wide.

Rose Heart stood in the doorway, furious.

"Oh, just 'getting something out of your room' from someone else's room? I'm not fond of sitting around waiting for selfish little bitches to take their sweet time while I stand around with a claw up my ass," she barked, rounding on Legacy, her slim claws digging into the floorboards.

Louisa stepped back, opened the window, and kept herself pressed to it, setting herself up for a quick escape. "Is this one of your little thief friends?" she said, nervously eyeing Rose Heart's dagger.

Legacy swallowed, leaning back to put some distance between herself and the dangerously pointed beak in her face. "Yeah, something like that," she said to Louisa, before turning her attention back to Rose Heart. "I was, honestly. I just ran into her on the way, and we decided to have a little chat. Sorry I have a social life, but you don't need to get hissy about it."

"Unbelievable," Rose Heart said, backing up to stand in the doorway. Her voice simmered. "The only impressive thing about you is how you make everything someone else's fault. You're seriously going to blame me for getting mad that you never tell me anything? That you can lie your ass off right to my face, turn around, and do whatever you feel like because when I call you out, suddenly it's my fault?" She grabbed the door handle. "If you want to be independent so badly, do it yourself—this whole job. See if I care. I'll be getting wasted somewhere nice and comfortable if you need me." She slammed the door, the thud echoing off the walls.

She was gone now, but the space she'd been standing in felt charged with a furious energy. The flame of an argument gone unresolved. Legacy felt it in her chest.

She turned to talk to Louisa but was only met with a barren windowsill, dust scuffed off the surface.

Alone, then.

This would make things much easier. Now she could deal with O'Hara without trying to cover her tracks the whole time and take the credit for this entire affair herself.

It was everything she'd wanted, the perfect setup for what she had to do, but she couldn't shake the nagging feeling deep inside that made her feel just a bit wrong.

# CHAPTER FOURTEEN
# A THIEF'S CROWN

L EGACY CREPT DOWN THE FAMILIAR castle halls, each step meticulous, calculated, and quiet as a mouse. Even with her hood over her head, shielding her from the world outside, it paid to be careful. Being invisible felt nice—even the portraits that felt like they'd been watching her every move before now looked past blindly.

It was such a useful spell that she wondered why more birds didn't have it. If it were common, there'd no doubt be equally powerful spells in place to protect these castles from invisible intruders. If it weren't, she shouldn't have been able to just get this power so easily.

Maybe magicians didn't often side themselves with criminals. Victor was cordial toward the Coyotes, but he was a black sheep in that regard. Most magicians were cold and uncaring to those outside their magical upper circle.

Vinmara had been like that. She took Legacy in as an egg, found nestled between mushrooms in the Shadow Forest, the kind of place eggs got left when their parents didn't take into account the biggest side effect of casual sex. Or when they divorced and the mother wanted no trace of her husband left, even in her children. There were a number of reasons, and she often found herself wondering which situation to be her own.

Vinmara was kind in raising her. She'd given her a place to live, food to eat, but once she'd gotten an apprentice with real magical ability, she'd struggled to hide her disdain toward Legacy for being unable to keep up. It was worse than outright anger that she tried so hard to hide it. The way her smile would drop when Legacy killed the plants she'd tried to grow, while Sepia's flourished beyond the bounds of nature. The way she'd swoon over Sepia's intellect and desire to learn and consume books at a rapid pace, whereas Legacy preferred lighting bugs on fire in the yard.

Legacy wasn't a perfect child, most weren't. The problem was that Sepia had been unnaturally talented, and being a normal child next to a prodigy was just as bad as being a failure.

Even at that young age she'd realized it, that she was going to be the lesser child no matter what, so she'd embraced it. As she grew into her teenage years, she talked back incessantly, stole from birds, bullied other kids, and locked herself away in her room while Sepia and Vinmara spent their family time together.

That was how Owl Wings found her. She'd tried to pickpocket him. Nowadays he had little patience for that kind of thing, but back then he'd laughed, realizing she was no true criminal, just a rebellious teen lashing out, and offered her a place in his new guild. It was a dream come true: a place she belonged that leaned into talents she had and things she was good at. No more poring over books she couldn't make heads or tails of, no more stupid chanting in hopes she'd awaken some hidden magical ability, just thieving, in a guild of birds who were all so bad at their jobs it damn near cured her inferiority complex.

She turned the corner, trying to remember the way to the king's room. She hadn't been there last time, she'd been to the treasury instead, but he'd be stupid to keep his crown locked up in there.

By Darivan, this castle was massive. She grew less cautious as she sprinted down corridors and dodged past a variety of royals milling about. They sipped their drinks and chattered, oblivious.

She slipped on the smooth marble floor, crashing into the ground with force. It made her wounds ache all over again, and she suppressed a groan. Other birds were looking around, confused, as they tried to find out where the thud had come from.

She wasn't stealing the crown just yet—she was going to make sure she had O'Hara along for that—but she had to scout the place first, find out where things were and what guards hovered in what areas.

She scrambled back to her feet and brushed herself off.

Where even was O'Hara? He'd been with her and Rose Heart leaving the tavern, but there had been no sign of him since.

That could be a problem, but she had to focus on the task at hand first. She sprinted up a large glimmering staircase, being more careful where she put her feet this time.

The castle was pretty, carved from marble and stone, draped in reds and golds to match the Golden Hearts' banner, and with swatches of stained glass windows in every room, but after seeing Victor's magical mansion, it almost felt lackluster. If it were her castle, she'd have hired a magician to make some books float around or something, maybe jewels if she felt really cocky, definitely some of those pretty floating light orbs. Torches had their own appeal, but those were everywhere, from cheap taverns to this very castle. If she had a castle, she'd want it to stand out.

Finally, at the top of a winding spiral staircase, and at the end of a long hallway, she made it to a room with massive doors carved with murals of lions and unicorns in the heat of some fictional battle. The handles themselves, she noticed, were carved to look like curled unicorn horns. A guard stood on either side of the door, with matching ornamental silver helmets on their heads, both looking bored. Each looked thin for someone of their status. Normal guards may just get scraps, but surely the royal ones would be better fed?

Well, it wasn't her problem anyway.

Now she had to figure out how to open this door without them noticing. Even cloaked in her invisibility, these weren't the kind of doors to just blow open in the wind.

Ah, the wind. It gave her an idea, and she stepped back to think. If she could remember the location to some degree, maybe there would be a window or even a balcony to sneak in through from the outside. She darted back through the hall, down the stairs, keeping her wings tucked tight to herself to avoid brushing anyone she moved past.

On the way out, she paused by the kitchen. The faint smell of a bready meal cooked earlier wafted through the air . Right now it was quiet, and very few birds were out and about in this wing of the castle. She knew from prior scouting that under a little trapdoor, one tucked behind crates of kitchen supplies, was the king's stash of treasure. It was a clever place, she had to admit, and if Naom hadn't told the others where it was, they'd have probably never guessed it was stowed away there.

None of the Coyotes were from the Golden Hearts' kingdom, much less ranked high enough to be privy to where the treasury was kept, so how Naom knew was a mystery, and one the Coyotes would never know the answer to.

Legacy crept in, holding tight to the counters and taking tiny steps to keep her claws from clicking against the floor. Right this moment, there was no one in here—the perfect opportunity.

Raiding the treasury wasn't in the plan from the start, but why not, while she was already here?

She flung open the trapdoor and reached down for the top rung of the ladder. Her claw wrapped around it, and she ducked in, closing the door softly behind her.

The ladder was long and slanted just enough for a bird to barely hold on without struggle as she descended into the narrow tunnel. It was an awful, inconvenient design, no doubt chosen on purpose to deter thieves.

She wasn't so easily chased away, however, and she'd already done this once before. It was all uncomfortably familiar ground.

Soon, the dark, enclosed tunnel opened up to a bright light, golden and stunning. The ladder ended at a ledge high above the treasure, and she stepped off it with a grateful sigh. It was something out of a storybook. Mountains of golden coins, jewels, necklaces, and more were piled in a room twice the size of the tavern she'd just slept in. The only thing it was missing was a massive sleeping dragon perched at the peak of the highest mound. No guards were inside, likely not allowed to stay so close to this mass of wealth for any period of time, lest they find a way to smuggle some of the smaller items out.

She jumped off the ledge, flapping as quietly as she could to descend onto the golden floor. It wasn't the first time she'd seen it, but she felt a fresh anger rise in herself anew. The king really just sat on all this, every day? He taxed his people all that, and for what? He had enough gold to buy himself another kingdom. Why did he need to take more?

No wonder Nensho was pissed. Farmers and ranchers were some of the hardest workers out there, doing more in a day than some did in their entire lives. If Legacy worked that hard just to have some king with enough wealth to literally bury his enemies take a chunk out of her profits, she'd be more than mad.

It was all greed, something she knew well as a thief. But despite that, she also knew hard work. Theft may not be the most honorable way to make a living, but it wasn't what this king did.

It'd be different if the funds actually went somewhere. Like Owl Wings, who used them to keep the guild fed and safe. But she'd seen the kingdom on her way in. Anything outside the castle was run-down, cracked, damaged, and old. All this gold and he couldn't pay someone to fix it? There was an air of ridiculousness to it that festered in her heart.

She'd barely begun sifting through the gold, trying to find the smallest things with the most value, when something moved out of the corner of her eye. A flash of color. She turned around and froze when she found herself locking eyes with another bird.

They were a small bird, with silvery gray feathers that faded off into blue at the ends of their wings and claws, their body dotted with white. The most striking feature was their eyes. Stark white and pupilless, like a pair of small pearls set in their skull.

"What are you doing here?" A girl, it sounded like. Her voice was strange and hollow.

Legacy didn't move, praying that she was talking to some other intruder in the empty treasury.

"You know what I am. Invisibility means nothing to me," the girl said, not breaking eye contact.

At least it looked like she didn't break eye contact—without pupils it was hard to tell.

"I do not see you, but I can hear you and your thoughts."
*Oh shit. Oooooh shit.*

This was a Dreamseer. That's what the weird vacant eyes meant. Legacy didn't know much about them, but she remembered a few key points now.

Dreamseers were blind and had special powers. Not all of those powers were known, but mind reading was one of them. Mind reading, future sight, some other creepy mental things in the same vein, were all possible with these birds.

Legacy wondered how this girl snuck in with her. The ladder wasn't exactly quiet—she was sure she'd have heard her following.

"I live among the rafters, part of the treasury, you see." The girl pointed up. Rafters of wood crossed high above her head, even way beyond the ledge Legacy had come in on. She wondered how all of this fit under the castle.

"Don't do that, it's weird as hell," Legacy said. It was one thing to know her thoughts were being read, another to hear them answered aloud. She spread her wings to take off. This bird wasn't here last time. Maybe she was a new security measure since the last robbery. If so, she wasn't doing much. Better to leave now in case that changed anytime soon.

"My name is Moon Eyes. I don't appreciate being reduced to a security measure. And I was here last time, I merely didn't move," Moon Eyes said, poising to fly as well. "I am no guard, but rest assured the real ones are awaiting you outside. I'd advise against taking anything at this point; it'll only incriminate you further."

Legacy didn't wait another moment. She bolted into the air, white wings beating furiously as she threw herself onto the ledge, scrambled up the ladder, and pushed her claws against the trapdoor.

It didn't open.

She pushed harder, claws nearly bending under the force. Nothing. Nothing but the rattle of a lock on the other side.

Still, she refused to relent, throwing as much of her body weight into it as she could until her body gave out, leaning limply against the ladder while she caught her breath.

*Think smart.*

Her heaving chest relaxed, and this time, she pressed one claw against the door with a gentle touch. Sparks flickered off her claws, then a puff of smoke, then a bright blue flame. The fire grew, darting between her claws and brushing against the door, waving in a beat to her breaths.

No dice. The door looked like wood, rustic brown swirled with all the age rings of a tree, but it didn't burn like it. It didn't burn at all, actually, just lit up a pretty blue while she hopelessly tried to torch it.

She extinguished the flame, then crawled back down the ladder to flop onto the ledge, defeated. Now seeing all that treasure just made her mad. No use grabbing any if she couldn't escape. That, and according to Mooney down there, guards knew she was in here. Getting caught with a satchel of stolen trinkets wouldn't bode well.

That is, if she ever got out of here in the first place. The guards probably thought they were real funny, trapping a thief down here in the treasury.

It wasn't as amusing to Legacy. She closed her eyes, curling up against herself in a moment of self-pity.

# CHAPTER FIFTEEN

# TRUST

As comfortable as the cold, solid stone ledge was, digging into her side, she knew she couldn't lie around doing nothing forever. Not when she had a job, no, two jobs to do. Steal a crown, steal a thief. It could be anywhere between near impossible or incredibly simple, depending on how she played her cards. *But it has to get done either way.* She stood up, the ache of both her wounds and her pride fading to the back of her mind.

She had to prove herself to Owl Wings, to Rose Heart, and the rest of the thieves, that she could do something meaningful. She wasn't content spending her life in the Coyotes as a second-best option to someone else. Unlike magic, this was supposed to be her lane, something she excelled in.

As she leaped off the ledge, she felt the air with her wingtips, allowing herself to hover above the mounds of gold as she tried to catch even the smallest breeze. A sign that there was an escape hole somewhere. The air was stubbornly stagnant, unmoving, and unpleasantly humid to boot. Next, she fluttered close to the walls, carved out from the earth itself in uneven lengths of gray stone. Nothing, still, until she got to the one section in the far reaches of the back of the cavern.

Visibly, it looked no different than any other section of wall, all unassuming stone and wood far above her head, but the sounds she heard told a different story. Just behind the wall, amid a pile of stacked stones and boulders, she could hear voices. She landed gingerly on the largest stone, talons almost slipping off the rounded surface as she pressed in close to the wall.

The words were muffled and impossible to make out, but it was undoubtedly the sound of birds chattering.

She jumped as a bird thumped down beside her and pressed uncomfortably close as she took her own space on the boulder. Mooney, again.

"Don't you have minds to read and shit? I'm busy. Bugger off," Legacy said, paying her no mind as she jumped down to push at some of the smaller rocks. They shifted, only to reveal more stone behind them.

"Moon Eyes," Mooney said, sounding miffed. "What is your purpose?"

"Yeah, I know your name." Legacy shoved her entire body weight against a larger boulder. "But if you're gonna read my mind, I'm gonna be an ass about it." She grunted in effort as it barely shifted a few inches. "And my purpose is to get out of here, obviously. Since some shithead moon bird made the guards trap me."

Mooney, or Moon Eyes or whatever, sat down on the boulder, preening herself comfortably while she spoke. "I did no such thing." A long silver feather slipped between her beak. "And that's not what I meant. Evidently you are here for something other than simple robbery." Her voice rang out, hollow and devoid of feeling but awash with meaning.

"That's none of your business," Legacy said, still trying to move the boulder. It was massive, and with how close the voices sounded, she had no doubt they were just on the other side. Besides, it was the biggest rock in this damn room—it had to be put here on purpose to block the exit.

"So you admit that you are?" Moon Eyes preened another feather, beak gently pulling together the barbules until they were seamless.

"I didn't admit a damn thing," she spat, getting more annoyed by the second. Mooney's weird voice, combined with this stubborn boulder, was throwing her entire motivational streak out of whack. She had a job to do. She couldn't afford to sit here idling.

"There it is again," Moon Eyes said, sounding wispy and far away. "The job you keep mentioning; what is it? It is strange for a thief to be sitting on top of a literal mountain of gold, yet you spurn it in favor of other things." She hopped off the boulder with surprising grace. If Legacy had never heard of the Dreamseers before, she'd have never guessed Moon Eyes was blind.

"I have never seen a thief so focused on other exploits that they'd turn their back to an entire treasury."

"I've got more important things to steal. Can't risk getting my tail caught over something as trivial as some coins when I need to come back to this place again." It felt like she was oversharing, but Legacy knew her mind was just being read anyway. May as well be honest and hope Moon Eyes took favor to that rather than bother being touchy about it.

"Mm-hmm, there is more to it, though. Strange to me that you would come back, as you were here before. Why not send a new thief? One unfamiliar to the guards, I wonder." She worded it like an idle musing, but it was a question, if not a direct jab at Legacy's attempt to skirt around the subject.

"Everything is strange to you since you spend your life camped out in a basement," Legacy growled "Ugh, it doesn't matter. Why are you even this interested? Either arrest me or not, but my motivations don't mean a thing."

"They do, because I sense your cause is a relevant one to me." Moon Eyes leaped up to perch on the boulder Legacy was trying to move, the torchlight on the wall above lighting her head up in a halo. "I know how to move that stone, as I was the one who set it there. Failsafe, if King Onyx, or any future king or queen, ever disfavored me, you see."

Legacy looked to the side, rolling the choice over in her head and inspecting it from every angle. This could be a blatant trap. It felt like one, like Moon Eyes just wanted this information out of her and would leave her caged down here regardless of whether she answered or not.

But… if she was being true, this could be a quick escape to get herself back on track, something she direly needed before she started feeling the effects of thirst. Hunger too. Her growling stomach was a painful reminder she hadn't eaten for several days now, not since she'd arrived.

In hindsight, it was strange. Why hadn't they been serving food at the tavern? She hadn't noticed it the moment of, but looking back, it didn't seem like any of the occupants were eating, and the bartender never made an attempt to sell her on anything. Nor had Rose Heart brought food back to their room.

Speaking of food… the King had to feed Moon Eyes somehow. Even if Moon Eyes did try and double-cross her, she could always wait for then and strike. It was a solid backup plan. *Fine, I guess I'll be humoring her.*

"Smart thief. Now, do tell, what brings you here?" Moon Eyes said, vacant eyes pinning her down. She felt open, raw, and painfully seen, like some kind of bug stuck up on a board by pins.

Legacy meant to tell her very little.

Instead, what she told her was everything. What she didn't say aloud her companion no doubt picked up along the way as her mind flashed through the memories of it all. Naom's death, her desire to prove herself, the mysterious prophecy, her run-in with the gang.

All of it spilled out, torn from her iron-clad mind with pliers of wit and a reassuring voice as Moon Eyes hummed along, a nod here, and a head tilt there, a honey-sweet "go on" there.

The plan was to just tell her the gist of it, but the more she talked, the more she said, sentences running into each other and crashing into unrelated subjects, all in a wild tumble of words that spilled out of her beak, leaving her breathing hard by the end of it, like she'd just finished some rigorous exercise.

"So, uh, yeah, that's that," Legacy finished awkwardly, trying to recompose herself.

"You've been wanting to tell someone how you feel for a long time," Moon Eyes responded, seemingly unfazed by the emotional outburst she'd just been force fed. "Jealousy, insecurity—it all drives you to self-ruin. Not everything is your fault, but not everything isn't, either."

"All that just to spit some cryptic bullshit at me?" Legacy said, miffed. "I thought you cared about the prophecy stuff, not a bunch of emotions you think I feel." She stepped back from the boulder, gesturing at it with an overexaggerated claw flip. "I told you everything— now get that thing out of the way."

Her voice had a bite to it, but underneath it quavered, unused to talking about things she normally kept buried in her heart.

It's not that she tried to keep it down inside, it's just that she had no one to tell. Owl Wings was the one she trusted the most, but she had to look good in front of him, and she wouldn't dare tell him anything that could come off as weakness. She'd tell Fortune, but Fortune was notorious for not seeming to care much about anything, and she usually just looked confused and uncomfortable when Legacy tried to talk about anything more emotional than what she had for breakfast. Legacy didn't blame her—she felt the same way a lot of the time—but it meant she really did have no one to talk about these subjects with.

The other thieves were a no-go. To prove herself to Owl Wings, she couldn't show weakness to them either. She couldn't offer them a scrap of information they could use against her.

Moon Eyes hopped off the boulder, standing in front of it and fixing her eyes on it. "That's the problem. You see everyone as the enemy, as competition."

Legacy was so transfixed by the boulder rolling out of the way on its own that she barely even registered the words coming out of Moon Eyes' beak.

"Nothing I say is cryptic. It is merely truth you don't want to accept."

On the other side of the boulder, a tunnel disappeared into an inky blackness.

Legacy wasted no time sprinting in, the darkness welcoming and freeing. She moved so fast she barely registered that the voices she'd heard on the other side were now gone, along with whatever birds had been speaking.

Moon Eyes spoke again, standing in the tunnel entrance, lit up in gold. Her words followed Legacy down the tunnel.

"Not all those you trust will be true, but you will never know your real enemies if you cannot trust at all."

# CHAPTER SIXTEEN

# IS IT CHANCE IF IT KEEPS HAPPENING?

THE TUNNEL WAS GLOOMY, DAMP, and unpleasantly cold in a way that reminded Legacy of the Shadow Forest. But the Shadow Forest was a host to countless forms of life. Animals crept under its shade, plants thrived in the moist atmosphere, and though the darkness felt endless, there was a comfort in knowing it always led somewhere.

The tunnel had no life, except the skittering of several bugs she couldn't quite see in the dying light, and the few sprigs of dry grass that poked between cracks in the stone. Proof that no matter how uninhabitable a place felt, something would find it favorable. Usually weird creatures, like naked mole rats or luminescent bats. It felt dry and devoid of feeling. It was cold, but there was no frost or breeze, just an oppressive chilliness seeping into her bones.

She had long stopped sprinting. Now she merely crept along, more hesitant by the step. Maybe this was the trap, and she was going to be stuck inside a stone tunnel deep in the bowels of the earth while Moon Eyes cackled behind a closing boulder. Suddenly she remembered the voices that had been on the other side.

Was that just bait? There were no birds here and no echoes from the tunnel ahead either.

No, she had to trust. She wasn't sure why she was taking Moon Eyes' sentiment to heart, but if there was ever a time to practice trust, it'd be now.

*Not all those you trust will be true, but you will never know your real enemies if you cannot trust at all.*

The final words clung onto her feathers like burrs while she trudged along, holding them tight to her heart as a security blanket in the gloom.

It was ridiculous. Just because she was cold to someone didn't make them an enemy. Rose Heart was just obnoxious to be around and painfully good at her job in a way that made Legacy feel hopelessly mediocre. She was still a Coyote, though, which meant she was far from an enemy.

The dark crept in closer, the last trickles of light fading as she found her steps blindly.

*Is this really how a good thief would treat a fellow guild member?* a voice in her head whispered. Her own. With no one around to talk to, her argumentative nature turned on itself, gnawing at its own legs like a trapped animal.

She powered onward. Something dashed alongside her feet.

*How about a friend? Would you feel betrayed if a friend acted like this to you?* her thoughts heckled, like ink spilled across her brain, seeping into the cracks, unable to be scrubbed out.

*She's not a friend, though. She's an asshole.* Legacy stumbled when her claws hit an incline, painfully recoiling before resuming her steps, more careful.

*But what if she considers you one?*

Her heart was beating so loud she could swear it was echoing off the walls.

*She went looking for you. You were gone, and she was worried about you.*

She took a deep breath, trying to steady herself.

*You wouldn't have done the same if it was her. You let her leave and didn't even try to convince her to stay.*

A minuscule gust of air kissed her cheek. It was either a sign of the end finally nearing or something breathing on her. The thought made her shiver.

*She may not be kind, but she's never wanted the worst for you.*

Her thoughts blew away at another gust of air, warm and carrying a smell of both dust and smoke. Pale light illuminated the path before her.

Her thoughts were gone now, banished into the recesses of her mind as she dashed forward with newfound energy, but the stain remained.

She was so excited to leave that gloomy, awful tunnel that she almost forgot where she was, coming to a sliding stop just before she bolted out the exit. It looked like a hole in the wall with some solid object blocking the other side, the back of what was maybe a bookshelf or some kind of cabinet. The only sign it was an exit was the halo of warm light seeping through the edges.

She flipped her hood over her head, ensuring she was unable to be seen. *Still have to be careful,* she thought as she pressed an ear against the shelf, straining to hear anything on the other side—a moving piece of furniture would no doubt draw attention.

Nothing, silence, not a peep from the other side.

She cautiously pressed the shelf only to find it was incredibly light and slid to the side with ease.

The room was, thankfully, empty. Torches lit the walls amber, and an empty plate sat on a lone table in the center of the room, but not a bird in sight. She crept in, holding tight to the wall so if anyone did come inside they wouldn't bump into her.

She had no idea where she was, but it must still be underground, if the cold stone floor and stale air were any hint. There was no door, only an empty archway at the end of the room. She slipped out, head swiveling left to right to check she was still in the clear. Being invisible helped, but it didn't make her invincible, if the near incident she'd just escaped from was any sort of indicator. To think she'd done all that just to get caught by some lone Dreamseer prowling the treasury. It was a ridiculous streak of bad luck.

Or maybe not. Every kingdom did have one Dreamseer, elected to guide them and serve as a delegate between the Dreamseers kingdom as a whole and the individual kingdoms of Camorthes. While the Dreamseers were supposed to remain entirely neutral to prevent any bias in their efforts to serve the greater world, it made sense they'd want a more personal connection within the kingdoms.

Most of the time they just hovered around the royals, out of sight and out of mind from the general public, which was pretty much what Moon Eyes was doing.

*I guess this one's on me.* She relented, knowing this wasn't something she could pin on luck alone. Really, though, was it her fault thieves also liked to be out of sight and out of mind in, coincidentally, the exact same place the Dreamseers did?

She sped through a few more rooms, all similar to each other. The same run-down, rustic style of furniture, stone floors, and torchlight, with only the furniture changing slightly between them.

She came to a screeching halt at a dim lit staircase.

It went in two directions. The wooden, worn, but well-kept stairs went up, scuffed by years of use. A warm glow emanated from above, inviting and a sign that the exit was that way. The other set was wood as well but aged far worse. They looked rickety, bowed, and unmaintained, disappearing down into the inky blackness of a stone-walled walkway.

A normal bird would take the stairs up, but she didn't want to risk being cocky again. The stairs going down would hopefully lead to some kind of basement area where she could slip out in a sneakier fashion.

With a final glance to make sure no one was around, she began the descent.

And a descent it was. The length of the staircase was nothing impressive, but the unstable nature of the stairs and the tight, claustrophobic stone walls made every step down take twice as long as it should have. One stair was missing, another was so poorly bolted to the wall it bowed under her step, sending a jolt of anxiety down her spine. The walls were so tight she couldn't even use her wings to catch herself if she fell, and it was hard to avoid knocking her shoulders against the torches pinned up on the walls. Thankfully they were yellow, a fire color weaker than hers, so they did little more than warm her.

When she came to the ground level, she paused and took a long moment to pray thanks to Darivan that she hadn't tripped on the way down.

The room she was in now was dark, massive, and had an uncomfortably low roof. The size was due not to the height but to how far back this narrow, tunnel-like room seemed to stretch. It went on countless wing-lengths ahead—so far she couldn't even see the next wall before it was swallowed by suffocating blackness.

On top of that, something about it felt strangely familiar.

The air chilled her as she walked, cautiously keeping an eye out for anyone else down here, but she seemed to be alone.

When she passed the first wall, she was met with endless rows of jail cells, and an explanation for why she remembered this place at all. This was where she'd been caged up after the incident on her last heist. The only reason she didn't notice it right away was she'd been blindfolded on the way in—and the way out when Owl Wings paid her way to freedom. Probably some security measure so escaped criminals couldn't have an idea of how to get out as easily.

The cells were mostly empty, and the ones filled were eerily quiet, heads turning to silently watch her as she walked down the rows. Pairs of eyes glowed in the dark, the birds themselves barely visible in the dusty gloom.

It stayed that way row after dreary row, eyes pinned on her back with no discernible expression. No murmurs or whispers, just stares.

How they even knew she was there, she had no idea. Her hood was up, so she was supposed to be invisible. Maybe it was all in her head.

She shook herself out, walking faster down the way.

She'd been here before, but she was sure it wasn't half this creepy when she was inside her dusty cell. *Maybe because nobody could watch me,* she mused nervously.

As endless as it felt, she eventually saw a wall emerge from the depths of darkness on the other side—another staircase, no doubt as rickety as the one she'd just come down and hopefully leading to an area less populated, if not directly outside.

Before she could dash up, a bird, almost invisible within the shadows of his cell, spoke. Her feathers stood on end for two reasons. One, because after such a long silence, any sound outside her own footsteps was a shock. Two, because she recognized the voice.

Though even if she hadn't, his penchant for self-identification would have told her who it was regardless.

"O'Hara sees a naive little thief who does not seem to understand that magical items don't work in the depths of hell." O'Hara cackled.

Ah, right. Of course the prison would have wards against magic. It didn't occur to her because she wasn't a magician, like a fisherman would see the clouds above and predict a storm, whereas a normal bird would just see clouds. This was surprisingly relieving, if only because it meant she wasn't going crazy and those prisoners actually had been staring at her. Normal behavior from birds with nothing else to do.

She wanted to keep walking, but the logical part of her knew she was seeing one of two much-needed items caged up in front of her. This could be useful.

She backpedaled a few steps to stand square in front of the cell.

Where the other cells had a torch to keep them lit, this one had nothing, just a slab of stone for a bed, a bowl of water by the bars, and a long-burned-out stub on the wall where a torch was supposed to be.

There was also a tall pole in the center, a pillar of stone carved to look somewhat like a strange tree branch bursting from the ground. It was hard to make him out in the shadows, but she could faintly see O'Hara perched atop it, a sturdy chain attaching him to its base.

It felt excessive, but then again, this was a prison underneath the castle. It wouldn't be good if criminals could circumvent the bars and run amok in the area with the most concentrated wealth in the Golden Hearts kingdom. She frowned as she remembered her own chains and her own cold, decrepit cell.

"How the hell are you already in jail? I just saw you not too long ago," she said. Probably not the most courteous greeting, but she was curious how he was this incompetent.

"O'Hara does not appreciate your tone. See, he was doing fine until a certain thief lagged behind and made him wait. Meanwhile, the guards saw my lovely ice-blood face and realized I was a wanted man." He spoke with his usual cheery lilt, but there was a slither of malice to his words, a warning that he blamed her for this, and that whatever meager trust she'd fostered was gone.

"So you just stood there like a dumbass?" Legacy said before realizing that was probably the worst possible response if she wanted to redeem herself.

No, she shouldn't have to redeem herself. It was his fault for standing there in a brightly lit street and for slipping up and doing whatever he did to become a wanted man in the first place. If he wasn't so damn untrustworthy, this would be easy.

"Very rude of you, considering O'Hara was waiting for you. If it's any curiosity, he did not know he was a wanted man until the guards told him," he said, expression indiscernible in the dark. Likely not of his own choice—the other prisoners probably all had the ability to light their own torches whenever they so chose. An ice-blood like him had no fire to work with, only cold, searing ice.

The fact that no one relit his torch told her just how often the guards came down here to check their prisoners, and slightly eased her sense of urgency at making a break for it.

"Ugh, whatever, I have places to be. Have fun in jail." He was important to her plans, but he certainly wasn't going anywhere—she could save breaking him out until later.

"O'Hara is not fond of chains," he said. She paused to catch his last words. "Perhaps we can come to an agreement."

It was a strange offer, given that she had no power here—no key, no lock picks, nothing to break him free right at the moment—but she considered it nonetheless. It could rebalance their dynamic, tip the scales in her favor again if she did something like this for him.

It was all about trust.

Maybe that's what Moon Eyes had meant, that she was missing out on great opportunities by not taking advantage of trust.

"Not much I can do from here, but keep talking," she said, keeping her back to him like she was still considering leaving. She wasn't, but it was the illusion that counted, the idea of making him more desperate so he would more likely agree to a deal that favored her.

"The guards, they carry a pair of keys on their ankles, one for the door, one for the chain. A flawed setup, really, but some poor soul a few cells down strangled himself on his chain, and the guards could not save him because their keys were hanging in their barracks, inside a locked chest, rather than on their person."

It was then it struck her that he still had his hat, the brim faintly lit in the glow seeping from the other cells. It was kind of funny, and she had to suppress a chuckle at the thought of the guards deciding to let him keep it on.

"Alright, here's my deal," she said, only half-turned to face him. "Help me with my job, just this one heist, start to finish, and I'll bail your ass out."

He seemed hesitant, though maybe it was just the fact that his eyes were hidden in the shade of the room and his hat made it harder to tell what he was thinking.

"Hm, O'Hara supposes he did agree to help you already, so, despite your horrifically sour attitude, and the fact that it's your fault he is here at all, so you really should let him go on a moral basis, he will help you with your heist."

Bingo. She smiled, finally turning to face him in full. "Sounds about right. Just hold tight while I go nick some keys."

Clearly the guards didn't come here often, but they had to bring food and water to the prisoners at some point, right? She bolted back down the hall of jail cells to where she started, no longer bothered by the eyes on her back. Once she got to the staircase, she situated herself in the shadowy corner, tucked tight to the wall as best she could. She pulled her cloak closer, making sure it covered most of her body. It didn't make her invisible, given the wards, but in a less magical use, the dark-brown fabric hid her white feathers, helping her blend into the darkness.

The hours crawled on by, like slugs inching their way across a forest floor, barely moving in the grand scheme of things as faster creatures darted on past, so much quicker they may well be in another dimension.

Nothing.

A fly zipped past her beak, clinging to the wall and doing the weird hand rub they often did.

More waiting. A heavy, oppressive silence draped over her like a heavy blanket while she waited with bated breath.

Footsteps sounded down the spiral stairs, beginning as a low thud high above that she felt more than heard, growing louder and louder as the bird descended. A lone guard appeared, burly and muscular, towering in height as the Golden Hearts birds did, with keys jangling against his ankle.

He didn't have a chance to look before Legacy was on him. She moved with urgency, clinging to his back and digging needle-sharp claws into his shoulders. She freed one claw to pull her dagger free and slice it clean across his throat.

Thieves weren't supposed to kill, if they could help it, but sometimes the situation couldn't wait for sneakier, smarter methods to come to mind. Sometimes you had to act right then and there and deal with the consequences afterward. *This is one of those situations,* she thought as she jumped off the bird just as his body thudded heavily to the ground, eyes dull.

It was only considered "banned" because some birds, such as Fortune, were far too quick to resort to the "no witnesses to snitch if no witnesses are alive" method, which only hurt the thieves in the long run. Especially if their client wanted the target short one sentimental valuable instead of deceased. Worse if the client became the suspect in the murder, and the thieves had to shut them up or risk having their name and identity slandered before not only potential clients but the law.

It was risky not just for the individual but for the guild's reputation as a whole, and that's what made it so looked down upon.

The guard choked out a wheeze, curved talons twitching as his blood spilled across the floor. A heavy copper smell permeated the air.

Legacy wiped her dripping blade off on his tawny feathers before sheathing it, watching his death throes apathetically.

It wasn't the first life she'd taken, and she'd long since moved past feeling any sort of guilt or remorse. It was a dog-eat-dog world, and you had to be some degree of selfish if you wanted to come out on top.

Selfishness, while often pictured a bad trait, was a quality she was hesitant to shake. She'd even go as far as to say she was fond of having it. It's what let her get ahead, what kept her soundly asleep at night when someone more empathetic would toss and turn in their guilt.

The guard was just doing his job, but so was she, and when they collided, she won.

That's all there was to it.

She hadn't always been that way, but when she and Fortune had been closer, the latter's influence was unshakeable.

She grabbed the guard's leg—it was pliant and moved easily, not yet stiff with rigor mortis—as she worked the keyring open and slid it off. Two small keys, both silver, shone in the dim light. One was slightly more worn, littered with scratches and imperfections, likely the one to the gate itself, as she imagined they unlocked that far more often than the one on the prisoners' ankle chains.

When she yet again approached his cell, O'Hara was smiling, his grin barely visible.

"O'Hara sees you have done as he asked. Now he asks that you let him go and he may be on his way to help you with your menial labors."

"Ugh, can it. I couldn't give less than a damn about you. I just need another thief because Rose Heart bailed on me," she said, sliding the more worn key into the gate. It turned roughly, almost getting stuck before the gate clicked open.

Hypothetically, she could release every prisoner in here, but that would draw way too much attention to herself, and she knew that no matter how happy they were to be free, someone would end up snitching on her for it.

It would also be total chaos, being that this place housed anything from tax evaders to serial killers.

She grabbed O'Hara's leg, and he recoiled. "Ah! O'Hara did not agree to be manhandled," he said, leg held comically tight to his stomach.

"Alright, be that way, then," she spat back, turning to leave.

"No, no, wait. O'Hara supposes you could manhandle him, just this once."

"Don't say it like that," she said, grabbing him again, more forcefully, and pulling his slender silver ankle close to unlock the chain. This one went far smoother, the key turned easily and the chain popped off with a clink.

He sprung free immediately, dashing out the open door and sprinting to the staircase in a blur of white and gray.

She would have thought he was abandoning her if he hadn't been yelling as he ran.

"Now let us escape this hellhole! O'Hara belongs in the bright sun and underneath blue skies, not in this musty basement," he shouted theatrically.

*Way to keep it discreet.*

Legacy sprinted after him, struggling to keep up. The distance was too short to warrant flying, and his long winterpie legs completely dwarfed her own. It took her two strides to make up for just one of his.

She wondered what it would have been like to be born a full winterpie. Hell, she wondered what it would have been like to inherit any features from the half ice-blood she already had. According to Vinmara, a magic spell was done on her egg to reveal her race before she'd hatched. Given her parents were nowhere around, she would have otherwise had no idea what she was.

Half winterpie, with only a white circle around her pupil to show for it, and half Long Shadows firepie, which made up the rest of her. The imbalance was so extreme she rarely bothered to tell others she was a hybrid, just claimed full Long Shadows blood unless someone questioned the white in her eyes. Then she'd say "oh, probably just a grandparent or something" and leave it at that.

Apparently, that's how it usually was with those kinds of crosses. Winterpie blood was famous for how recessive it was, and usually it ended up dwarfed by anything else. It was the reason they stood as the one kingdom who had actually outlawed cross-kingdom relationships. While the other kingdoms had varying opinions—from indifferent, to disliked, and everything in between—in the Frozen Winds it was a punishable crime.

These stairs were worse than the last, and every step felt frighteningly hazardous, except the ones that weren't there at all.

Still, she was right about this staircase leading outside, and the duo made a hasty escape.

# CHAPTER SEVENTEEN
# REPRIEVE

Legacy and O'Hara emerged from inside one of the many weathered pillars surrounding the castle. It leaned worryingly sideways, with bricks missing or askew and an air of a place that hadn't been kept up in years, if ever. It was set far in the back, the massive eyesore tucked away behind what she assumed were the royal gardens and shielded by trees with wide green leaves.

She exited quickly, wanting to be as far from inside that sketchy tower as she could. O'Hara lagged behind, looking side to side with confusion set in his brow.

"O'Hara doesn't suppose you could take the cloak off? He cannot see you, and he knows this will be quite the job if his comrade's whereabouts are unknown," he said, facing a tree that was nowhere near her.

*Almost forgot about that.*

She slipped the hood down, still baffled at the lack of feeling that came with it. There should be something, a magical tingle or a buzz in her ear, anything to let her know when it was working and when it wasn't. Having to rely on the reactions of others could be detrimental, and even if Victor's magic was supposedly near unbreakable, it was defeated by that ward over the prison, so she felt she had the right to be cautious.

"Why do you even talk like that?" she said. O'Hara jolted, then turned to face where she was actually standing. "It's so inconvenient. I know your name. You don't have to say it every damn time."

"It is a winterpie thing you would not understand," he said, trotting along the wall that connected to the pillar, looking it up and down for a discreet exit.

"All I understand is that that's bullshit," she remarked, scanning the wall herself. It was endlessly tall, a massive gray structure looming high over her head. Flying over it would be stupid, now that the guards knew O'Hara's face. Even from a distance, his white feathers would stick out in stark contrast to a kingdom of birds colored in browns, red, and golds.

"Ah, well, O'Hara was raised by wolves, you see. He cannot shake their manner of speech." He pressed his claws against a spot on the wall, but nothing happened.

"Wolves aren't real," she said, following him. She'd read the phrase "raised by wolves" in a book once, and there was the Wolf Thieves Guild, but the creatures themselves were nothing but a myth. From what she'd

heard and read, they were massive, dangerous creatures, alike to dogs but ten times the size and with an
unquenchable thirst for blood.

The last part sounded a bit like vampires, and she
wondered if wolves might not be vampire dogs.

"Hm, you are no fun. Mayhaps O'Hara enjoys
hearing his own name, and that is all." He sighed,
shoving at another stone. It stood unyielding beneath
his talons.

"Yeah, I can see it. 'Sides, I know it's not that in-
grained in you—I heard you slip up in the canyon when
you thought I was a ghost." She overshot him, looking at
the base of the wall as she walked for any sign of a hole
or maybe a drainage ditch of some kind to crawl out of.
The grass was cool and dry, crunching under her claws.

"Ahm, you heard no such thing," O'Hara said,
refusing to look her direction. "I think you imagined it."

*Coy bastard.* She had no retorts for that, but it didn't
matter, as just then, she stumbled on an indent in the
ground, it was muddy on the edges with water flowing
through. Damp strands of grass hung over the stark
edge, not naturally formed in the earth but cut through
by birds and their tools.

The grass was bright green, flourishing with
moisture.

The drainage ditch stood about her height, and
where it met the wall, metal bars came down to rest
just on the surface of the water.

She grimaced. It was an exit alright, but one she'd
have to swim through.

"Get over here; found our way out. Then we can
crash a night and grab something to eat." She pointed

a sharp claw at the water. "You go first." It looked like a safe way out, but it wouldn't hurt to make him test it.

"O'Hara sees what you are doing, and he is not content to be a guinea pig. Feel lucky he is indebted to you," O'Hara said. He then grabbed his hat, held it tight, took a comically deep breath, and threw himself into the water. The clear surface broke with a loud splash, droplets spraying Legacy in the face.

He moved awkwardly, head going under repeatedly, and it looked more like he was jumping along the bottom than swimming, but he made it through the grate without drowning. Winterpies were supposedly good swimmers, so someone had either lied to her, or O'Hara was a special case.

As soon as she saw him hauling himself up to shore on the other side, she dove in.

The water was cold, a freezing shock so sudden she had to suppress a gasp when she plunged in, but once she adjusted, it was easy to propel herself along. As soon as she got to the grate, she dipped her head under for a brief moment, then emerged on the other side.

Pulling herself out of the water proved to be a feat, her cloak sodden and trying its damnedest to drag her back in, but she dug her claws into the grass fronds and hauled herself out.

She shook herself violently, trying to dispel some of the water that soaked her feathers through. They were smooth and oiled, and in rain or a light spray the drops would just roll off, but being completely submerged was not what they were meant for, and now she looked like a soggy wreck. She shivered in the air at a chill that cut to her bones—in part because of her drenched status but now that she was outside the wall, she could see the sun dipping below the horizon.

The sky enveloped the vast world in front of her, hazy purples and golds in the air casting a pink hue on the rolling hills and sprigs of stray heather. Silvery clouds dotted the sky, outlined in the sun's light. The city ended here, and the only buildings were farmhouses dotting the countryside, wheat fields stretching on endlessly.

A lone tree perched on a nearby hill, branches stretched wide in every direction and the base nearly the size of the tower they'd just come out of. It looked near tall enough to touch the sun, heavy branches brushing the clouds.

"We could sleep there, I guess," she said, pointing to it.

"O'Hara hesitates to agree with you, but he will for this."

Birds were meant for trees anyway. It would be fine, and in the morning, she could try her hand at finding something to eat out in those fields.

Her dreams were a formless mishmash of the events that had just transpired: Moon Eyes and her creepy stare, the fight with Rose Heart, everything about O'Hara, all collected into one emotional roller coaster that she woke from with a gasp, blue eyes flying open. Then she promptly forgot the details, as often happened with dreams.

The wind buffeted her stomach from her place high above in the branches of the tree. Her claws dug into the rough reddish-brown wood, keeping her locked in place even in the deep throes of sleep. The thick green leaves around her were lit up by the rising sun, casting speckled shadows across her feathers.

Down far, far below, so much so it was faded and muddled, O'Hara slept in a hollow at the trunk. He'd stated something about "winterpies do not content themselves to sit in trees with little bugs and the like," which was ridiculous. But she supposed he did come from a land of glaciers and ice, with almost no trees to be found except pines too dense to sleep in. He said it was the bugs, but he was probably scared to perch so high on something that swayed with every breath the wind took.

She chuckled as she bounced off the branch, diving down so fast the tree's rough bark blurred into one smooth red line. Her wings stayed tight to her body until the last second, when she flung them open to catch herself on a drift of air before alighting in front of the trunk.

Sunlight filtered into the hollow, casting her shadow sharp against the back wall. Nobody was inside, and she felt a pang of regret for trusting O'Hara to keep his word. He was a thief, as sleazy as she was, and if it were her, she'd have run off too. She turned around with a heavy heart, only to collide with a mass of white feathers. "Mphh!" She spat, backing up. "What in the hell?"

"O'Hara has utilized his excellent hunting prowess to bring breakfast—he hopes you are grateful. If you are not, he will steal your lover." On his back lay two jackalopes, thin and bloody but big enough to give the pair the energy they'd need for the work ahead.

A pang of hunger gripped her stomach.

"I don't have a lover, meathead, and I'm not into your type, so don't get any ideas," she remarked, grabbing one of the jackalopes off his back. It flopped down in her grip, fresh and still bleeding. She took care to avoid jabbing herself on its antlers.

"O'Hara is disgusted you would ever assume he likes or enjoys your presence. He is here only out of obligation and brought you a meal because he assumed you're incompetent at feeding yourself." His tone was snide. He had a strange way of talking, and outside the way he spoke about himself in the third person, as well as the rapid-fire pace he spat out words, he never looked truly upset. Even his insults and meaner remarks had an air of amusement to them, like he found everything funny.

It grated on her patience and almost made her miss the bite that Rose Heart had. It was sharper, meaner, but it felt honest, not like this weird, amused facade O'Hara put up.

Worse if it wasn't a facade, because that meant he just didn't take Legacy seriously. The thought made her stomach roil, and she torched her jackalope with a little too much enthusiasm. The edges curled and tiny plumes of smoke dissipated into the air. Now her meal was burnt and bitter, but it was still edible.

"Where are you even from?" she asked, tearing into the furry creature. The hunger in her gut took her mind by storm, allowing her to ignore the aftertaste of charcoal. "You talk real weird, not like any bird anywhere I've ever been, which is most places." She didn't specify further, not wanting to give him any details to use to skirt around her question, as he often did.

She'd been to most of the eastern kingdoms—the Frozen Winds, the Burning Talons, the Long Shadows, and the Golden Hearts. That left the Sunlit Clouds, Solar Eclipse, and Dreamseers kingdoms as the only ones left untouched. But she still knew birds from those places. Misfire was hatched in the Sunlit Clouds, Rose Heart in the Solar Eclipse—O'Hara was undoubtedly not a Dreamseer—and none of them spoke the way he did.

"O'Hara does not need to tell you that," he said, taking a bite of his painfully raw jackalope, blood dripping onto his pale chest. "But he will anyways. O'Hara was born into magic."

She waited for him to continue.

He didn't, just took another bite, beak squishing the tender meat as he tore it to shreds small enough to swallow.

"Uhhh, that's it? Magic?" She had a vague idea what he could be getting at, but still. Was it literal? A metaphor? A lie? Gods, he was frustrating.

"Magic, yes. The families of posh, rich, goddess-blessed birds all competing with their silly bloodlines. Alas, despite his father and his mother being so blessed, O'Hara drew his straw short and ended up in the underground. The place where the gamblers and smugglers crawl to make their homes among the dishonest."

*He's like me.*

"Which family was it?" she pressed, though she had a couple of guesses. It definitely wasn't the Hir Lanas. He was the same age, if not younger, than she was, and she'd have seen him or heard him mentioned before.

Not the Mir Elves—they were the only family removed from the fight of magical bloodlines and notably only had five family members at any given time. She wasn't sure what that was about. They were a strange group.

Fer Vyr was a no. They were all non-winterpies and quite proud of it.

That left Del Vero and Ser Vynn. Both near equal in power, and both mostly winterpies.

"O'Hara wonders why this matters, but he is a self-reject of the Ser Vynns. Have you ever heard of Victor? O'Hara is his nephew, son of his brother Virgil."

It was a rhetorical question. Everyone knew Victor. Her neck feathers spiked up in surprise.

"Oh, I—I never would have guessed. Sorry for the questions. It just seems kind of funny we were both raised by magicians."

"You too? Funny indeed, though let us leave it at that; O'Hara is not fond of his blood."

*Strange,* she thought as they continued their meal in silence. But something nagged at the back of her mind that she couldn't quite pull free. Not pertaining to his story, she understood that more than well, but a feeling of camaraderie that didn't sit right in her stomach.

It felt like she'd raised a meat rabbit, and now that the time was coming to put the cleaver to its neck, she was hesitating. It was a warm, happy feeling that felt like it could get in the way of her goals.

*He's not a friend,* she had to remind herself, *he's a sacrifice. Remember your selfishness.*

# CHAPTER EIGHTEEN

# THREE THIEVES

LEGACY FINISHED PLUCKING THE JACKALOPE bones clean of every meat scrap and string of sinew before tossing them aside and standing up. She faced the city with a determined crease in her brow. With the massive wall of the castle in the forefront of her vision, she could barely make out the tops of taller buildings and spires beyond it.

Today was the day: time to steal a crown. She leaned over O'Hara, claw raised to bonk him on the head. Before she could wake him, a red dot in the distance caught her eye. A deep crimson bird flew low over the hills, straight toward the pair of thieves.

She reached for her dagger but stopped when the bird came close enough that she could see their features. Leaf-green eyes, deep-red feathers turning to bright cerise-pink at the wings and tail, and little feather growths sticking out on the chest and head.

O'Hara stirred, awakened by the tense air.

Rose Heart landed gracefully, long wings brushing the ground with a *whoosh*. Her face curled in a frown.

"Before either of you even says a word," she said, shooting daggers to O'Hara as he opened his beak, "I'm not here because I care about either of you. I'm here because, after a period of thinking—"

"Hah, didn't know you could do that," Legacy interrupted. O'Hara cackled.

Rose Heart paused for a long moment, jet-black claws digging into the ground as though she was imagining the soft grass to be the face of a certain someone. Maybe two someones.

"Because, after a period of thinking, I realized you two cracked eggs couldn't organize a piss-up in a brewery," Rose Heart said, voice scathing. Legacy had a hunch it wasn't what she was going to say originally, but she had the better sense to keep her beak shut this time.

There was more to Rose Heart's expression than annoyance, something tugging at her features more akin to disappointment. What did she expect, a party to welcome her back after storming off? If she wasn't so immature that she'd abandon her fellow thief, maybe she wouldn't have set herself up to be let down like that.

The words rang hollow inside Legacy's head, but she didn't understand why. It was Rose Heart's fault—really, what was she expecting? An apology?

*Oh...*

Legacy stole a glance at the red bird's face, just now realizing no one had spoken for an uncomfortable stretch of time. It wasn't just disappointment, not in the usual way one could be disappointed, over small mishaps or maybe someone not performing up to snuff, like during their training. It was a letdown, sad sort of expression, like she'd offered a treat to a stray cat and it just darted away into the alleys without a second glance.

The feeling made Legacy uncomfortable, like her feathers were crawling with insects, so she spoke to fill the space.

"So, are you here to join us or just stand there like a dunce?" It came out meaner than she meant, or maybe she was finally noticing the bite to her own words.

"You are truly, painfully insufferable. I want nothing to do with a thief who wants nothing but the worst for me, but I realized that this would reflect poorly on me if I let you take all the credit." Her eyes narrowed, green slits burning a hole into Legacy's forehead, voice lowering to a sinister growl. "Unlike you, I can put our differences behind us to get a job done—something you should learn if your precious daddy Owl Wings is ever gonna see you as anything more than a number in the ranks."

Legacy lunged at her, body moving before her mind as she dug her talons into the meat of Rose Heart's shoulders, throwing her to the ground with a surprised yell. Rose Heart was far taller, but Legacy had surprise on her side, and now she held the upper hand as the two began battering each other in a flurry of dagger-sharp claws, slapping wings, and beak jabs.

O'Hara stepped back a few paces, dumbfounded. He reached up to hold the brim of his hat in one claw, watching the fight with shocked interest.

Legacy rolled just before Rose Heart jammed a claw toward her eye, using her smaller body to try and dodge between Rose Heart's legs.

Now that the surprise wore off, Rose Heart easily snagged her claws on Legacy's cloak, pinning the smaller bird to the scuffed grass and pressing a claw against the wounds on her neck, newly scabbed over and raw.

Legacy kicked and struggled, trying to regain her footing, but the ache in her neck forced her back down, and she lay defeated in the dewy weeds.

Before she could speak, Rose Heart grabbed her beak, holding it tightly shut.

She spoke with a soft fury, like the low hum before a storm rolled in. Enough to get her point across but not enough O'Hara could hear, regardless of how much he strained to listen.

"I'm done with you and your childish antics. Darling, I have done nothing but try to help you again and again, and again, but what do you do in return? Where have you ever tried for me? I don't need us to be friends, I don't want us to be friends, but I do want a fellow thief who can shut her beak for two Darivan-damned seconds and learn to play nice long enough to get a job done."

Legacy struggled, one last feeble attempt to break free, but Rose Heart's grip was firm, using the full force of her body weight as leverage.

"Owl Wings made me the Master Thief, and you know why? Because I'm not self-absorbed and bent on blaming my problems on everyone around me. Because when I fuck up, I own up to it instead of tripping over backward trying to justify myself."

Legacy averted her eyes, looking at the grass beside her instead. It swayed in the breeze. Rose Heart jerked her beak sideways, forcing Legacy to look her in the eyes.

"You keep telling yourself it's happening because life isn't fair, because I'm prettier, because I'm a better thief. You know what? That doesn't have a thing to do with it. It has nothing to do with anything. I'm just not a self-absorbed asshole."

Rose Heart let go, brushing off her feathers and shaking the dust free. Her expression was one of cold indifference.

Legacy got up and turned her back to her fellow Coyote, too ashamed to look at her, or O'Hara, who'd been creeping closer as best he could. She kept her shoulders hunched tightly to herself.

When Rose Heart spoke again, her voice was softer, almost kinder. It made Legacy sick. "It was a horrific event, what happened to Naom, and a convenient scape-goat for you to pin your struggles on, but it doesn't mean anything. Our jobs are hard, thieves die, and sometimes you can't look any deeper into it than that."

"So come on, dear, let's steal this crown and get on with the job."

Three thieves flew in silence, wings buffeted by the breeze and the rising sun warming their backs.

O'Hara was the first to dare break the silence, cheery voice grating after the stretched minutes of empty air.

"O'Hara does presume you know how to get inside the castle?"

It was a question but also an opening, an invitation to speak after she'd kept her beak shut for what felt like hours.

For how odd he was, O'Hara had a surprising charisma about him, a way with words that hinted at an intelligence hidden underneath his outlandish personality.

*Only hinted, though,* she huffed to herself. He was still ridiculous.

"Uhhh, yeah, I was lookin' for that yesterday," she said. "I think the king's gotta have a balcony somewhere near the top. I can get in that way." She paused, thinking. It was broad daylight, and the three were blatantly out of place in this city, but that had never stopped them before.

They could wait for nighttime, but then the king himself might be in the room, and he'd previously been a renowned warrior. Not the type of bird to get in a fight with, not if she wanted to keep her neck wounds from being opened up *again.*

Hopefully he wasn't wearing it, or else sneaking in would be for nothing.

She flung up her hood and dove for the balcony, splitting off from O'Hara and Rose Heart as they landed in the streets below, tiny specks of red and white darting along in a sea of oranges, browns, and yellows.

Several balconies stuck out from the tallest spire of the castle, of varying sizes and decorated in various ways. One seemed more ornamental than the rest, draped with ribbons and lush, exotic plants. The kind of thing only royalty could afford.

She landed on the railing silently, pinning her wings to her body as she crept, step by step, to the door.

Before she went in, she pressed her ear to it, listening for any noise inside.

Nothing. As it should be. The king and queen were busy birds, after all, and probably had more important things to do than loaf around in their room in the middle of the day.

She rested a claw on the handle, golden and swirled in beautiful ornate designs.

It felt too easy. This was the king and queen of the Golden Hearts kingdom, not some working-class family; how were they content to live so unguarded? Sure, she had invisibility on her side, but there were wards against it in the prison, and Moon Eyes in the treasury, meaning whoever was in charge of security considered magic a potential threat.

She opened the door, the sun behind her casting a stark shadow on the polished oak floor.

It looked… like a royal bedroom. The furniture was all unnaturally clean and kept, carved with an attention to detail she'd never seen before. The fabrics that made up the rug and the covers on the bed looked pricey. She didn't know a pillow could look expensive, but every single one in this room whispered luxury. Nearly unused at that. Royalty had to be too busy to bask in the luxury of their overpriced cushions too long, but the slips of time they got between work had to be heavenly.

No crown, though, not on the vanity or poking out of the closet. Nothing. What was there were plants. There had to be a potted plant on every surface available, different species of them hanging down from pots suspended on the ceiling or growing up from ornate porcelain pots resting delicately on the ground. The pleasant floral smell that hung in the air was familiar and comforting.

She darted to the bookshelf and started sliding books out, seeing if any were victims of the old "hollow book" trick, used for storing sentimental items discreetly. None were big enough to hold a crown, but blackmail would work just as well.

Halfway through the second shelf, she grabbed a large red book, and the lack of weight almost made her slam it up into her face. *Score.* She flung it open so fast the binding creaked in protest, and was met with a small string of glistening pearls.

They looked familiar, but she couldn't quite place why. Just like the smell of the room. She pocketed them either way, shoving them into one of the many small pockets hidden in her cloak. They were expensive but nothing to waste time over. The blue book next to it was also a cache, with a small golden key inside. *Whatever it's for, it'll be worth holding onto,* she thought as she slid it into her cloak.

She grabbed the next book, continuing down the line until she slid the last green book into place.

There were no more valuables to be found, but what she did notice was the content of the books. A lot of them were about nature, plants, and the other environments of Camorthes, but an equally large amount were about criminals. Specifically, thieves and assassins. The books ranged from wild assumptions about how guilds of either kind operated, general advice given by criminals during interrogation, and an array of other books with similar content matter. Some even had loose sheets of confidential police reports sandwiched between the pages like bookmarks.

They looked new compared to the rest of the shelf, which showed its use. The little tears in pages and bent corners betrayed how thoroughly read they had been in their short lifetime.

She grabbed a few that seemed particularly informational and silently turned them to ashes between her claws, just to get them out of the claws of the royals. They didn't need to know all that.

Next, she tried the vanity, pulling open drawers and digging through carved jewelry boxes. Lots of pearls, again, and a few rings, but nothing that screamed king or queen. This felt like the same stuff you'd find in a particularly rich noble's home.

Footsteps echoed outside, and she went rigid. She dropped everything she'd been holding and dashed to the closet. She threw it open, the thin wood door almost catching as she slid inside, then shut it behind her.

Inside the closet was painfully cramped—she felt all sorts of strange fabrics and articles of clothing dangling against her face from where they were hung up. Underneath her was a disorganized pile of clothes strewn across the closet floor with no rhyme or reason. That familiar scent hung in the air heavier than before, something mossy and nice. She breathed it in but stopped mid-breath when the bedroom door creaked open.

# OH, MY PRINCESS

FOOTSTEPS, LIGHT AND DAINTY, CRASHED into Legacy's fears. She pressed herself deeper into the clothing pile, hoping whoever it was would grab what they needed and leave.

They did; the only problem was that whatever they needed was in the closet. She huddled deeper into the clothes in a futile hope it would keep whoever was here from touching her. She was invisible, as long as they didn't touch her, she should be fine.

The doors to the closet slid open with force, bright light burning Legacy's eyes.

When they finally adjusted, she saw Louisa standing there with a dumbfounded expression.

Dumbfounded quickly became furious, Louisa's yellow eyes hardening in a glare. "Ugh, so I was right about you! You are just some sick stalker pervert!" she shouted.

Legacy's first thought was *how can she see me?* Her second was that if she was going to be caught, she wasn't going to be caught as some creep.

"I—wait, no, it's not what it looks like," she blurted, stumbling over her words. She had a third thought: *why was Louisa even in here?*

"You're sitting in a pile of my clothes, in my room—what is it supposed to look like? What else could you possibly be doing?" Louisa said, claws tense. "I really thought you were better than that."

Well, that answered the question, sort of. So this was the wrong room, but it still felt strange Louisa would be this close to the king and queen. There was an answer somewhere, but her brain fizzled out before she could think of it.

"No, honestly, I was here for someone else, I swear it," Legacy said, then realized that sounded worse. "I mean, I wasn't here to dig through someone else's clothes," she backtracked as the glare from Louisa burned deeper. "I was, uh… I was on thief business, that's all."

"Freaky, perverted thief business. You best have a good explanation for this or I'll start yelling. See how the guards treat you when they find out you've been peeping on their princess."

Legacy's heart skipped, mouth agape.

So that's why she was right next to the king and queen.

She was their daughter. Which meant this was a fuckup of proportions Legacy couldn't even fathom.

"I-I'm not peeping!" she shouted feebly.

Legacy wasn't sure why she was justifying herself. Maybe it was because Louisa had an air of virtue, of innocent nobility, that made Legacy feel the fact that she was a dirty street rat hunkered down in her closet all the more. Whatever it was, more words came out in a river, oblivious to whether she wanted to speak them or not.

"No, no, I'm not a pervert, please, really. Just let me explain and also get out of this closet, because I feel like it's not helping my case."

The crown was out of reach now; may as well try and save her dignity.

Louisa being a princess was something that, by all means, should have surprised her, but it didn't. Not as much as she'd thought it would.

It felt right, like all the chapters of a story clicking into place at the very end. Louisa was clear-spoken, kind, and carried herself with dignity only befitting a royal. Now that Legacy knew what she was, it was hard to believe she could have ever been anything else.

Louisa stepped back but held her ground in a way that said *if you try anything, you're done.* "Alright, then, tell me what you could have possibly been doing other than stealing my clothes? And don't feed me all that about how you're here for my valuables. My parents are one room away, and they've got way more than I do." She stalked forward. Legacy only now noticed her massive, curled claws, dangerous in a way that was hidden by their innocent baby-blue color. She was dainty and slender, but she was a Golden Hearts bird through and through, with the muscles and claws and overwhelmingly powerful presence to match.

"Hah, uh, funny story, actually," Legacy said before she could stop herself. "That's where I meant to go. See, believe it or not, I'm not a royal, so, uh, I've never been up here before."

Louisa's eyes flattened in a straight, emotionless line, looking less impressed by the second. It stung worse than any insulting shout from Rose Heart or crude lecture from Owl Wings. "Mm-hmm, likely excuse," she said, drawing in a breath to call the guards.

"I just need your dad's crown!" Legacy blurted, because she hadn't dug herself into a deep enough hole already.

It was the worst thing she could have said—though it felt like she was coming up with worse ones by the second—but it got Louisa to exhale her breath in quiet shock rather than screech for the guards, so it was somewhat of a win. Life was all about seeing the bright side of things, and all that.

A long silence drew between them, Louisa's eyes open in round *O*'s and Legacy frozen mid-self-removal from the closet.

Then Louisa started laughing. It sounded out, gleeful and airy, bouncing off the walls of the room.

It was better than being pissed, but it also was painfully similar to when Nensho laughed at her not too long ago. It was starting to feel a little patronizing. Was she really so hard to take seriously?

Her brows knitted in annoyance, and much to her surprise and displeasure, Louisa only laughed harder. It was starting to feel excessive.

"I'm sorry, but you're a real dear," Louisa said, still chuckling between words. "Now, what in Camorthes do you need that crown for? It's nice enough, but the rest of his jewelry is worth a lot more."

Every bone in her body recoiled at the thought of sharing guild plans, but something about Louisa seemed genuine, and in her gut, she felt she could trust her. Maybe it would backfire, but Moon Eyes' words still rang clear in her head, bouncing off the walls of her brain until it became stifling.

She had to learn to trust.

She couldn't bring herself to open up to her fellow thieves, not yet, but starting with an outsider was easier. Then, if things went south, she could just disappear back into the shadows. An easy out.

"Well, it all started with that gang," she began, rattling off her entire mission and reason for being here in one incoherent flood of words. Louisa listened intently, eyes locked on Legacy with a force so strong she had to keep glancing around at the plants and the floor to avoid her burning gaze.

"You, uh, you look real into this considering it's your dad I'm tryna rob," Legacy said when she finished. Louisa's eyes absolutely sparkled. Pale yellow with glimmering curiosity and intrigue overflowing from them. It made Legacy want to keep talking, just to see that interested face all the more, but she had to stop somewhere.

"Oh!" Louisa said, breaking face. "Sorry, sorry, it just all sounds… really cool? Maybe that's weird, but ever since I found out Skyflake was an assassin, and I ran into you, I've been looking into you types a lot. Hearing it from you yourself is fascinating."

"Well, I did see your books—guess that explains those," Legacy said, a warmth in her cheeks. She'd never been looked at like this before, like she was something to be admired, like she was something *interesting*. It made her skin itch and burn in a way she didn't quite understand. More so because this was the same bird who'd been about to throw her out on her ass just minutes ago.

"Ah, I didn't know you saw those. That's embarrassing," Louisa said, scratching at her chest as she looked to the side. "Well, anyways, I guess I see why you're here now. It'll make my dad real mad, but it'll get the gang gone, right? So it'll help in the long run?" The way she said it sounded like she was trying to talk herself into something, asking herself more than Legacy.

Legacy nodded. "Sure will. Get them out of here, then I can take off and be done with this place."

"Oh…" Louisa said, quiet. "A-anyways, I can help you. I know it's my dad and all, but…" Her beak moved like she was going to say something else, but she trailed off. "I can help, just with this. Just to get the gang out of here," she said, though it sounded like a quick cover-up for something else.

Maybe she wasn't as trustworthy as Legacy thought.

Or maybe she was, Legacy assured herself. Maybe she just had reasons she didn't feel like sharing. It was fair enough. Legacy hadn't told her about the prophecy or anything beyond "give Nensho the crown and she'll leave."

For now they were even, and that was enough.

"So, can we just turn the corner and get into your parents' room? I've got a couple buddies on the other side drawing the guards away, so it should be all clear," she said. From inside the room it was hard to hear if any alarm had been sounded, but supposedly, if Rose Heart and O'Hara came through, there was an "accident" involving a lot of fire in an area with a lot of alcohol.

"Sure can. They keep their door locked, on both the balcony and inside, but I have a key to get in from when I was younger," she said, drawing a book out of the bookshelf. She opened it up and gasped. "Oh, Darivan, no, it's not—"

Legacy fished the key out of her pocket, holding it up sheepishly. "Sorry about that," she said as Louisa snatched it from her grasp.

"Diyos and Darivan you are such a thief. Ugh," Louisa said, but the words had no bite.

"It's what you love about me though," Legacy said coyly, chuckling as she slid outside the door and into the hallway.

"Pretty strong words for a pain in the tail like you." Louisa snickered, following close behind.

The hallway was long and beautiful, illuminated by the massive window-like arches on either side, sunlight shining through them to light up the marble floor. The first time she ran through here, she hadn't even noticed Louisa's room tucked away on the opposite end of the hall, just above the stairs.

The two sprinted along, claw clicks echoing off the vast walls. They came to the end, where the massive doors that led to King Onyx's room sat. No guards were present, and the only sign of life was a dull moth fluttering about.

Louisa stuck the key in the slot, while Legacy impatiently jumped from foot to foot.

A sinister voice sounded out from behind them.

"I don't think so, *thief*."

# CHAPTER TWENTY

# ASHES TO ASHES

LEGACY WHIPPED AROUND, REALIZING WITH a start that her hood wasn't up. It must have come down while she was in Louisa's room, and now she stood bared raw to the world.

"The world" being the bird at the other end of the hallway, who stalked forward with a dangerous hiss in his voice. His feathers were mottled sky blue and dark navy, and half of his face was contorted into a red, charred curl of flesh. The sun shone down on him, casting a deep shadow from where he stood to the opposite wall. It didn't seem to touch him, his frigid feathers impervious to the warm light.

"You got away the last few times, but now you won't be so lucky. This time the guards who saved you are rotting outside!" he screeched, then lunged at Legacy.

She hit the ground before she could fathom any sort of reaction, scrambling back to avoid a second blow from his ridged talons. They gleamed like daggers, sharpened to deadly points.

She scrambled to her feet, body still weak from her wounds. "What the hell—what are you doing here?" she shouted, barely dodging out of the way as he struck again, claws slamming into the marble floor where her head was moments before.

He was a whirlwind of movement, all flying claws and heavy wings lashing in a plethora of directions.

Legacy backed away and dodged left, trying in vain to unsheathe her dagger.

"Skyflake?" Louisa said, golden eyes wide as saucers. Her voice was almost swallowed by the sound of clicking claws and heaving breaths.

Skyflake paused. The few seconds felt infinite while Legacy struggled with her dagger. It snagged on the cloak, fighting her pull with sentient ferocity.

"Louisa? You're here with *her*?" he barked, jabbing a claw in Legacy's direction. The cloak couldn't tear or give—it was too high-quality for that. She found herself wishing for her scratchy, cheap, tearable cloak. The kind that would have given her back her damn knife.

It reluctantly tugged free. She flashed a wild grin as she pulled her dagger out, brandishing it proudly.

Louisa shot between the two before either could strike, her height apparent as she dwarfed both Skyflake and Legacy. "It's over. I told you to stop coming here, and don't you dare lay a claw on her," she spat at Skyflake. Her body blocked the sun, casting an outstretched shadow toward Legacy, who stood bewildered behind her.

"I can handle myself," Legacy snapped, leaping over the girl in a streak of red, her claws missing Skyflake's face by mere inches. "Just stay out of this." It came out harsher than she intended, and she caught a glimpse of Louisa's face falling.

Legacy slashed her knife at the assassin, the air whooshing between them as she missed again.

It's not that she was opposed to having Louisa protect her. It was just—

Skyflake slammed a claw on the ground, icicles shooting up from where they struck. One came close enough to graze her throat as she sprung backward. Her throat felt warm, a tingling feeling escalating to something unnaturally hot.

—It was just that this was criminal business, the kind of squabble that should be restricted to the unclean dredges of society. Not something a pristine, shining bird such as Louisa should touch. It might stain her.

Legacy's throat burned as she shot a blast of cyan fire toward Skyflake, singeing his back. He howled in pain, and Louisa flinched. The princess's claws twitched like she was dying to get in the middle but was conflicted on whose side to take.

Skyflake retaliated, slamming into Legacy's side and throwing them both to the ground. More icicles sprung up, one only a breath away from her neck.

If Legacy were the princess, she'd have run, hidden in her room, maybe leaped out the window and soared into the golden hills, as far away from this mess as she could before it got her tangled up in matters she didn't belong with.

But Louisa was a better person. She wasn't the type to run. She wasn't the type to abandon others, even if they had nothing to give. She was stupidly selfless.

Skyflake rolled on top, pinning Legacy to the floor with ridged claws, constricting her throat. She spat at him, sparks flying from her beak, but the pressure was too great to allow any flame to escape.

Legacy was rarely so aware of her own inadequacy as when she was with that princess

No, it wasn't that she was blind to it. It's that she only let herself look inside and peek at the flaws she could slap a bandage on or brush under a rug of excuses and blame. Things like her temper, which she could pin on Rose Heart for aggravating, or her shortcomings as a thief, which weren't quite so short, she just set the standards high enough she could point and say "Yeah, that's my biggest issue" when she was forced into any kind of self-reflection.

She struck Skyflake with the muscled weight of her wing, the shock of being hit on his blind side loosening his grip.  Her obsession over her skills as a thief was a diversion, an easy, tangible problem that felt legitimate enough to fall back on but not so self-incriminating that it made her look like a total asshole. Something that could be remedied with practice.

She flung him off, his body, despite being larger than her own, flying across the floor with little effort. He felt thin, the bones underneath his feathers giving her a place to grab as she jumped on top of him and stuck her dagger against the side of his cyan neck.

"Let me go," he hissed, voice strained as she pressed the knife flush against his trachea. "Let me go… and I'll tell you something about your little guild."

She paused, the knife edge obscured by the smooth feathers of his throat, frozen in place—much like Louisa, who'd faded into the background as she watched in fear.

*What could an assassin know about the Coyotes that I don't?*

"I wasn't just killin' your little friend for the hell of it." He made an attempt at struggling, muscles tight as he tried to throw Legacy off. He failed, collapsing limp and defeated back onto the floor, and only then continued his frantic whispers. "Let me up, and I'll tell you exactly who paid to have her crushed into mist."

Legacy hesitated. Her grip weakened.

Skyflake kept talking, the skin at the edge of his mouth curled in a sneer. "That was their words, y'know? They didn't just want her throat slit, they wanted her gone, wiped off the face of Camorthes."

She wanted to kill him. He was here, in her claws, throat against her knife, but his words gave her pause. They shouldn't. He could be lying to save his skin, but what if he wasn't? It always felt strange, the incident that happened. Not just because of the normally petty conflict rising to violence, but because *Skyflake* was the one who did it. He looked young and unfamiliar out of the few faces of New Moons she'd seen. He definitely wasn't their leader or any sort of authority.

If they were going to take it a step further, if it had been an attempt to provoke the Coyotes, would they not have made it more obvious? If she hadn't caught him, or if he hadn't slipped up and let himself be seen, even if only for a moment, she'd have never even known he was one of the New Moons.

None of it sat right.

Skyflake could be a liar, but maybe, between whatever lies he told, there would still be a truth to glean.

Her blade loosened, close enough to stop him if he tried to run but not so close he was strained to speak.

She didn't want to believe him, but it all fit uncannily into place. The pieces of a strange, morbid puzzle she'd shoved under a dresser and forgotten about.

"Tell me," she said, "and you can leave."

A sick grin split his face, one side of it lost to the reddened burns that scored his head.

"It was one of your own," he replied.

She choked on a breath.

No, he had to be lying.

This wasn't the truth. This made no sense.

"A traitor among thieves; is it so hard to believe?" He chuckled, the smug laugh of someone who'd watched his enemy drag themselves through the mud by their own neck.

"Now let me go, and I can tell you more." His muscles tensed as he prepared to stand up.

Legacy drove her dagger through his throat, the blade splitting cerulean feathers, then skin, then bone, a sickening crunch as his head flopped, limp, to the side.

His legs kicked feebly, not with life but with the after-death twitches of someone whose soul was gone while their body struggled to keep hold of it.

He wasn't going to tell her more. Legacy knew that game far too well. Feed someone a tidbit of the truth and then string them along until you can weasel away. She'd heard enough.

Backed against the door, Louisa watched with an empty expression. It was the kind of confused, lost stare of a person who wasn't sure how to react. The look of someone who was way in over their head and only now realized they'd passed the point of no return.

The silence stood long and suffocatingly unbroken.

# CHAPTER TWENTY-ONE
# DUST TO DUST

L EGACY STOOD STILL FOR A long time, feet planted like roots in the marble floor. She stayed unmoving even as the sound of footsteps echoed behind her, louder and louder as whoever it was scaled the staircase. Her heart beat frantically, each thump crashing into her chest from the inside.

Two birds came out of the stairwell. Legacy heard their footsteps, two sets sprinting in her direction, but she stayed solidified in place, too paralyzed to turn and look at them. Blood dripped from her dagger onto the floor. Her breathing came out staccato, hitching on the tightness in her throat. Louisa was just as frozen, staring at the floor in a daze, the key halfway inside the lock next to her hanging head.

She didn't look sad, as one might expect at seeing a past lover slaughtered in front of them. She just looked overwhelmed.

"What in Darivan's name is the holdup," one of the newcomers, none other than Rose Heart, shouted. Her voice was sickeningly thick poison in Legacy's ears. It bounced off the walls and escaped into the wind-chilled air outside, leaving a poignant ringing in its wake.

Legacy's muscles tightened. Beneath her bloodied claws, Skyflake's eye stared back at her, glassy and unseeing, like the eye of a fish strung up at the wharf markets.

"O'Hara thinks you complain about him a lot for someone who's taking sweet time on her half of the job," O'Hara added, voice shrill in the quiet.

The air was dusty, the faint breeze blowing in spritzes of pollen and stray dirt even as high up as the tower was.

Legacy found it in herself to look back at the two, feeling lost.

Rose Heart came closer. Her long claws clacked against the stone as she pinned Legacy under a scrutinizing green gaze, only broken when her eyes flicked to Skyflake's corpse, bleeding out onto the marble.

The blood was thick and stuck uncomfortably to the soles of her feet.

Legacy craned her neck to look out the window, shoulders stiff and body rigid.

The sun burned so bright she had no choice but to look away. It scalded her brain, an oppressive warmth radiating from her eye sockets and throughout her head. She looked instead at her shadow stretched across the ground, the long claws of shade contorting her figure into something reminiscent of how she felt inside. The marble pattern spread out like veins.

It was all so much to take in. Funny, how the simplest spoken sentence could change the trajectory of everything.

A traitor.

One of their own.

One of them.

A thief.

Maybe it wasn't Rose Heart or O'Hara, but it could be.

She swayed in place.

Rose Heart dashed over, her scornful expression falling as she reached to rest a claw on Legacy's back. "Darling, are you okay? You look faint." She brushed her claws down Legacy's side, grazing skin-deep wounds through the soft cloth and battered feathers. "He didn't hurt you too badly, did he? You don't look all that roughed up."

Legacy pulled away like she'd been struck, blue eyes wide.

Rose Heart recoiled. Her claw twitched like she wanted to reach out again but thought better of it.

"Could be a concussion. Or a head thing," O'Hara added, voice distant from where he hung back by the stairwell. "O'Hara will get the crown; you get her back to the tree, the inn, or wherever you think best. Personally, O'Hara prefers the tree, as he is now banned from the inn."

Her head felt fuzzy.

"No," Legacy finally sputtered, legs weak. "No, I can do it. I'm just winded, that's all. Get out of here.

I'll do my part." The warm sun burned the areas of her face where the feathers thinned, an itching, crawling sensation on her skin.

It couldn't be true. It shouldn't be. But if it was, she'd been right not to trust. She'd never wanted to be right less in her life.

Rose Heart, Louisa, and O'Hara all exchanged glances, filled to the brim with secrets.

Then, the two thieves left as a pair, dashing down the stairwell with a few hesitant glances back. Skyflake's body, a forgotten object, cooled in the shadows of the arches. Dried blood hung on to the edges of his frayed feathers.

It struck her, strangely, that he bled like any other bird. Thinking about an ice-blood made her envision something a little more… frigid on the inside. Something jagged and cool to the touch. Then again, it was just a nickname. They called the firepies "fire-bloods," and she was sure they bled lukewarm liquid.

The venompies were more up in the air. She hadn't been burned by venomous blood yet, but they had less predictable powers. Some had little fangs, some had barbed tongues, a select few even had feathers poisonous to the touch. Toxic blood was hardly a stretch. But none of that was important right now.

Louisa came to stand beside Legacy, who watched her companions leave with a stare.

It was a comforting presence, even though Louisa was just as shaken.

"They really care about you, huh?" Louisa said. Her voice was wispy and quiet, but there was a conviction to it that empty consolations never held.

"I'm sorry I killed your boyfriend" wasn't what Legacy meant to say, but it's what came out of her beak.

"You're dodging the subject," Louisa said, trotting over to the large door and leaning her weight against it while she pulled. Legacy trailed behind, in the same forlorn manner as a lost dog.

The aged door creaked open hesitantly. It blocked the glaring sun and cast a cool shadow over the two.

"Not on purpose," Legacy said. It still wasn't something she wanted to talk about, not until her brain felt less like a scrambled breakfast, but she really did feel the tiniest bit bad about killing Skyflake. Not because she gave a damn about him, but because she did give a damn about Louisa.

She wasn't sure when that had happened, actually, but she had no reason to argue with herself on the matter.

Louisa huffed. "Did you not hear what I said before? He and I are over. We have been for a few weeks now. He kept creeping up here trying to get me back, but I'm over it."

The two slid into the room, Legacy clinging tight to the shadows, Louisa sauntering in like she owned the place. Because, technically, she did. The air smelled of mint so strongly that Legacy could taste it on her tongue.

"Just like that, really?" Legacy asked. It probably wasn't right to pry, but it felt weird to throw away a relationship so casually. Not that she was an expert; she'd never been in one, only a few flings here and there. But Louisa didn't seem the type for flings, or for throwing herself into the arms of any charming guy who came her way.

The thought made Legacy's stomach churn, and she focused on digging through the drawers of a massive ornate vanity instead. They should act fast. The guards were no doubt close to coming back now, but she found herself moving slowly as she rifled through necklaces and bracelets, wondering if she might not be able to pocket a few. Dalarite, senestone, diamond, and more, set in metals just as rare. Any one of these was enough to afford a month's worth of dinner.

She slipped a senestone necklace into her cloak, the clover-green jewels glittering deep within her shadowy pockets.

"It's... well..." Louisa's voice faded off, and she paused to sift through a nightstand, haphazardly sliding things aside and making a great deal of noise as she scraped jewels and metals against the bottom of the drawer. "I mean, you saw the books, the ones in my room."

"Sure did," Legacy said, cringing as Louisa slammed the nightstand with a loud crash.

"I wasn't with him to be with him," Louisa continued, sliding across the bed to move to the other nightstand. Why she did that, Legacy wasn't sure. It didn't look big enough to house a crown.

"It was about the freedom, the... the thrill—"

"I didn't think you were into that sort of casual thing." Legacy snickered.

"Ugh, not the obscene kind!" Louisa shouted, flustered. "I mean, it's exhausting, being cooped up in here with my parents every day of my life. There are so many rules, so many codes of etiquette that I'm supposed to follow, even if I'm alone. I'm an adult woman, yet I feel like a hatchling." Her voice softened as she pulled something out of the top drawer. "I was going to run away with him." It glittered gold in the torchlight, small in size, and adorned with only one small onyx in the center. Fake modesty. A way to make the king look like one of the people rather than a force high and mighty above. If only his people could see the treasury he perched on. "He was supposed to be my escape from here, but when I found out he was an assassin…"

"Not into a life of crime?" Legacy said, sauntering over and leaning in close to get a good look at the crown. It was disappointing. Hopefully, Nensho was telling the truth when she said it wasn't the value that mattered, because compared to anything else this man owned, this wasn't too impressive. And she wasn't going to dare touch down into that treasury again.

Standing this close to the other girl, she could smell a trace of flowers. Rose, lily, dahlia, all clinging to her feathers like a sweet perfume.

"Ah, it's not crime as a whole. It's being an assassin, specifically." Louisa handed the crown over to Legacy.

Their claws lingered together for just a touch longer than they needed, before the light-gold circle dropped into Legacy's grip. "I don't like it here. I hate being a princess, I hate living with my parents' claws around my throat, but… I do like being a healer. That was my own choice, you see. To join Skyflake in a group whose sole purpose is to end lives while mine is to save them feels…"

She didn't finish her sentence. She didn't need to.

"I know what you mean. He didn't seem like the greatest guy, either, but I might be biased." They both laughed, walking toward the balcony together.

Then the two left, Legacy following Louisa's lead as they leaped off the balcony and into the wide blue sky, the silence between them comfortable and warm.

Legacy landed at the entrance to the tree hollow, heart beating cruelly against her chest. The sun, now high in the sky, shone between the leaves far above, speckling the ground she stood on. The shadows twisted and turned, shivering as they moved about like they had a mind of their own.

There was no sign of O'Hara or Rose Heart.

It was for the better, she told herself.

She felt that, in her current state, she was far from ready to see either of them again. Her only consolation was that Skyflake said *traitor*, singular, which meant it couldn't be both of them.

The grass rippled in the wind, waves of soft green spanning for miles. When she was with Louisa, her anxiety had taken a respite backstage, but now it was crawling back, making a home nestled deep in her chest.

*Even if it was multiple, it wouldn't be those two together,* she tried to assure herself. Rose Heart would never be that comfortable around a male, and O'Hara felt too independent to be a traitor.

The idea alone was unfathomable, but if Legacy were a traitor, she'd try a little bit harder to be less of a nuisance in the process. The point was to blend in, after all.

"So, are they showing up any time soon?" Louisa said, looking around with wide gold eyes. A breeze tried to steal her words, making them hard to decipher. Legacy leaned in closer, head cocked so that the sound might reach her ear slit better. "Shall we check the inn?"

"Oh, uh, yeah. They should be here any moment," Legacy mumbled, lost in thought.

Alone was a different story. One bird could still be any bird.

O'Hara was unlikely. Not only did he seem like the type to run away instead of solving his problems, but he also wasn't one of the Coyotes, and it felt weird for a member of another guild to have such a big problem with Naom. For that reason, she felt pretty confident crossing him off the list, among her other reasons. But Rose Heart…

She did gain from Naom's death. Immediately after, she'd become the Master Thief. It felt like no coincidence that it was timed so close to Owl Wings' old age, and his mentions of complete retirement.

But what if it wasn't? She flipped through names in her head like she was skimming files.

Fortune was unlikely, for similar reasons to O'Hara. She didn't even bother to hide her blatant rebellion, and if she wanted someone dead, she'd do it herself instead of hiring an assassin. Hell, she'd probably drag the body right to Owl Wings and show him.

Cottonmouth, as the overseer of all the guilds, was the most likely to want anyone dead for any reason. She wasn't fond of keeping birds she didn't like around, and it wouldn't be the first time she made someone she disliked disappear.

But employing an assassin? That wasn't her style, and even if it had been her, Skyflake would have had no reason to make a big deal of it. It was only traitorous when someone other than Cottonmouth did it, after all.

That crossed her off. And just to make things easier, she mentally checked off anyone not among the Coyotes. There was simply no reason for them to want Naom gone—no gain, nothing. If there was, she could get to that after considering her more likely suspects.

"I think I see them! Look, by the wall," Louisa chattered, pointing toward the castle's walls. The sun lit them up burgundy, the bricks warm and inviting.

Legacy looked up, spotting two figures flying toward her from the wall, one pink and red, one white as snow. They cast swiftly flying shadows on the ground underneath themselves, barely beating their wings as the wind pushed them along. They'd be here in minutes.

She breathed deeply in… and out, collecting herself. But her worried thoughts swept back in tenfold.

Judgement was a suspect, undoubtedly. She wasn't sure what he'd gain from Naom's death, but he was so unknown that the possibilities were endless. His friend Thistle was equally suspicious.

Legacy once heard that cheaters were more likely to suspect their partners of cheating, and she wondered if the same could be said of traitors.

Thistle thought everyone was out to get him; maybe being a liar himself was why. His blatant hatred of Owl Wings, Cyrill, and seemingly any authority figure set up a solid motive on top of it. It was different than Fortune's rebellion; his was out of what seemed like a genuine fear of being stabbed in the back.

Rose Heart landed, her gentle descent barely damaging the grass and weeds below her feet. O'Hara thudded down beside her, squashing the plants in his wake.

"Your head feeling any better?" Rose Heart asked, coming in close but stopping herself before she was close enough to make physical contact. They'd been fighting the last time they'd had a "normal" conversation, but Rose Heart's worry seemed to overshadow her annoyance, for now.

"O'Hara does not care about her head; it was already scrambled. He would instead like to get a closer look at that," he said, pointing a silver claw at the thin crown in her talons.

She held it closer, flashing him a glare. "Don't even think about it."

"He just wanted a peek." O'Hara sighed, fake hurt. "So, what is the next part of this supposed heist? And will O'Hara be of any help this time? He feels that, for how much you begged him to be a part of this, he spent most of his time following Rose Heart like a lost puppy. He did about as much thievery as one, too."

Her forcibly relaxed breathing went out the window at that as a bolt of anxiety shot through her lungs, piercing her heart. All the commotion, the crown, the traitor, Louisa, had led her to forget the dirtier part of her plan.

The others looked confused, but she pulled herself together with a half-assed grin.

"Yep, the next part is where you come in. You and Rose Heart just gotta follow me, and I'll explain as we go." The thumping in her chest should have been excitement, anticipation, the culmination of everything she planned to do going just as she wanted it to go. For once in her life, she was doing everything not just right but better than right. She was single-handedly doing the biggest thing the Coyotes had done in years, with far less effort than she'd ever expected.

So why did she feel like there was bile in her throat?

# CHAPTER TWENTY-TWO

# A MISTAKE IN THE REFLECTION

FOUR BIRDS FLEW TOGETHER—RED AND white, red and pink, white, and purple—in a formation that consisted of Legacy up front, leading the way, Louisa at her side, and the other two only a few wingbeats back. The wind was gentle today, doing little more than offering a soft cushion to float their wings on. No clouds drifted in the sky, just an endless blue as far as the eye could see.

The weather, the timing, it was all perfect.

The only deviation from the plan was the princess in their ranks, but if that was the only unexpected factor, Legacy would take it.

High over Legacy's head, the sun hung in the center of the sky, a large glowing chandelier that lit up her feathers in a saturated glow.

The bile in her stomach hadn't subsided. If anything, it grew worse by the minute. It rose, burning her chest and her throat, choking her breath and making her tremble down to the tips of her wings. Her body felt warm and wrong, a separate entity from her mind. The smell of wheatgrass strangled her.

Why the uneasy feeling? Her mind couldn't help bouncing between thoughts and accusations. She didn't like O'Hara. He wasn't a friend. He was a pest. He was a nobody, an unwilling martyr who would die to save the world. If their quest was what the Dreamseers claimed.

And the chance was slim, but maybe he *was* the traitor, and she was doing everyone else a favor by doing this.

She beat her wings. Far below, her reflection shone in a clear spring, sparkles of light dancing on her image. Hopefully she was remembering the way to the cliff correctly. These fields tended to look the same, all barely different spans of various identical crops stretched for miles on end.

No, it had to be Rose Heart. Who else had any reason to kill—

"O'Hara! Get your ass up here. Are those wings just decorative?" Rose Heart snapped, voice abrasive on Legacy's brain.

"O'Hara thinks you need to slow down and enjoy life once in a while. Maybe then you will have fewer age lines in your face."

Louisa laughed, looking at Legacy with a gleeful smile. It fell when Legacy barely caught her eye and just looked on ahead. Her brows were creased in thought.

The spire of stone peeked over the horizon, unmistakable and odd. A single talon reaching toward the stars, frozen in time.

"There it is," she mumbled, words lost on the breeze.

Louisa sidled up to her, wings beating dangerously close to her own. The smell of flowers filled her nose.

"Hey, you look kind of out of it. Is there something else going on?" Louisa said, voice as low as she could keep it without being impossible to hear. Behind her, O'Hara and Rose Heart were too busy bickering to notice.

"No, it's fine. Just tired."

"I don't buy that for a second. In fact, it's pretty insulting that you thought I would," Louisa said as she glided on the wind, barely needing to beat her wide wings to stay up. "I don't just heal physical wounds, and I know what it looks like when someone's not feeling right in the head. I just want to help."

Legacy relented. "Just... let me do this, and I'll tell you afterward, yeah?" She hoped this would buy her enough time for a convincing lie. Or maybe just a twist of the truth, because it felt wrong to lie to Louisa completely. Not just because she was a good person but because she was smart enough to see through Legacy's bullshit more than once now.

The cliff came up quickly. What was a gray speck on the horizon now loomed like a pillar to the gods before her. She lifted her wings to let herself drop onto the ledge, the wind, gentle as it may be, throwing her off-balance and making her land crooked.

Hopefully Nensho found her quickly, because she hadn't thought up much of a plan for stalling O'Hara until she arrived.

Her gut twisted painfully when she looked at him, still lost in his bickering with Rose Heart.

She'd seen many dead bodies in her time. Countless cooling corpses who'd met their ends in a variety of gory ways, or maggot-infested decayed birds never given a burial, and by now she felt desensitized. But seeing a man still alive, still talking, and knowing he was going to die before sunset was a new kind of sickening. It was different than the horror of Naom's squashed body.

Maybe it was just because she was seeing him alive and animated, or maybe it was because it was her fault he was going to die. That this was her choice. That she had every bit of power just to tell him—tell him to run and never look back. Tell him he could live to see another day.

Did the traitor feel like this with Naom? Did they spend every day watching her, sick to their stomach, knowing an assassin would be killing her on their behalf? Were they able to talk to her face-to-face without their chest constricting so violently it felt like they were being throttled?

A thought hit her. It was sudden but so glaringly obvious she wondered how it took her this long to make the connection.

*Am I any better than the traitor?*

It didn't matter what the traitor felt, really, because in the end they still had Naom killed. And it didn't matter what Legacy felt, because she was going to kill O'Hara anyway. Remorse meant nothing; remorse didn't bring back the dead.

*But I am different. I'm doing this for the guild, not just me.* But the words rang hollow in her mind.

She turned to O'Hara, trembling. She could be better. She had to be better. Maybe she wasn't the kindest bird in Camorthes, and maybe she was selfish, but she wasn't cruel.

"O'Hara, you have to run."

O'Hara looked rightfully confused, staying planted in place though his wings lifted just a tad. "O'Hara would prefer to fly, actually, as there are few places to run." He gestured around at the small ledge.

"Don't play fucking coy. Just run, go, now! Or else you'll die," she screamed, trying to hammer the point through his thick head.

Louisa and Rose Heart looked at her like she'd grown a third eye. O'Hara raised his wings but stayed put. "O'Hara thinks this joke is strange and not very funny."

"Nensho is coming!" she yelled, shoving him toward the ledge. "Nensho is coming, and she... she's going to kill you when she does." Her words were tattered, coming out disjointed as she shrieked herself breathless.

Before anyone could move, before O'Hara could fly away, before Legacy could yell again, there was a sound on the wind. It was the deep, heavy beat of wings.

Everyone's heads turned as a dark figure thudded down on the end of the ledge. Navy-blue feathers blotted out the sun, a hulking figure silhouetted against the daytime star. There was a straw hat on her head and a sprig of wheat in her beak.

Legacy dropped the crown, which made a glittering clatter as it fell.

"You're out of time, little thief. I'm here to take what you owe."

# CHAPTER TWENTY-THREE

# THE SUN IS BRIGHT, THE STARS NOWHERE TO BE FOUND

O'HARA FROZE, KNOWING THERE WAS nowhere to run now.

Nensho was large, but her wings were double the size of any of the thieves and would carry her along twice as fast, twice as far. Another bird landed beside her. Copperhead, the venompie from before. His tinted glasses hid his eyes, but Legacy could see a smile on his beak.

"Hmph, I thought you were gonna put the crown on him—that woulda been funny," Nensho said, stepping forward to stand chest to chest with O'Hara. He shrank back, trying to hide in the shade of his hat.

"Now, tell me where you put the necklace," she barked, grabbing his throat with a massive talon, pinning his slim body to the stone in one smooth movement. His hat went flying, careening across the stone. Out of the corner of her eye, Rose Heart's body twitched, like she instinctively wanted to lunge forward, but stayed put.

O'Hara kicked and struggled beneath Nensho, but it was no more fruitful than a rabbit kicking at the jaws of a wolf.  Despite his situation, he still found a way to contort himself to look at Legacy, eyes wide and glossy.

"You... you did this?" he whispered, before his face twisted in fury. "O'Hara is not some object to be handed over! He helped you, and for what? To be passed around like a ring, or a necklace, or a *crown?*"

"Oh, shut up," Nensho said, putting more pressure on him. "Just tell me where you put the damn necklace. You know the one."

He mumbled something, but Legacy didn't hear it. It must have been what Nensho wanted to know, because she smiled crookedly. Copperhead lingered at the edge of the cliff, keeping his distance.

Legacy tried to tear her gaze away from the winterpie, only to be met with a worse sight: Louisa and Rose Heart. Both looking at her not in anger, not in disappointment, but in betrayal. Two pairs of eyes bright in the shade of the cliff.

"I can't believe you. I cannot fucking believe you," Rose Heart hissed. The sun made her eyes glow leaf green.

"I... I thought you were better than that," Louisa stuttered, averting her eyes to the stone she stood on.

Legacy turned over a million ways to apologize in her head, throat murmuring with unsaid words. Her heart burned like a torch, lighting up all her mistakes in stark shadows on her rotten insides.

In a weird turn, the sickening nausea from before dissipated, leaving cold indifference in its wake.

No apology felt right. Nothing she could say would fix this. No words would save O'Hara.

What she did instead was whip around, claws first, at Nensho.

It felt like throwing herself at a brick wall. There was no give, no softness. Even her feathers felt like stone, but Legacy clung tight, digging her claws into Nensho's shoulders as the massive bird thrashed around, trying to throw her off. O'Hara scrambled to his feet and leaped into the air, but to her surprise, he lunged for Nensho as well.

*Why the hell isn't he running? This is his chance. My life for his.*

"Go, for fuck's sake, go!" she shouted.

Her claws slipped, and she crashed to the ground. Eagle talons slammed her face down so hard it rattled her brain against her skull. Blood oozed down her cheek. As she struggled to her feet, she saw Copperhead scrambling to hold himself up fighting Louisa and Rose Heart, golden tongue flickering as he waved side to side. The sun reflected in his glasses.

"O'Hara is not staying for you," he spat back, taking a swipe at Nensho's chest. It didn't break feathers, but it left icy tendrils on the fringes, seeping in to freeze her skin.

Legacy dodged another blow as Nensho swung at her, darting between her legs with wily grace. With O'Hara distracting her from the front, Legacy was able to dislodge her own dagger and aim it for the back of Nensho's neck.

The strike glanced off, navy feathers and small blood droplets flying, the wound not deep enough to kill. It wasn't even deep enough to slow her down. As Legacy opened her beak to shoot flame at her, Nensho turned with astonishing speed, using a giant shoulder to send her flying across the ledge.

Her head struck stone, and she felt the reverberations all the way down her spine. From where she lay, she could see Copperhead gaining an edge on Louisa and Rose Heart. He dodged and weaved between the two, alternating with snapping blows from his beak.

Louisa looked exhausted, her own attacks haphazard and weak. Rose Heart was trying to cover for her, but she had a deep fang mark in her back, no doubt a venomed bite, and it made her falter.

Copperhead bled from his neck but still had the strength to batter Louisa in a flurry of blows.

O'Hara was faring no better, having been thrown to the ground, with Nensho looming over him.

Legacy pulled herself to her feet, realizing she had a choice.

There was no right answer. Louisa, Rose Heart, O'Hara—they'd all come here on her command. They'd all put their trust in her only to have it shattered by her betrayal.

But O'Hara was the sacrifice. He was the one she'd dragged here to kill. He was the one she should rightfully save. A way to go back on her mistake, a way to redeem herself.

A way to prove she was better than the traitor, before it was too late.

Forget Owl Wings, forget the quest. Why did she even care about pleasing him so much? Because she felt like she owed him? Because without him, she'd be a useless, ornamental nothing?

Well, even handed her ideal life on a platter, she'd still found a way to throw it away.

She leaped forward, throwing herself into Nensho's side. Big as she was, the surprise caught her off guard, and Nensho staggered.

Beneath Legacy's claws, O'Hara lay bleeding in the dust. He looked over her shoulder, then looked her in the eyes.

"I… I'm sorry," Legacy stammered, chest heaving. "I fucked up, I fucked up. I should never have done this."

"O'Hara knows what it is like to make a mistake. Though he admires your attempt at retribution, he thinks you should save the princess." He paused to take a wispy gasp of air. "She has no part in our dirty world," he said, making no move to get up. Quite possibly, he couldn't. A deep wound scored his side, reaching down the feathers of one thigh and ending at the scales of his leg. Crimson rivers flowed down into an ocean.

"O'Hara is sad you would turn on him like this, but he hopes we can make amends in the next life," he whispered.

Legacy had no time to reply as Nensho recovered, tossing her aside and lunging past her toward the broken winterpie, slamming her massive talons into his chest.

As she recovered, Legacy locked eyes with him one last time, the weight of her mistake heavy in her soul.

He closed his eyes.

Then she turned around, sprinting toward where Copperhead and Louisa were fighting. The two rolled on the dusty stone as they tried pecking and whacking each other with flailing wings. Rose Heart lay unmoving a few wing-lengths away.

Legacy grabbed Copperhead by the neck, hauling him off Louisa with a force she didn't know she was capable of. She slammed his head against the ground, glasses falling off his face. Behind them, his pale-yellow eyes burned with fury.

His feathers were singed along the edges, and he reeked of smoke.

Whoever it was hadn't hurt him, but Legacy knew her fire was stronger than either of the others.

Her throat simmered, not with the sick bile of before but with the birth of a flame. Blue lit up her throat as she opened her beak, shooting a blast of sun-bright cyan fire into his face. He screamed and screamed, but she didn't stop until he went silent, his charred body limp on the ground. The iridescent sheen of his feathers was long gone, lost to the layer of ash on what was left of him.

She breathed heavily, heart racing and throat cooling. Past the corpse, she could see Louisa frantically doing something to help Rose Heart, who lay still, but her head was too fuzzy to process what.

The silence was oppressive, and she realized that Nensho had gone quiet.

She turned slowly to look at the giant bird, her body feeling like it was packed full of lead.

Nensho no longer bristled or tensed, just stood on one leg, casually twirling the king's crown in her claw. It glittered in the sun. The straw hat still sat on her head, no worse for the wear.

A white body lay before her, with feathers stained crimson, and a black hat a few wing-lengths away, the sunlight highlighting the tiny speckles of dust across its surface.

"The deal's done, thief," Nensho said, as transactional as if she'd just sold a fine cow or a woven carpet. "While I don't much appreciate that little stunt at the end, I'm a woman of my word, and I'll leave. Just stay out of my path in the future, yeah?"

She stepped over O'Hara, offering a claw in a shake. There was a new wheat stalk in her beak.

Legacy felt distant, like her head had taken a walk without her, but she reached out and shakily shook her claw. The grip was steadying.

It was strange. She should be mad. She should be *furious* that Nensho had killed him.  But you wouldn't berate a dog if you were the one who'd shoved the rabbit in its mouth.

Nensho killed him, but she'd given every warning in the world that she was going to. Legacy couldn't be mad at that. She was mad at herself that she'd fallen for it. That she'd let herself be roped into this sick game. She couldn't even say she'd been tricked. It was all her choice. She'd damn near been given a checklist, and she'd fulfilled it to the letter.

"I really didn't think you'd do it. You're a bold little thing," Nensho said, a glint in her eyes as she fiddled with the crown.

Then, with a last rueful glance at Copperhead's body, she took off, her deep-blue wings blowing dust up around her in her wake.

# CHAPTER TWENTY-FOUR
# WHAT IT TOOK TO GET HERE

LEGACY DIDN'T MOVE FOR A long time.

For minutes long as hours she stood in the cooling wind, feeling it beat against her chest. It tugged on her cloak, the bloodstained fabric rippling.

O'Hara's body lay still, his soul long departed but his blood still warm. She stood over him, watching the clouds so she didn't have to look at the body at her feet.

Rose Heart was hurt, she knew that, but she was no healer. There was nothing she could do to help. Better to let Louisa handle it.

All the thinking she'd done over the traitor and for what? What did it even matter? She herself was no better. Maybe the traitor wasn't even trying to betray the guild. Maybe they thought they were doing what was right, maybe they thought they were doing what was best, and by the time they'd realized it was a mistake, they were in too deep.

Naom and O'Hara. Equally dead. Equally betrayed.

She still wanted to find the traitor, not because she feared they'd turn on her, but because whoever it was would understand.

She picked up O'Hara's hat, turning it in her claws. The inside had little white down feathers stuck along the lining. Then she set it on his head, covering his bloodied face with the wide brim.

"I'm sorry," she whispered, then left to check on Rose Heart.

Her companion was still lying on the dirty stone, but her eyes were open, and though she looked bleary, she was alive. Venompie venom was strong, but Solar Eclipse 'pies were incredibly resistant.

Louisa stood over her, relief on her face and wounds scattered across her body. She was breathing heavily. When she saw Legacy, she averted her eyes.

"Here to help? Or are you here to finish us off too?" Rose Heart croaked. Weak as she was, she still managed to flash her fellow thief a scathing glare.

It struck Legacy then, that neither Rose Heart nor Louisa knew why she'd had O'Hara killed. For all they knew, she was out to get them all.

"No, no, not at all," she stammered. "It was a mistake. It was all a mistake." It wasn't what she wanted to say, but she wasn't quite sure what that would have been anyway.

The most sickening part was that she knew, having been given the same choice, not one of the others would have sacrificed her.

"Too late to fix that one now, isn't it, darling?" Rose Heart said, head falling back to the ground. Louisa rushed to cushion it.

"Yeah, you could say that," Legacy replied, unsure what else to say. What could she, really? This was beyond salvaging. Might as well go straight to acceptance.

"Why did you do it," Rose Heart asked, her voice barely a whisper.

Louisa grabbed her beak and gently held it shut. "You need to stop talking—it's just going to make you tired, and you're a bit big for me to carry if you pass out."

"I could help," Legacy said.

"You might drop me," Rose Heart mumbled through her closed beak. Legacy winced.

"Anyways, the venom just has to run its course," Louisa said, soft-spoken. "It's going to feel awful, but you'll be okay; just rest a minute." Then she looked at Legacy and pointed a stern claw at the golden fields. "You should leave."

"I—"

"Get out of here," Louisa said again, a bite in her words.

Legacy obliged, leaping off the cliff and letting her shaky wings carry her into the sky. Clouds floated past her, soft and gentle. They brushed her wingtips and filled her lungs with damp, cool air. She breathed in deep, drowning in the feeling.

The flight was long, but it felt like mere seconds. The aches and pains in her body were absent, and she barely felt the chill of the spring wind as she powered along blindly. The only indication of time passing was the sun as it climbed higher and higher, then fell behind her, lighting up her wings in a golden sunset. The moon peered prematurely over distant hills, anxious to rise before night truly fell.

Kalin put up no fight on her arrival, the gate guard too high or too drunk to realize she wasn't even a Golden Hearts bird.

She went back to the tavern because she wasn't quite sure where else to go. The smell walking in was rancid but familiar. The rickety wooden walls and creaky stairs greeted her like an old friend as she shambled to her room, picking the lock with ease and collapsing on the cushion inside. Through the window, the sun's fading light set below the city.

The stress of it all left her winded, her body weighted and leaden as she sank into the bed. She curled in on herself, dirty wings pulled tight to cover her face and block the light. Her cloak hung heavy over her body.

She didn't want to sleep. It felt wrong. Like she didn't deserve the luxury of rest, but primal instinct fought her self-deprecation and beat her into a restless slumber.

～◎✦ ✦ ☾ ✦ ✦◎～

White eyes haunted her sleep. Pale, glowing, and distant in the depths of an endless black tunnel.

Moon Eyes emerged from the shadows.

Legacy tried to back away but was met with an unyielding wall against her spine.

The Dreamseer cocked her head, tilting it just a bit farther than something natural should ever do.

"You need to wake up," Moon Eyes said, voice echoing as though it were spoken from the cave walls and not her mouth.

"I-I don't know if I can," Legacy replied, shaking.

"Wake up."

Legacy jolted. The cave fell before her eyes, replaced with worn wooden walls, a moonlit window, and a bird vigorously shaking her awake. "Ah! What in… What the, the hell?" was the best sentence her freshly woken mind could conjure.

"Oh, thank Darivan, I almost thought you'd gone comatose," Louisa said. She looked rough, missing chunks of feathers and covered in blood and dirt. One of the pearl strings on her face hung loose, the pearls only held together by the tiny knots between them.

As much as Legacy liked her as a clean, unsullied princess, this was a good look for her.

Legacy stared at her blearily, not sure what was happening. Her heart was still racing from a dream she'd forgotten the details of.

"Uh, take your time, I guess," Louisa said, sitting on the cushion beside Legacy. "Sorry to wake you up like that, I just… I just want to talk. About what happened, I mean—I don't mean to rush you." She kept rambling, words clearer as Legacy got a grip on her consciousness. "It's just that this is time sensitive. My parents are probably worried sick that I've been gone so long. Last time I snuck out with Skyflake, they'd even called a search party."

Legacy stretched out, more tired than when she'd fallen asleep. Her muscles ached. "What is there to talk about?" she said.

Louisa looked straight ahead, eyes fixed on the wall. Legacy followed her gaze—the two inseparably close yet worlds apart.

"Why you did it, I guess. That's a start," Louisa said. She sounded sad and distant.

"Does it even matter to you?" Legacy asked in reply, eyes darting to her companion. "You're a princess. Someone who's gonna move on and never see any of us again. I couldn't care less if you leave thinking I'm some kind of traitor."

Saying the word out loud felt strange. A label that kept peeling up at the edges and trying to fall off no matter how many times it got pressed back down.

"Don't turn this around; we're talking about you right now," Louisa snapped, but the bite in her words was more of a mournful nibble. "Just, just tell me why. Please. So I can put it to rest in my head. Even if the answer is that you're really a horrible person. I need to know."

"Even? So you think there's a chance I'm not?"

"There's always a chance. I may not have known you for very long, but I consider myself a good judge of character." Louisa reached out, flicking a small golden flame from her claw. It bounced in the air, sizzling away before it reached the floor. She still wouldn't meet Legacy's eyes. "A healer's job is to cure everyone equally. I've seen the foulest members of society, the killers, the rapists, laid up in beds right alongside the heroes and martyrs."

"And you were with Skyflake because… you're a good judge of character?"

Louisa laughed but quickly stifled herself. "Ugh, just stop dodging the question." She turned around to face Legacy, grabbing one of her small claws in her own. "Just tell me; it's the least you can do after dragging me into this."

"I've always felt inferior," Legacy started. Louisa's grip felt warm, and she found herself leaning into it. "Ever since I was young, I've always been the second best to someone else. Never bad, but never as good as them. I thought that leaving my first home, leaving behind my first shortcomings, and becoming a thief would finally give me a chance to do better."

She released Louisa's claw, standing up despite the pain in her body. Her blue eyes focused on the window, at the moon staring ambivalently back, and the stars speckled like wildflowers.

"But I didn't. I still failed. I still managed to be second best, and I'm still not good enough. My own area of expertise and for what? Nothing. Somehow, in a skill set I've mastered, I'm still not the best. A lifetime of practice to be some background character. So when Nensho… when Nensho made me an offer, an offer that would prove my worth to not only Owl Wings, but the others…" Legacy's shoulders hunched, brows crashing together in anger. Her tense claws left scrapes on the wood. "How could I refuse?" she hissed. "None of them ever helped me, none of them ever noticed me, so why shouldn't I throw one of them under to further myself?" She laughed, high on her own manic energy. "It's all they've done to me. Really, I'm just returning the favor."

Louisa's expression looked like she was trying to work out the answer to a riddle, equal parts interested and confused. It was to be expected. She had no idea about any of this. She knew nothing of Legacy's past, and she knew nothing of the stakes in a thief's life.

"I think you're wrong," Louisa said.

"What do you know, Princess? You sit on your ass all day with fresh food and clean water every meal, with Mom and Dad holding a dainty little safety net out for you if you ever do screw up. You have no idea what it's like to have your entire life riding on being better than the people around you," Legacy said, bristling.

Louisa, by some miracle of Darivan, didn't even twitch a brow. Instead, she stood up slowly, calmly, and walked to the window. The moon outlined her slender body. "I wasn't talking about that," she said. "I mean when you said they don't care about you, that's wrong. I saw you and them," she continued. "The way they worried over you when you were hurt. The way they'd tease you. Whether you want to believe it or not, they loved you."

It stung, even more so because Legacy knew she was right. *Why does she have to be right?* This would all be so much easier if they'd hated her, if they'd always expected the worst, and if she'd just lived up to their expectations.

"It makes me feel sick," Legacy whispered, bristled feathers flattening against her back. "Is that the answer you wanted?" The question was why, but she knew this wasn't just about the reason. It was equally about if she regretted what she'd done. If she felt remorse.

"I know. I saw you try and take it back, just a few tragic seconds too late," Louisa replied. "That's life, though. Mistakes have their consequences. You can't always fix things once they've gone too far."

"But," Louisa continued, reaching up to press a palm against Legacy's chest, "you did try. You did try to fix things, and when you couldn't, you did the next best thing."

Legacy looked her in the eyes, lost in the golden glow as she kept talking. "I know you aren't a bad person. Maybe not a great one, but you aren't malicious, merely… shortsighted, and a little selfish."

"More than a little," Legacy said, chuckling to try and lighten the atmosphere.

"A lot selfish," Louisa corrected, smiling, "but your answer was what I expected to hear, which is to say what I *wanted* to hear."

"So this is it?" Legacy placed her own palm over Louisa's, feeling her beating heart through their joined claws.

"Hm," Louisa hummed, a coy smirk on her face. "Do you want it to be?" The stars danced in her eyes. Outside, the moon was dipping below the city, casting a comfortable, alluring darkness across the room. The lone candle on the wall was unlit.

"I-I wasn't aware I had a say in it," Legacy stammered, averting her eyes. She felt the other bird's grip tighten.

"Let me join you, then. You wondered why I wanted to know all this? It's because I want to go with you," Louisa said.

"Ah—You… I mean…" Legacy fumbled her words, still recoiling from her own emotional revelations, not yet primed for this conversation.

"Thieves don't kill, unlike the assassins guild Skyflake was in with, and I was wondering if you might be in need of a healer. Seeing all the trouble you get into, I'm sure it would do you all some good," Louisa said, then paused. She pulled her claw back, leaving a cold spot on Legacy's chest. "Unless you have one already… then it's back to the castle and a lasting goodbye."

"We don't!" Legacy blurted, grabbing Louisa by the shoulder, like she was afraid she'd fly away and never come back. "No healer for us, just some spit and prayers. I'd have to… I'd have to ask Owl Wings first, but I'm sure he wouldn't be against it. I mean, he let Misfire in, so the bar is on the floor." Thinking about Owl Wings gave her a surge of energy. Despite all the pain, the loss, all of it, she'd done it. The Kirran had left. The Golden Hearts kingdom was cleared because of *her*. He had to be happy with this, maybe enough to let Louisa in.

"Do you know where Rose Heart is?" she asked. It was just hitting her that she hadn't seen the thief since she'd been injured the other day.

"A great time to be talking about other girls," Louisa said flatly. "She's in the tree hollow. She's doing fine now that the venom's worn off."

"Ah, sorry, I didn't mean it like that," Legacy said hastily, grabbing her small collection of belongings and packing them neatly into her traveling pack. "I just… if you're coming with me, and what you said about your parents is true, it's best we collect ourselves and get out soon, yeah?"

"If you're ready," Louisa said, a nervous smile on her face. It was a lot, leaving her family behind, her city, everything she'd lived for until now. Legacy thought it was pretty brave.

"Always ready," Legacy said. "Now, let's get out of here before your dad shows up. I don't really want to meet him."

CHAPTER TWENTY-FIVE

# UNTHREADING OUR SORROW

WHEN LEGACY SET FOOT IN the tree hollow, eyes barely adjusting to the dark, all she saw was the back of Rose Heart's head. The other thief was staring at the wall, solemn and unmoving. The growths on her head bobbed gently in the breeze, the cool claws of wind weak in the wooden cavern.

"Rose Heart?" she said, voice loud in the silence.

The other thief said nothing; she didn't even twitch a feather, just stayed as still as the dead.

"I think you should explain," Louisa whispered, backing up. "I'll stay out here to give you a moment."

248

Legacy nodded, walking in to stand next to her companion, head held low. "I know you're upset; I understand."

"Upset?" Rose Heart hissed, body stiller than a statue. "That's a small word for what I'm feeling right now, *darling*."

"I know what I did was wrong, I know," Legacy pleaded, reaching out to lay a claw on Rose Heart's shoulder.

"I sure hope you do." Rose Heart pulled away, eyes narrow. "Does this have to do with what happened at the castle? Ever since then you've been acting strange. No, not just strange, outright absurd."

Her panic over the traitor seemed silly now. They existed, sure, but who was she to take the word of an assassin? Maybe Naom had done something horrible and had it coming. Maybe Skyflake lied about the whole story to divide the Coyotes. Or maybe it was a stupid personal matter, a stolen lover or something similar that posed no threat to the rest of the guild. Whatever it was, she was in no position to judge.

It still felt better not to tell Rose Heart. Whatever the traitor's intentions, it wasn't worth stirring the pot. Not to mention once the traitor, whoever it was, found out they'd been discovered, things could go awry real fast.

It wasn't worth the trouble. Not until she knew more.

"Ah, yeah…sorry. Been a lot on my mind since the Goldblood heist, I guess. I just… I just didn't want to fail another one. I didn't think any of what I did through," Legacy said solemnly.

Rose Heart said nothing, and for several minutes, the girls stared at the tree interior as a pair, like it was somehow going to speak in their stead.

As non-sentient walls tended to do, it said nothing and left the silence open for the thieves to fill.

For a moment, empty silence. Then Legacy took a deep, chest-filling breath and started to speak.

She didn't talk about the traitor, but she did talk about everything else. She started with her childhood, the very beginning. Maybe it wasn't important, but why not?

Her egg had been abandoned in the depths of the Shadow Forest, found nestled in a patch of mushrooms and moss. There were no parents to be found, either dead or they'd abandoned her. As frowned upon as it was, it was a common way to deal with the aftermath of a fling for parents too queasy about just crushing the egg and child within.

She'd been found by Vinmara Hir Lana while she was on a hunt to gather ingredients for her spells and potions, and by some Darivan-guided miracle, the mosses she needed were the ones housing Legacy's egg.

*Oh, you poor thing*, she'd said in that sweet, maternal way elderly women often spoke. Not that Vinmara was *that* old, but she was older than she was younger. Then she'd taken Legacy home to Elyton, with plans to foster her until her own parents posted missing signs or she found a couple wanting a child. There'd been no such luck, and fostering turned into a halfhearted adoption. Halfhearted, not because Vinmara didn't care for Legacy but because the rest of her family was unhappy with her raising an entirely non-magical child over hatching her own offspring.

So Vinmara tried and failed to win Victor's heart, then gave up and took an apprentice. Sepia was the same age as Legacy, same height, damn near a gold-feathered twin, but she was a prodigy.

Vinmara tried to love and raise them equally, but it never worked out. Legacy would rather sneak out and harass the locals or steal from tourists than deal in any sort of magic. Even the things a bird with no magical ability could do, like making potions or researching spells, didn't interest her in the slightest.

It pushed her and her mother apart, and when she'd recovered from her teenage rebellion, they never bothered to make amends. Instead, Legacy ran away, with a brighter future in her mind than being a side piece to someone else's story.

Rose Heart stopped her at this point, a question on her tongue. "Second best? Don't tell me that's how you've felt?"

"I'll get there," Legacy explained, before launching into her tale again.

She'd lived alone for almost a year, making her way through life by hiding in gutters and sniping gold from the occasional passersby—she'd met Fortune during, and the two teamed up because they were both young criminal runaways. She skimmed that part of the story, this wasn't about her and Fortune.

One such passerby was a man with tan and brown feathers, carrying himself with heavy bones and sore joints. *An old man*, she'd thought, *an easy target, and he's got some nice gold earrings to boot.*

He was so easy to back into a corner and rob it was almost comical. Until he'd flipped the script and suddenly had *her* back to the wall and a knife to her throat. Rather than kill her, he said he was impressed with her abilities and offered her a place in the Coyotes. He said it was a better place for someone with her skill set than the streets.

"Huh, that's surprisingly similar to how he recruited me," Rose Heart said. "Not identical, but close. Do go on."

The two were still watching the wall, afraid to meet eyes, but the atmosphere felt lighter. A bug skittered down the bark as she continued.

In the Coyotes, things were good, until she fell into place in the guild and found that her place was far lower than she thought she deserved. Maybe it was egotistical. Maybe she misled herself into thinking being a Coyote would fix all her problems, but after everything she'd gone through, coming to a guild that specialized in a talent she had and finding she wasn't even the best there was… rough. With Naom, she'd let it slide because she'd been there far longer and was much older.

"But you…" Legacy said to Rose Heart, "you joined just before I did. We've been there damn near the same time, yet somehow I feel like I'm leagues behind you," she whispered, claws tight in the dirt. "The Goldblood heist was my first chance to prove we were at least equals, and I blew it."

Rose Heart was looking at her now, not happy but not seething either. She looked strangely neutral, like she was putting the pieces together in her brain before the emotional aspect had time to settle in. "So… where does O'Hara come into this? Why was his sacrifice supposed to help you? How could that ever have done more than if you'd just talked to me?"

"Nensho gave me a choice when she caught me," Legacy explained. "She said I could be let go if I brought her that necklace he'd swiped from her. Some kind of sentimental thing, I guess, but whatever. That's why she was mad."

Rose Heart tilted her head.

Legacy barreled on. "I told her... I told her I could do her one better. I said I could bring her the thief who took it if she promised to leave the kingdom. It felt like an easy out, a quick way to checkmark this mission, you know?"

"And make you look good. Because you were the one who came up with it," Rose Heart said. "Not to condone anything you've done, but I am starting to see what happened. It makes sense, in your weird, awful way of doing things. So let me guess, she asked for the crown with him, and that's how we ended up where we did?"

It sounded so much worse when she summarized it like that.

Legacy nodded, quiet.

The same bug skittered up the wall a second time, the shiny blue shell darting around before disappearing into a crack in the wood. It felt like more of those bugs were scrambling around inside of her.

"Can I ask you a question?" Legacy finally said.

"I don't see why not," Rose Heart replied. She was watching the bug as it peered out from the crack, but her head was tilted to hear Legacy.

"Was it all in my head? That you all hated me, that I was alone, that if the places had been reversed… you would have done the same to me as I'd done to O'Hara." Legacy's voice cracked. "Was I imagining all that?"

Rose Heart stood up, stretching before she walked to the entrance of the tree hollow. She motioned for

Legacy to follow. "Let's talk about this in the fresh air. The sun's rising, and I'd hate to miss it."

They both passed by Louisa, who gave Legacy a small, encouraging smile.

# CHAPTER TWENTY-SIX

# THE SUNRISE IN OUR EYES

THE NIGHT WAS MELTING AWAY, the once-black darkness fading out into a rich blue-green. The clouds were lit up tangerine in stunning contrast. A flock of geese speckled the sky far past the rolling hills.

Rose Heart and Legacy stood side by side in the waving grass. It brushed their claws, with the longer, wilder strands tickling their stomachs. The air was cool and smelled like morning dew.

"So was it, then?" Legacy said, staring into the sky with a heavy look in her eyes. Dried blood still stuck to her cheek, and her cloak felt uncomfortably damp on the fringes where it brushed the weeds. "Was it all in my head?"

"Oh, darling," Rose Heart said, looking at her companion with a smile, "you're a crazy bitch, you know that?" Her eyes were green and bright, shining with the rising sun. She looked so… alive, so real, with the damp fronds of feathers poking up from her stomach and the inner corner of her beak curled coyly.

"Ah, what?" Legacy said, startled. Not by the words themselves but by the way they were said, with a carefree fondness that harbored no cruel bite underneath.

"Crazy, and always have been, but it's what makes you fun." Rose Heart continued with laughter in her voice, "Of course it's all in your head. I may be… more of a bitch myself than I intend to be, but really, it's not out of maliciousness. You just have a habit of provoking people and then blaming them when they snap back at you."

"I… hm." Legacy wasn't sure what to say back. She had no argument, not one that wouldn't ironically and horribly prove Rose Heart's point right here and now. "I guess so. It's stupid, though. What a stupid thing for someone to die over."

She didn't understand how she was standing here, being treated like an equal. It didn't feel deserved. It felt wrong, like a cloak that hung just a bit too uneven and a bit too long to sit on her shoulders quite right.

"You need to talk to others," Rose Heart said. "You need to learn to lean on them, not just ball it all up inside. That's why O'Hara died, because not only are you selfish, you're so afraid of talking to anyone else that he ended up a victim of your repressed inferiority complex." The words were cruel, but her tone was far from it. She said the words flatly, no less factual than a statistic. "That's why the Boss likes me more. It's not luck. It's not some mystic force out of your control. It's because he knows I'm not too scared to go to others if I need it. He knows I put the job first, even if it makes me uncomfortable."

"I've never… I've never seen you do that," Legacy replied. She fiddled with the grass between her claws, the sunrise growing too bright to stare into any longer. It was orange and consuming, and she found herself wishing it would stay put for just a moment longer, that it would hang on to the horizon for just another hour before it disintegrated in the cool morning air. She breathed it in, trying to catch what she could of the smell before it whisked away.

"Well, no one ever makes a thing of announcing their emotional conversations to the world. At least, I don't." Rose Heart chuckled. "But honestly. You think it's stupid, but it can be dangerous to let those feelings go as unchecked as they were." She reached out, touching a black claw to the white spot on Legacy's chest. She still shook, the aftereffects of the venom making her unsteady. "I can't forgive you for what you did to O'Hara… But I won't spend our time in the Coyotes together hating you for it either. Just promise me you'll never do this again, darling. That's all I'd ask."

Legacy breathed in the dewy air, feeling it cool her lungs and soothe the ache inside. "I promise. I'll do better, or at least I'll try."

"Thank you," Rose Heart said, her voice a whisper on the wind. This was more than Legacy had ever hoped for, after what she'd done. It wasn't forgiveness, but it didn't have to be. Better than that, it was a chance to improve herself, a chance to make sure nothing like this ever happened again.

In this moment, it felt clear to her why Rose Heart was the Master Thief. It wasn't her talent. It wasn't just what she'd said minutes prior. It was because she could, amid all her passive remarks, still act as a lifeline. She could spit and hiss and throw a fit over anything, but at the end of the day, she really cared about the Coyotes. She would never betray them.

Legacy could say that with confidence now. Rose Heart was not the traitor. She couldn't be, because she actually gave a shit. If she didn't, she would have cast Legacy aside in a heartbeat. She would have said "just get back to work" with a snide turn of her head and left her fellow thief to put herself back together.

Now that the guilt was fading, not gone, not even close, but subsiding enough that it was no longer a constricting snake around her soul, she felt the absence of O'Hara more than ever.

For all his faults, he'd become a welcome presence, a mediator in their group to lighten the mood in his own weird way. He was just like Legacy, really—another confused bird making his way in the world as best he could.

She breathed in deep, closing her eyes for a moment before opening them again. This would hurt for a long time, but there was nothing to be done now but staunch the bleeding and get on with her life.

She turned away from the sunrise, shrugging her shoulders to try and get some blood flow through them in the stiff chill. "Are you ready to go home, then?" she said with a smile on her face. Rose Heart nodded, arching her wings over her back in a similar attempt to warm herself up. Either one of them could have used fire, but that felt too incandescent for this moment.

"I hope you don't mind the princess I'm bringing back with us," Legacy said, sheepishly leaping into the air before Rose Heart could protest.

# CHAPTER TWENTY-SEVEN

# SHADOW'S EMBRACE

LEGACY FELT HER WINGS DROOPING with soreness as she powered into an unlucky headwind, consoling herself with thoughts that her guild wasn't far and she just had to keep going a little longer.

The trip back home was as pleasantly uneventful as it had been on the way there. More so, even, because the trio traveled with the knowledge that the Kirran would leave them alone if they did cross paths. An unexpected ally gained from unfortunate circumstances.

Ally was a rough term, but they weren't an enemy, so that was something.

The thought reminded her of Moon Eyes' words, something she hadn't considered in a while. Not that she'd had much time for ruminating lately.

*"Not all those you trust will be true, but you will never know your real enemies if you cannot trust at all."*

It reminded her of Rose Heart, and the weird, convicting trust she'd felt at the end of their conversation the other day.

She'd made the decision to trust Rose Heart, and it revealed a truth. Not a big truth, not the kind that sent a bird back on their tailfeathers or left them with a gawking beak, but the kind of small, subtle truth that offered a soothing breath to an anxious mind.

Rose Heart cared. That was the truth. In her weird way, she cared, and that meant the world in the face of what Legacy had learned prior. Someone was an enemy, but it wasn't the Seducer of Kings, the Thief with a Silver Tongue.

It was less inspiring to think that she'd have to repeat this if she did want to weed out the traitor. Making friends with Judgement or Thistle seemed damn near impossible, and she wasn't sure she wanted to try.

No, she could be content with what she had now. She was no detective. If she were, she wouldn't be robbing other birds and making connections with gangs. The traitor would reveal themselves eventually, or they wouldn't, and Skyflake would be proved a liar, but she could pass this on to Owl Wings and let him deal with it. He was the boss man, after all.

She still wasn't going to tell the others. This wasn't an issue of trust but of knowing how poorly the Coyotes were at dealing with any sort of conflict. The last thing she needed to do was spill this and have someone get stabbed, Thistle leave, and watch a scene akin to something you might see when a barn catches fire, and every animal collectively forgets about the gaping exit in front of them.

The trip was long, but she was sure she could find something else worth thinking about. Like how she was going to explain the tagalong princess to the Boss.

To Legacy and Rose Heart, this kind of traveling was old hat, but they had to make twice as many stops to accommodate said princess.

"Aren't you a Golden Hearts bird, darling? I'd have thought you better at the long-distance thing," Rose Heart remarked when they stopped for the third time that day to rest and recover by a creek, Louisa panting heavily.

"Ah, yes," Louisa tried to say between breaths. "I am, really, but… I've never flown quite… quite this long… before." Her wings were massive and built for gliding, but her body was accustomed to the cushy life of always having food and water at her beck and call. Most stops were so that she could take several worryingly large beakfuls of water in at once before moving on.

She was doing that now, submerging her entire face in the creek, drawing up an absurd amount of water, and throwing her head back to let it slide down her throat. Her face feathers, normally dainty and well-kept, were soaked through and dripping onto the pebbles by the shore.

"You know you can go like three days without water, right?" Legacy remarked, standing on a large stone in the center of the creek. "You don't have to stop every time you're a little thirsty."

"I thought it was four days?" Rose Heart added, having stretched herself out by the water in a catlike, relaxed way.

"No, no, I'm pretty sure it was three," Legacy said, unsure. She shrugged. "Eh, who gives a shit."

"Ugh, that sounds awful though. Besides, we aren't in any real rush, are we?" Louisa quipped back, submerged up to her chest in the water now. Was she not worried about ruining her jewelry and clothes?

What Louisa said was true: the job had been done in record time—Misfire had taken this long on much simpler jobs before—so there was no reason for anyone to make haste.

So, much to the thieves' dismay, the frequent stops continued.

It didn't help Louisa that, even after having the mission explained to her, she didn't quite grasp the severity of what was going on. To her, this was just another generic thief job, not something abnormal. There really wasn't a rush (or else they would be rushing) but Legacy was anxious to share her victory with Owl Wings.

Louisa was also unhappy with the elements, which were especially apparent in the contrasting warm days and chilly nights of spring. She pressed in increasingly close to Legacy every night they stopped to rest, shivering. *You're a firepie. Just make a fire,* is what Legacy would have said to anyone else, but she liked the warm body against her own. So, for once in her life, she decided to keep her beak shut. She also didn't mention that maybe if Louisa didn't drink water like she was trying to drown herself, she'd be a lot warmer.

A few nights in, Legacy even offered to share her cloak for them both to rest under together. It wasn't very big, since it had to be short enough not to snag on the ground or get under her feet when she was wearing it, but she was content to let Louisa take the majority of it.

"I presume I'm not invited to this," Rose Heart said while she pecked at a freshly killed peryton beside the cuddling birds. The bloody heap at her claws was picked apart daintily, the feathers and fur carefully moved aside to get to the best meat without making Rose Heart look too barbarian.

"Get your own girlfriend," Legacy said. It was a bit presumptuous—she'd never had an actual conversation or confession or anything of the like—but she was pretty sure friends didn't often sleep like this, pressed together underneath a tiny cloak in what was a mild chill at best.

Louisa didn't protest this, and she was definitely still awake. That had to mean something.

"That's your thing, babe. I'll hold out for a handsome man," Rose Heart said, staring dreamily into the trees. Legacy wondered how she thought she was ever going to fall for a man when every man that came too close got bit and shooed away. Maybe one with a high pain tolerance would eventually win her heart.

Legacy just sighed at that and closed her eyes as she leaned in closer to the princess. In all fairness, she was rough around the edges too, and she'd still found a partner—hopefully, crossing her claws over it, because Owl Wings could always chase Louisa out.

The bubbling water soothed her to sleep.

The trickiest part of their journey was the jaunt through the Shadow Forest. If Louisa was bad at flying her own home territory, she was abysmal at one for the opposite-bodied Long Shadows 'pies. Where Legacy could dart between tight branches and find her way with ease in the hazy light, Louisa kept colliding with collections of branches, tumbling over roots, and getting her feathers mussed up. There was a point where she started to look more tree than bird, for all the sticks and leaves stuck to her.

The cold also crept in, more aggressive in the twenty-four-hour shade than it was over the Golden Hearts Plains. It was a breath of fresh air after the warm wheat and grass smell.

Legacy ended up cracking and telling Louisa to light a fire, but the ex-princess was scared she'd burn down the forest.

It wasn't possible, not in spring, at least. Everything was way too damp from the leftover winter frost. Late summer… maybe. If there was an unfortunate drought that lasted an unfortunate amount of time.

The trees were resilient, though, having grown accustomed to housing kingdoms of an arsonist race. Even dry, it would be a feat to burn more than a few yards before it fizzled out.

That night, as Legacy and Louisa lay close together, Legacy found herself leaning over to preen her companion's silky blue-purple feathers. Her cloak was long cast aside, resting abandoned on the moss beside them. They'd tried sharing it, but it was uncomfortably damp from the wet plants and only made them both colder.

She ran her beak over each ridged surface, pulling together the barbs that held each feather's delicate form. Previously battered and worn, they now came together in a smooth, interlocking collection of plumes. Louisa shivered under her touch, reaching around to tug at the small red feathers on Legacy's neck.

It was less of a returned favor and more of an invitation.

That night, she found herself glad Rose Heart was sleeping high above their heads, blissfully unaware of anything transpiring below.

Or so she thought, until the next day. As they were packing their things to take off on the final stretch of their journey, Rose Heart gave her a coy, knowing grin. "Couldn't wait until we got home?"

Legacy's face burned, and she kept her eyes focused on her bag as she stuffed the remainders of dried meat and changes of poultices for her wounds. "None of your damn business," she said.

Louisa only laughed, gleeful and lighthearted.

And so their trip came to a close. That next day, they made a straight shot to the Coyote den, with no stops in between. Not for water, or rest, or anything.

Louisa didn't even complain, the thieves' excitement finally rubbing off on her as she powered through treetops and even managed to keep her collisions with shrubbery to a minimum. The end to their journey laid tantalizingly near.

# CHAPTER TWENTY-EIGHT

# RETURN TO NORMALCY

THE COYOTE DEN WAS A small, easy-to-miss thing, hidden from prying eyes in the orange stone valley of the Paradise Mountains. It was right on the border of the Golden Hearts and Burning Talons kingdoms, making the trip through the edge of the Shadow Forest feel unnecessary.

It would be, for any normal bird, but it was a deliberate detour done to ensure that any birds watching the border left them alone when they touched into the Shadow Forest, rather than follow them straight to the Coyote den. The scenic route was always safer.

Far below the three birds, at the bottom of the valley, a river flowed. It was normally small and thin, like the world's veins barely visible through the surface of its skin, but in springtime, it swelled with snowmelt from the Burning Talons mountains.

Today, the shore was barely visible, the dark, wet rocks peering their heads just above the surface along the side, with small waves slapping against them. Bubbles of foam clung to their bases.

Legacy landed at the entrance first, steeling herself for what would happen when she walked inside. Two sets of footsteps followed her like shadows as she led the way in, the familiar dusty air coating her lungs and clogging her nose. Pleasantly unpleasant, in the way familiar things could so often be.

For a moment, there was nothing. Just three birds standing side by side on a rocky outcropping, unsure of how the next hour of their lives was going to play out. Deeper in the cavern, she could see Judgement on his spire, Fortune playing some kind of card game with Misfire, and Thistle taking a drink from the pooled water at the lowest part of the cave.

Misfire was the first to notice the girls, and he waved a claw in greeting. Fortune turned her head to follow what he was looking at, and her eyes went wide when she saw not two, but three birds.

Misfire called out as he leaped off the bridge and flew to the ledge. The rest of the guild, picking up on the commotion, was fast to join him. Thistle stretched his shoulders and fluttered over, joined by Judgement, who leaped off his spire with a smooth beat of his wings.

Fortune showed up alongside Misfire, having moved so quietly it was impossible to know when she'd taken off or landed.

The four Coyotes, comfortingly oblivious to what Legacy had done, crowded around her, Louisa, and Rose Heart with varying degrees of interest. Only Judgement stayed back, clinging to the edge of the raucous crowd with detached disinterest.

Everyone was standing together on the ledge, save Cyrill and Owl Wings. The sun filtered in through the holes in the ceiling, casting weak shadows on the stone. The noise was suffocating despite the crowd being quite small.

"Who the hell is this?" Fortune asked, louder than everyone else and thus the easiest to understand. Louisa winced at her words, not yet knowing that Fortune rarely meant harm. She just had a tendency to talk like she was pissed off.

"Smart move, marching a stranger right into the guild," Thistle remarked. "Now she knows where we live." He was an outlier in his unwelcoming demeanor. The rest of the Coyotes seemed excited, peering around each other with bright eyes, not daring to come too close but not wanting to be so far as to struggle to hear her.

"I think she's alright," said Misfire, pushing in just a bit too close.

"You would, you damn creep," Fortune said, leaning against a stone spire with faux disinterest. Unlike Judgement, however, her golden eyes were still trained on Louisa.

Legacy wasn't sure she liked the look on her face. It was curious, but there was something unreadable to it. Like a dog watching you get just a little too close to its food, while it waited for you to get close enough to bite.

"Oh, hello. It's a pleasure to meet all of you," Louisa said, smiling. She didn't sound nervous, and by some grace of Darivan, she didn't even look fazed despite the many criminal eyes pinned on her. Even Legacy had cold feet, and she knew these birds.

The ex-princess looked visibly out of place. Her new coat of messy feathers interwoven with leaves and twigs was far from enough to cover how she carried herself, her kind demeanor, and that strange lilt to her voice that only royals seemed to have. She also had her various accessories: the pearls on her face, the rings on her claws, and the small white slips of cloth hanging from her ankles. Things no thief would wear. Nor most civilians.

"I was hoping to speak with… Owl Wings, was it?" Louisa continued, scanning the crowd and picking apart each bird mentally. It hit Legacy then that Louisa actually had no idea what he looked like. It was a strange realization, that he, or that any of the Coyotes, were such strangers to someone Legacy felt so familiar with.

It made her chest swell with pride. Maybe it was because she was finally doing something worth the attention, maybe because she'd just come in with a beautiful girl on her wing and could tell everyone "this one's mine" or maybe she was just proud of herself for making it home. Mistakes or not, the first mission was a success, and she was buzzing to tell the Boss.

Unfortunately, said Boss was nowhere in sight, and neither was Cyrill.

"They're up in his room," Judgement said.

"Yeah, he's been giving himself gray feathers over this damn prophecy." Fortune chuckled, pointing a gold claw to the tunnel across the bridge.

"So… is she one of us? Or is this, like, some kind of hostage situation?" Misfire said, trailing behind the girls as they trotted across the bridge. He stopped when Rose Heart turned her head and flashed him a searing glare. Her head feathers bounced with the snappy movement.

"We're about to find out…" Legacy said, her anxiety warring with her excitement deep in the pit of her stomach. She had to plan this perfectly. She had to lead the conversation with their success so that Owl Wings was happy enough that he had no choice but to recruit Louisa. She had to explain fast or else he'd get impatient and just talk over her, but she couldn't explain *too* fast or else he'd miss what she was trying to say.

Twenty paces down the hall, she knocked at his door.

Nothing happened, and she raised a claw to knock again, only for the door to slide open with a resounding creak. *Be patient*, she reminded herself.

Inside was a familiar scene. Owl Wings leaned over the massive stone table in the center of his room, papers scattered around him and a half-empty glass of some kind of dark liquor by his side. Heavy bags pulled at his eyes, and he didn't even look up when the door opened. Cyrill was standing by his side, looking as normal as he ever did. He glanced up, catlike yellow eyes darting toward the doorway, hanging onto Louisa for a drawn-out second, then flickering back down at the table.

"They're back," he whispered to the Boss.

"I know that. I'm not going blind yet; just hold on two seconds while I figure this out. Then I'll deal with 'em," Owl Wings said, distracted. She noticed a book was open next to him, bearing a page with disjointed celestial scribbles. "Not my fault these damn Dreamseers make everything so hard to figure out. They could have given me a checklist. Or instructions that weren't in fucking hieroglyphics."

"They have an additional accomplice," Cyrill added.

"An additional— Huh?" Owl Wings' head snapped up at that, eyes going wide when he saw Louisa.

"We, uh, we did the mission, Boss," Legacy said, shifting her weight nervously.

"First, tell me who the hell this is and why she's standing in my room. I've already told y'all not to bring more hookers in here," he snapped.

"Hey, I'm not—" Louisa started.

"I'm sorry, more?" Rose Heart hissed.

"No, no, it's not like that," Legacy said quickly, hoping she hadn't screwed this up too badly. "She… she was a princess, and now she wants to join us. She's a doctor and good at healing so we wouldn't have to keep fixing our—"

"Quit rambling. She's in, mostly because she's already seen the place, and the bar is so low it may as well be in the fucking void," Owl Wings interrupted, spinning a quill in his claw. He slammed the quill down, ink bursting from the nib. "Now, forget that. Tell me how the job went."

And just like that, Louisa was a Coyote. In typical Coyote fashion, there was no ceremony, no questioning, just Owl Wings saying things and everyone else going along with it. It kept things simple.

Legacy looked at Rose Heart, nodding to encourage the other to speak.

It was Legacy's fault they'd succeeded, but it felt wrong to take the credit for what happened when she'd done it in such a piss-poor manner.

"We succeeded," Rose Heart said simply. "We found the problem: a gang tormenting the kingdom with a leader who had it out for the king. Thanks to Legacy, we were able to scare them off. Done and done."

"And that's all?" Owl Wings said, skeptical. Next to him, Cyrill was using a cloth to gently wipe the spilled ink off the table.

She didn't blame him. "Done and done" was not commonplace for this guild. It was usually "done with a few hurdles and pitfalls along the way, and also someone's in jail."

"That's all," Rose Heart said, words clean-cut and leaving no room for doubt. "I'm as surprised as you are."

"We can tell you more later," Legacy added. "But it wasn't… as grand scale as we thought. It went fine." It did not go fine, and while it wasn't hard, per se, the sacrifices it took to actually make Nensho leave were… unpleasant. Better if he didn't know it took a thief's life to pull it off.

"Hm," Owl Wings said, thinking. He didn't look entirely convinced, but he never really did. "In that case, rest for a while, show the new girl around, and then get back to work until I scrape together what comes next."

"Louisa is my name, sir," Louisa said, bowing her head.

"Don't call me sir. Now, get out of my room," he said, shooing them out with a wing.

Before Legacy could follow, Owl Wings stopped her.

"Legacy," he said. "The next job is in the Shadow Forest. You want in on it?"

She thought about it for a moment, keeping her back to him. It sounded more like a demand than a question, and she knew if he'd asked before this entire escapade, she'd have jumped on the offer. It made sense, after all.

She'd done this job with relative success, and she looked enough like a pure Long Shadows 'pie to fit right in.

But her body was sore, littered with half-healed wounds, especially the ones on her neck. They were hidden deep within her feathers, but she knew they'd scar.

And inside… her heart ached in a nagging, awful way. She'd succeeded, but the success hung on her heart like a bag of rocks.

It could serve to prove herself further. A way to show that this wasn't a one-off lucky occurrence. But the last time she'd pushed herself to prove her worth, everything had gone to shit. O'Hara's face flashed in her mind. His wide, betrayed eyes stared holes on the inside of her brain.

"I'm sorry, Boss. I don't think I'm ready to jump back into this yet. Try Fortune. She was raised there too," Legacy said, then left before he could say anything in reply. She walked down the hall, head held high. She could relax now, as much as a thief could. Her job, as messily done as it had been, was done, and the rest was in the claws of the other Coyotes.

She could grieve and recover on her own time. There would be future chances to prove herself, but this wasn't one of them. If there was anything she'd learned, it's that she needed to stop trying so hard. It only served to tear her apart on the inside.

She walked across the bridge, down the entrance tunnel, and stopped to stand on the small ledge jutting out of the entrance. The bright moon was suspended in the vast night, and she closed her eyes to bask in its cool glow. In body, she was alone, standing solo with nothing but the moonlight at her side, but she'd never felt less lonely. Inside the den, there was Louisa, and Rose Heart, even Fortune.

Her shadow stood in front of her, cast onto the stone by the warm light inside the guild.

High above, the stars glittered, docile and beautiful. Things could change, but right at this moment, below the endless sky, things were almost okay.

# END OF BOOK 1

S ET ABLAZE, AND BY EXTENSION One for Sorrow, is a culmination of support from those around me. First and foremost, my family. My mom, who gave me books like The Grimm's Fairy Tales when I was at the ripe old age of "in elementary school" because she thought they were child friendly, which no doubt fed into my love of dark yet animal centric stories. My dad, who was traumatized by Watership Down when he was a kid and had to see his daughter grow up to create that exact brand of cute animals doing awful gory things. (I also have to thank him for finding a lot of books and authors for me, a lot of my literary inspirations were suggestions from him) They've both been paramount to Set Ablaze becoming a reality, having given me their endless love as well as a lot of help financially to make this book a tangible thing.

A massive thank you to my grandparents and extended family, who've been there every step of the way. Grandma Connie, who supports my art and shares my deep love of animals. My Grandma Silvana read all the mini stories and drabbles I wrote with interest. Grandpa Jorge, who I stole my sense of humor from. I hope he, myself, and my brother have a lot more future road trips together to come.

Speaking of my brother, I appreciate him too. I doubt he'll see this because he'd probably shrivel up and die if he tried to read a chapter book, but he's been a constant menace in my life that deserves acknowledgment.

I also have to thank my friends. Carousel and Dani, my best friends from high school who've stuck strong since. My friends I've met online in my years running my online account for Set Ablaze (especially the ones who've been theorizing and tracking my art, and motivating me to get these books out so I can finally give you guys some answers).

A special thanks to Jaime Ricciardi. She both beta read for me and drew the absolutely lovely cover, and even made me a little mini Legacy plush that now sits next to me when I write. She has a fantasy book series of her own, The Dreamfarer's Tales, and I highly recommend checking it out.

Last but definitely not least, my partner, who's a fellow writer working on a comic of her own. She helped with the beta reading and also did about 99% of the work on the wiki while I fooled around on the sidelines.

You're all the reason this was possible, and I'm ecstatic to have you along for the ride.

S ET ABLAZE STARTED WEIRD. IT was born out of the site Deviantart, where I used to post and share my art during The Dark Ages (middle school), as a little roleplay group between some friends and I. You can't find the group anymore, it's been long deleted, but it lives on in spirit. Back then it was never meant to be anything more, but after a long stretch of time following me leaving Deviantart and working on a different story (a kind of semi sci-fi fantasy tale, also with bird characters), I revisited the concept. While the story itself was in shambles, the foundation felt like something real, something fun that I could mold into a very tangible tale. And so I did, and so now we have Set Ablaze.

Some of the characters from the original roleplay group live on. Fortune, Nensho, and Legacy were such characters, as well as some we haven't met.

The story doesn't end here, not by a long shot. Two for Joy is the next in the lineup, and I've already started the first draft between bouts of editing One for Sorrow.

Between book releases, you can follow updates on the progress as well as see the art I make on my Instagram @cr0wfeathers

Above all else, Set Ablaze is supposed to be fun. If you come out of reading this at least somewhat entertained, I'll have succeeded.

Best,

**SILVANA MILLER**

When a book of mine gets bought, I oftentimes don't
see where it ends up. I have a collection of pictures of
the times I catch people sharing it or telling me they
read it, but outside those it's normally a sale and then
it's out into the void.

Reviews: the good, the bad, and the ugly, are a way
to tell me you read what I made. Whether they offer
useful criticism for future books, or just express
how it made you feel, few things are more key to an
author. So if this book impacted you, leave a review
about it! It helps me, and I love reading them.

# OTHER BOOKS
# BY THIS AUTHOR